SERI

ED

Ed Gorman became a full-time writer after twenty years in advertising, and is acknowledged as being one of the worlds leading writers of dark suspense. He is the founder and editor of Mystery Scene and lives in Cedar Rapids, Iowa with his wife, novelist Carol Graham. Amongst his other novels are *Cage of Night*, *Night Kills*, *The Long Midnight* and *The Poker Club*.

Praise For Ed Gorman

"Books like this are what inspired me to become a writer in the first place."
—DEAN R KOONTZ

"Gorman has a way of getting into his characters, and they have a way of getting into you"
— ROBERT BLOCH, author of *Psycho*

"Gorman pulls things off with sleek bravura, reclaiming the field from the legions of cardboard cutout serial killers"
— TIME OUT

Other Titles by Ed Gorman

The Long Midnight
The Poker Club
Night Kills
Cage Of Night
New Improved Murder

Ed Gorman

SERPENT'S KISS

CT Publishing

First published in Great Britain by CT Publishing, 1999.

This edition 1999 CT Publishing.
Copyright © Ed Gorman 1999

A CIP catalogue record for this book is
available from the British Library.

ISBN 1-902002-09-1

9 8 7 6 5 4 3 2 1

Book design and typography by DP Fact & Fiction.
Printed and bound in Great Britain by Caledonian
International Book Manufacturing, Bishopbriggs, Glasgow.

To a man who understands the rigours of friendship, Rex Miller.

SERPENT'S KISS

1966

When he was dying, there in the street, the ambulance still on its way, he started crying.

The cop who'd shot him, kneeling next to him now on the quiet back street, felt embarrassed for him. The cop hoped when his own time came, he didn't start blubbering. Pretty goddamned embarrassing with all these people around.

Anyway, what was this sonofabitch crying about? He was the one who'd escaped from a mental hospital named Hastings House and then brutally stabbed three teenage girls.

But the killer started to sob, and hold his stomach where the cop had shot him. Blood bubbled in the corner of the man's mouth.

And so the cop, cursing, said, "Hold on; you'll make it."

But the man knew different, of course. And so did the crowd of poor black people who'd gathered shoeless in the ninety-degree midnight of the ghetto. Some teenagers had bottles of wine stuffed inside greasy paper bags. Others toked openly on joints. One plump young woman breastfed a tiny, shiny black infant.

The man looked up at the cop and said, with great effort, "I didn't kill them."

The cop couldn't help it He sneered. "Somebody saw you, man. You went right into the women's toilet and grabbed that teenage girl. And an old woman saw you."

"It was me physically. But spiritually it was somebody else."

It was me physically but it wasn't me spiritually. Right. These fuckers always had some crazy story.

And the stench; this foul, greasy odour the man gave off. What was the smell anyway?

"Feel my stomach," the dying man said.

"What?"

"Feel my stomach."

"Jesus."

"Please." And the man weakly took the cop's hand and guided it to a place just below his sternum.

And goddamn. The cop felt it.

Something twisting inside the man's stomach. Something alive. Coiling and uncoiling.

9

The cop jerked his hand back as if he'd been burned.

"He dead, ain't he?" a young boy said peeping down into the man's face.

The cop looked up at the kid and scowled. "You go stand back on the kerb, you hear me?"

But the kid kept leaning over and peeping down at the man. Blood bubbled from the man's nostrils and mouth and dripped from his chin.

The cop just kept staring at the man's stomach right above the wound.

Something was fucking in there. Moving.

"He dead," the kid said again, but he finally moved back to the kerb.

By the time the ambulance came the man's stomach was still and the cop would be damned if he'd say anything about it to the ambulance attendants or the man from the Medical Examiner's.

He had felt something moving in there. No shit. Honest.

The cop didn't want to end up at Hastings House himself.

Today: Tuesday, April 25

A MALE NURSE named Claiborne was the first person to notice that a patient named Dobyns was missing. Claiborne was on the third floor of Hastings House to deliver 100 mg of Thorazine to a delusional patient who had been somewhat violent earlier in the day.

The time was 9:02 p.m.

Claiborne's first assumption was that Dobyns had gone one of two places: the TV room (several of the patients had expressed an interest in HBO's presentation this evening of *Chariots of Fire*) or the library. Before his somewhat lengthy stay here, Dobyns had been an English professor at a local college. While the library didn't offer a sophisticated reader much to choose from—the selection ran heavily to romances, mysteries that emphasised puzzles instead of character, science fiction that was mostly about an intergalactic lawman named Rick Starman, and westerns in which the horses were at least as smart as the people—even patients as cosmopolitan as Dobyns found the library a nice place to sit and relax. Only when you noticed the bars on the windows was the effect spoiled somewhat.

Dobyns proved to be neither place.

The time was 9:08 p.m.

Claiborne had one more place to check before he allowed himself the luxury of anything remotely resembling panic.

Claiborne had lately noticed Dobyns going into the chapel from time to time. A nondenominational nook where religious items from all the major faiths but Hindu could be found, the chapel afforded patients total silence and solace. There was even a small stained glass window high on the west wall.

Dobyns was not in the chapel.

The time was 9:12 p.m.

Two hours previous, Security Chief Andy Todd had been readying himself for the short drive home and his first nondietary meal in three months (he had been taking medication for high blood pressure) when his office phone rang and one of his men had informed him that today's violent and ongoing rainstorm had played hell with some of the security lights that sat on metal poles above the electrified fencing. (Todd had spent his first ten years in security working upstate at the prison; he was right at home at Hastings.)

"The goddamn sonofabitchin' job" as he had called it to himself had taken till now to finish (three electricians at God-only-knew how much per hour had clung to the metal poles like drowning men to life rafts getting the lights to work again) and had left him damp and rumpled in the process. Andy Todd was a man who liked to look sharp in the khaki, army-style uniform he had chosen for himself (his men had similar uniforms but theirs lacked bold brass buttons and the absolutely meaningless but quite impressive insignia Todd wore on his right arm).

He was just leaving when the phone rang.

"Todd here."

"Andy, it's Claiborne."

"Hi, Jeff. 'Fraid I'm in kind of a hurry. I'm two hours late for dinner and you know how the missus gets." Actually, Todd noted, Jeff Claiborne couldn't tell you diddlysquat about anybody's missus. He was manly enough but gay, and while that didn't bother Todd all that much (he had a brother he suspected was the same way), it didn't exactly make Claiborne an expert on women. "How can I help you?"

"I think we may have a problem."

"What kind of problem?"

Claiborne paused. "We've got a patient missing."

Oh, dear sweet suffering Jesus, Todd thought, the image of roast beef (nice fatty roast beef) and mashed potatoes with lots of gravy and a big helping of pumpkin pie fading sadly from his mind. "What floor?"

"Third."

"Who?"

"Dobyns."

"Holy shit."

"Right," Claiborne said. "That's what I was thinking."

Dobyns was a genuine crazy. He had managed to spook the

12

entire staff.

Now he was missing.

Wonderful.

At this rate, Andy Todd was going to get off his medicine for high blood pressure around the year 2347.

"I'll be right up," Todd said.

"Sorry about your dinner."

"Thanks," Todd said, thinking once more about guys like Claiborne and his brother. How could they do it to each other in the butt, anyway? Todd had haemorrhoids and it was painful enough just applying Preparation H let alone screwing around back there.

Snapping off his office light, he moved his 220 pounds down the hall to the elevator. This one felt bad. He wasn't sure why. He just had an instinct was all. It felt very bad.

The time was 9:18 p.m.

"If he took anything, I don't know what it would have been," Jeff Claiborne said. Piece by piece he threw the contents of Dobyns's bureau drawers on the tightly made single bed pushed against the wall.

Comb, toothbrush, half used tube of Colgate, Gillette Foamy shaving cream, Santa Fe aftershave, dental floss, Ban roll-on, and a single Trojan condom in a sleek red pack.

"What the hell you think he had that thing for?" Todd said.

"Told me he thought he might get lucky with one of the nurses."

Todd shook his head.

"Well, that's what he said, Andy. Hope is what people live by, even in nuthouses."

Todd glanced around the room. "Don't use that goddamn word anywhere around Bellamy. You know what he did to Dolan for calling it a loony bin."

Dolan had been fired summarily, his perks, including health insurance, cancelled at once.

"Sorry," Claiborne said. A stocky, thirtyish man with a rugged head and shaggy blond hair, Claiborne usually wore a smock that got him mistaken for a doctor. The black horn-rimmed glasses didn't hurt, either.

13

"Let me try the other two floors," Todd said, "See if Unger or Lumley know anything about this."

Each floor had its own security guard around the clock.

"Shouldn't you call Bellamy?" Claiborne said as Todd started out the door.

Todd paused in the doorway and grinned. "You really want to see me get my ass whipped, don't you, Jeff?"

"But I thought—"

"I'll call Bellamy as a last resort. After I've exhausted every other possibility." He shook his head again. "You know what that sonofabitch would say if I told him we couldn't find Dobyns?"

"Pissed, huh?"

"Pissed? Are you crazy? Pissed isn't the half of it." He swept a beefy arm out to the corridor. "You keep looking around up here, all right?"

"Sure, Andy."

With that, Andy Todd left Dobyns's room.

Nothing useful had been found.

The time was 9:29 p.m.

As he sat in the guardhouse at the front gate, sipping decaf coffee and listening to a night call in show about alien abductions, Frank Dvorak kept thinking about what he'd seen in the back window of the laundry truck.

A face.

He'd been sure of it.

Then why the hell hadn't he done anything about it?

The question could be answered in two words: Heather Moore. Ever since Frank had been transferred to the night shift here at Hastings, Heather had shown definite signs of becoming restless. By now, it was pretty obvious she wanted to start dating other guys and drop Frank who, she had lately been hinting, was too old for her anyway. Frank was thirty-two.

They had been in the middle of one of their marathon phone arguments three hours ago, just at dusk, when the laundry truck pulled up to the gate from the inside and beeped. The

14

laundry service usually did its pick-up around this time and Frank hadn't thought much about it. How the hell could he think about *anything* with the battle raging over the phone, anyway?

The white panel truck had just pulled between the open gates when Frank had glimpsed the man's face. Instantly Frank had flashed on what most likely happened. A patient had climbed into one of the laundry carts the driver loaded up and somehow managed to get into the truck without being detected.

Just as the truck had been leaving the grounds, the patient had sat up and peeked through the window.

Right at Frank.

Frank had wanted to do the right thing, of course, but just as he'd seen the guy, Heather had gone into her sly story about the cute new guy at the insurance office where she worked. This was obviously the guy Heather planned to start dating anytime now. If she wasn't already.

So there you had it. Frank *should* have hung up right away and called Andy Todd pronto.

But he'd been so pissed at Heather, so intent on finding out this cute guy's name that—

So now he sat in the guardhouse sipping decaf and listening to tales of alien abductions.

If only he could be so lucky to have an alien ship swoop down and pick him up and take him somewhere out among the stars. No more worries about Heather or cute new guys at the office. Or the kind of mistake he'd made by not calling Andy Todd at once.

The time was 9:31 p.m.

Andy Todd had guards on the respective floors walk him around. They searched everything, including toilet stalls, closets, stairwells, and nursing offices. Nothing.

It was at this point that Ames, one of the guards whom Todd had taken into his confidence, said the unthinkable. "You checked the floor below, right, Andy?"

"Right."

"And the floor above?"

"Right."

"Where the hell could he be?"

They were having diet Pepsis in the staff lounge. Andy was also gnawing on a Clark bar from one of the lounge's seven vending machines.

"He couldn't have got out of this building," Andy Todd said. "It's locked up tight. That leaves me no place else to look." He frowned. "That leaves me picking up the phone and calling Bellamy and telling him Dobyns is missing."

"Uh-uh."

"Uh-uh? If Dobyns isn't on the first floor and isn't on the second and isn't on the third, then just where the hell could he be?"

"The tower."

"The tower?" Andy Todd looked at the other man as if he'd just suggested that George Bush owned a complete collection of Liberace records. "The tower? Nobody goes into the tower. Not you; not me. Hell, I've never even seen Bellamy himself go into the tower."

"It's a thought. It's the only likely place left."

The tower. Jesus God. Hastings had been built in Victorian times, when the architecture ran to sprawling estate houses with turrets and spires and widow's walks. Off the east end of the building rose a four-storey tower that, so far as Andy Todd knew, had been shut down. The windows were boarded up, the elevator that led to it had long ago been closed, and the door to the interior stairs was bolted closed and padlocked with a Yale the size of a catcher's mitt. Among the staff there was, of course, great speculation about what had once been in the tower—there was even the kind of urban campfire talk that passed for ghost stories, tales of lights shining in the windows and horrifying screams being heard on the wind.

"No way he's in the tower," Andy Todd said, polishing off his Clark bar.

"Then where the hell is he?" Ames said.

"By now he could be back in his room. Lemme check."

Just as Todd got up to grab the receiver from the wall phone, the thing surprised him by ringing.

"Todd here."

16

"Andy, this is Frank at the front gate."

"Right, Frank. I know where you are. I assigned you there, remember?" Dvorak had an irritating way of belabouring the obvious and with one of Bellamy's prize fruitcakes strolling around somewhere, Andy Todd was in no mood. "So what can I do for you?"

"Wondered if we could talk a little."

Todd sighed. "You still want May off for vacation?"

"This time it ain't about vacation."

"I'm real busy, Frank. Could it wait till tomorrow?"

There was a pained pause. "One of the patients got free, didn't he, Andy?"

"How'd you know about that?"

Another pained pause. "Something kind of happened earlier tonight, Andy."

"Oh, yeah?" Andy Todd was preparing himself to get violently, explosively angry, high blood pressure or no high blood pressure. "Like what?"

"Well, maybe I saw something."

"Such as?"

"This face."

"Yeah?"

"Yeah, Andy. I can tell you're gettin' pissed. I can feel it over the phone." Right now Frank Dvorak sounded as if he were about six years old.

"You screwed up, didn't you, Frank?"

"I'm real sorry, Andy. I was arguin' with Heather and—"

"What happened, Frank? About this face you mentioned?"

Pause. "I know you're gonna get even more pissed off when I tell you, Andy. I mean, I know how you are."

Andy had to hold in the rage or Dvorak would take all night getting it out. "Tell me, Frank. Tell me fast. That way maybe I won't get so pissed."

"I saw somebody in the back of the laundry truck. You know what I'm saying, Andy? Like the patient hid in the laundry cart and stowed away inside the truck and rode right out to freedom. You know?"

"The laundry truck left here about six o'clock."

17

"Yeah, 'bout six."

"You waited three hours to call me?"

"I'm afraid I did, Andy."

Andy Todd then gave himself permission to slip into warp drive. He called Frank Dvorak so many names so fast and so loud that neither man could be sure of what was being shouted. All both of them knew was that it was awful, awful stuff. And Andy knew it was not exactly what the doctor had in mind when he said Andy should take things easier and not get so excited.

Andy Todd hung up by slamming the receiver back onto the cradle three or four times and so hard the whole phone started to tear from the wall.

"He got out in the fucking laundry truck," Todd said to Ames who was sitting there watching the show his boss was putting on. "The fucking goddamn laundry truck."

The time was 9:46 p.m.

1

THE JOCK ON KFAB had just pronounced it 10:07 a.m. —"ready with more of the hits you want to hear"—when the man in the back seat of the Yellow cab realised that he had no idea who he was.

No idea whatsoever.

He leaned forward, trying not to show the least trace of panic, and said, "Excuse me."

"Yeah?" the cabbie said, his brown eyes suddenly filling the rear-view mirror.

And then the man realised: *How can I say it?*

Excuse me, sir, but I don't happen to remember my name. Do you happen to know who I am?

And realising this, all he could say, his voice nervous now, was, "I was just wondering if you had the time."

"Like the guy on the radio said, 10:07."

"Oh. Right. Thanks."

And slumped back into the seat that smelled vaguely of vomit and slightly more so of disinfectant.

This was impossible.

Impossible.

He was merely a man—a nice normal man—riding along in the back seat of a taxicab and he'd merely forgotten his name.

But only temporarily. The way you forgot who you were dialling sometimes. Or the date of your birthday.

Or—

"Here you go," the cabbie said.

"Pardon me?"

"I said here you go."

"Go?"

"This was the address you gave me."

"It is?"

This time the cabbie turned around. He was this little guy in a blue Windbreaker and a white shirt. Shiny bald with freckles along the ridge of scalp bone. "This is where you said you wanted to be left off."

"Oh."

The cabbie stared at him. "You all right?"

"Yes. Sure."

"Because you don't look too good."

"I don't?"

"Kinda pale."

"No, really, I—"

"Maybe you got a touch of the bug that's goin' around. My old lady's got it and—" The cabbie shook his head miserably. Then he put his hand out. "Ten bucks, please."

"Oh. Right."

For a terrible moment, he thought he might reach inside his pocket and find it empty.

But there was a small fold of crisp green new bills. He counted out twelve dollars and gave it to the cabbie.

"You take care of yourself," the cabbie said.

"Thanks."

He was halfway out of the rear door of the cab when he realised that he didn't remember giving the cabbie this address. But he had to have given him this address or else why would the cabbie have stopped here?

He said, "May I ask you a question?"

The cabbie regarded him in the rear-view again. "Sure."

"This address."

"Uh-huh?"

"This is the address I gave you?"

"Sure thing, chief. I always write 'em down. And I wrote this one down same as always."

"I see."

"4835. Ain't that right?"

"Uh, yes."

"So anyway, like I say, you take care of yourself."

And get the fuck outta my cab, asshole. I got other fares to worry about now.

So he got out.

And the cab went away.

And here he stood, sniffing.

Actually, it was a perfect morning for sniffing, and enjoying. This was the Midwest at its most perfect apple blossom weather, the temperature in the seventies even though it was still morning, and the wind at ten miles per hour and redolent of newly blooming lilacs and dogwood. Girls and women were already wearing shorts and T-shirts with no bras, breasts bouncing merrily beneath the cotton. Dogs appeared in profusion, tugging masters behind them; everything from Pekinese to wolf hounds were on parade this morning. Babies in strollers waved little pink hands up at him and a couple of college girls in an ancient VW convertible gave him mildly interested glances.

At one time the Italian Renaissance buildings of this area had been beautiful. This was back in the days when the neighbourhood had been largely populated with young middle class families who couldn't yet afford houses. These apartment buildings had shone with respectability, the pedimented windows and arcaded entryways not only fashionable but elegant.

Now the neighbourhood was given over to student housing, serving the sprawling university several blocks north. Middle class aspirations had long since fled, replaced now not only by students but by those who preyed on students—drug pushers, hookers, muggers, and merchants who automatically marked everything up 20 percent more for the college kids.

From open windows came a true cacophony of musical styles—heavy metal, salsa, jazz, and even country western. Students today were much more eclectic than his generation of the sixties had been when the official music had run to the up-against-the-wall lyrics of the Jefferson Airplane, the Doors, and the Stones.

If he couldn't remember his name, how did he remember music he'd listened to over twenty years ago?

Trembling, he started across the street.

He stood in front of the place, looking up at the arched entranceway and remembering... nothing.

He knew he'd never seen this place before.

Then why had he given the cabbie this address?

The front door opened. A young black woman, pretty, slender, came down the stairs carrying an infant. "Hi," she said.

21

"Hi," he said.

She saw the way he was looking at the entrance and said, "May I help you with something?"

He shrugged. "I just want to make sure I've got the right place."

She laughed. "It's the right place unless you're selling something." She pointed to a discreet sign, black letters on white cardboard, NO SOLICITORS.

"Oh, no," he said. "I'm not selling anything."

She laughed again. "Then this is probably the right place."

She hefted the infant and walked on, looking eager to be caught up in the green flow of the perfect day.

He stood there a few more moments and then went up the stairs.

The vestibule smelled of cigarette smoke and fresh paint. The hallway had been done in a nice new baby blue.

He went over to the line of mailboxes. He checked the names carefully. None looked familiar.

He tried once again—it seemed pretty ridiculous, when you thought of it: *What's my name?*

He dug his hand into his right pocket. He felt two quarters and a dime. He also felt a key.

When the key was in his fingers, and his fingers in front of his face, he saw the number 106 imprinted on one side of the golden key.

He looked at the mailbox marked 106: Mr Sauerbry.

Who was Mr Sauerbry? Was he Mr Sauerbry? If he was, why didn't he remember?

The inner door opened. A fat man in lime-green Bermuda shorts and a T-shirt that read OLD FART came downstairs leading a pretty collie on a leash.

"Morning," the fat man said.

"Morning."

He could tell that the fat man was suspicious. "Help you with something, pal?"

He wasn't sure why, but it irritated him to be called pal. "No. Just looking for my friend's apartment."

"Which apartment is that?" the fat man said. The collie was

22

yipping. He wanted outside with the green grass and yellow butterflies.

He said, too quickly, "Number 106."

The fat man lost his expression of suspicion. Now he looked curious. "You actually know him?"

"Who?"

"The guy who lives in 106."

"Oh. Yeah. Sure. As I said, he's a friend of mine."

The fat man pawed at some kind of very red, crusty skin disease he had on one of his elbows. "Nobody's ever seen him."

"Really?"

"Not one of us. But we've always been curious."

This time, the dog didn't merely yip. He barked. In the small vestibule, the sound was like an explosion.

"Needs to piss," the fat man said. Then he smiled. "Matter of fact, so do I. But I guess I should've thought of that sooner, huh?"

And with that, he nodded goodbye and let the collie jerk him down the vestibule stairs and outside.

Two minutes later he stood in front of 106.

The apartment was at the far end of the hall. Warm dusty sunlight fell through sheer dusty curtains. For a moment he felt lazy and snug as a tomcat on a sunny bed. He wished he knew who he was. He wished things were all right.

He looked both ways, up and down the long rubber runner that stretched from one end of the hallway to the other.

Nothing. Nobody coming. Nobody peeking out doors.

He inserted the key.

How had he come by this key, anyway? Exactly what was it doing in his pocket?

The key worked wonderfully; too wonderfully.

He pushed open the door and stepped inside 106.

The smell bothered him more than the darkness.

Unclean. That was all he could think of. His brother and he had once found a mouse that had died in the cellar. Over a period of hot sticky days, it had decomposed. He thought of that now. Of the way that little mouse with its innards all eaten

23

out had smelled.

But if he could remember his brother… why couldn't he remember himself?

The second thing he noticed was the darkness.

You wouldn't think, on so bright a day, that you'd be able to keep an apartment this dark, even with all the paper shades and curtains pulled down.

But it was nearly nightlike in here.

He reached over to turn on a table lamp. The bulb blew, blinding him temporarily.

Shit. What the hell was going on here?

It took long, unnerving moments for his sight to return.

He felt helpless and stupid.

Gradually, it did come back, of course, his sight, and so he walked through the three rooms and a bathroom and all he could think of was Aunt Agnes, how even into the 1980s she'd kept her little tract home looking just like the 1950s, complete with blond coffee table and big blond Philco TV console and lumpy armchairs with those screaming godawful slipcovers with the ugly floral patterns.

This apartment was like that. And given the heavy layer of grey dust on everything, he doubted it had been cleaned since the 1950s, either. . And then the thought: *Who was Aunt Agnes? If I can remember her…*

He had the sense that he'd just stepped into a storage closet that hadn't been opened since the last time President Eisenhower had been on the tube…

Why have I come here?

On one of the blond end tables there was a telephone, one of the ancient rotary models.

He went over and picked up the receiver and thought: *Who am I going to call?*

And then, automatically, he dialled a local number.

The dial tone was so loud it seemed to be digging a tunnel into his ear.

Four rings.

On the fifth a very pretty female voice said, "Hello?"

He said nothing.

"Hello?" she said again.

And again he said nothing.

Who was this? Why had he called?

"Hello?" she said. There was something desperate in her voice now. And then she said: "It's you, isn't it?" And her voice was softer. You might even call it tender. "It *is* you, isn't it?"

He wanted to say something.

He had this sudden, inexplicable urge to cry. To sob. He felt overwhelmed with grief.

But why? And who was this woman exactly, anyway?

"Richard," she said. "Richard, please just tell me it's you."

And then he hung up.

He sat down in a dusty armchair and put his face in his hands. Again, the urge to sob. It was almost as if he wanted to vomit. To purge himself.

He looked at the phone. In the curious brown curtain-closed darkness of the musty, dusty room, the phone looked almost alien. How queer, when you thought about it, that you should pick up this small instrument and a human voice would come through it.

He put his head back against the chair and closed his eyes. He thought of what the fat man in the OLD FART T-shirt had said. That nobody had ever seen the man who lived in 106.

Was he the man who lived in 106? Somehow he doubted it.

And then he saw the envelope.

It was a regular manila envelope, with a metal clasp close, an eight by ten.

He saw it in his mind.

And he saw what was inside.

That was when he jerked forward in the chair and opened his eyes.

He did not want to see, to know what was inside the envelope.

The only way to avoid this was to keep his eyes open. To somehow forget all about the manila envelope.

He stood up and started pacing.

He should leave this apartment. Leave quickly.

But go where?

If he did not know who he was, how could he possibly know where he was going?

In the cinnamon coloured darkness, he paced some more.

This went on for ten minutes.

Meanwhile, on the street, girls laughed and babies cried and cars honked and buses *whooshed* past.

If only he could be a part of that.

That bright, giddy flow of spring life.

Be gone from this musty smell of death; and the sudden queer chill of the living room as he turned and looked through the gloom at the bedroom.

Of course. That's where the envelope was. The envelope he'd seen so clearly in his mind.

In the bureau there.

Top right hand drawer.

Just waiting for him.

He tried not to go. He tried instead to go to the front door and put his hand on the knob and let himself out into the warm streaming sunlight and the sweet balming laughter of children.

But instead, he went farther into the odd darkness of this place, deeper and deeper till he passed the brass bed and the solemn closed closet, and walked straight to the bureau and put his hand forth and—

The manila envelope was there, of course.

Waiting for him.

He reached in and picked it up and then he gently closed the bureau drawer and walked back to the living room.

With great weariness, he went to the armchair he'd been sitting in and sat down once more, a great sigh shuddering through him, his blue eyes sorrowful, knowing the images they would soon fall on.

He made quick work of it, then, knowing there was no point in putting it off any longer.

He unclasped the envelope and slid the photographs out.

The surface of the black and white photographs was glossy, silken to the touch. Given the clothes the women wore, and the hairstyles, these photos had obviously been taken in the thirties. But that made them no less shocking.

He looked away at first.

They were even worse than he'd imagined them.

But once more, after turning his head for long moments, he knew it was no use.

He stared at the photos again.

Carnage was the only word that could describe what his eyes settled on now.

Two or three young women, naked, their faces hacked up— one of them had had her nose ripped away—and their breasts cleaved off, leaving only bloody holes.

In the centre of a stomach a hexagram had been bloodily carved, and in another an obscenity had been cut into a forehead.

Sickened, he sank back in the chair.

He knew better than to close his eyes. His mind would only conjure up the photographs again.

But he knew he was not done with the envelope quite yet. With the photographs, yes.

But waiting inside the envelope would be a sheet of paper… He had seen this in his mind, too.

And so once more, he sat forward, and jammed his hand inside the envelope and pulled out a small piece of white writing paper.

In the centre of it was writing in ballpoint pen.

He had to hold the paper close to his face to read it.

MARIE FANE

He knew instantly who she was, and why her name was here.

Despite himself, he raised one of the photos and studied it again.

Marie Fane was alive now, but soon enough she would be one of these dead and savaged women.

And he did not have to wonder about who her killer would be.

A sullen black youth in leg irons and handcuffs being led to a police car raised his left hand and flipped everybody the bird. *Cut to:* Three SWAT team cops kneeling down behind a car as a

27

beefy white man swaggered across a night-time parking lot firing two handguns at them. *Cut to:* a pretty teenage girl sobbing about her addiction to crack cocaine. *Cut to:* a mayor's aide running to his car obviously trying to outdistance the reporter who kept yelling questions at him about an alleged contractor payoff and cover up.

The one thing all these pieces of videotape had in common was the presence, at the end of each story, of a tall, redheaded woman in her mid-thirties. While nobody had ever called her beautiful she did have a vivacious intelligence that made her unabashedly sexy both on camera and off. Her full mouth was by turns wry and sombre, her green eyes by turns comic and vulnerable, and her voice by turns ironic and sad. She signed off each piece the same way: "This is Chris Holland, Channel 3 News."

Now, a Chris Holland four years older sat in a small editing room in the back of the noisy Channel 3 newsroom smoking one of her allotted three cigarettes a day, and editing a videotape.

What she was putting together was called an audition reel. Reporters take their best stories, edit them together, and send them out to potential employers, i.e., TV stations around the country. Maybe the reporter is a city type who suddenly longs for a few years in the boonies; maybe the reporter is trying to survive a bad divorce and feels a change of scenery will stave off putting the old head in the oven; or—and this is the most likely scenario—the reporter feels it's now time for him/her to take that shot at working in a bigger and better market—trade in Des Moines, say, for Chicago or Terre Haute for LA. Or, if you've just been fired, trade in your present situation for just about any place where the currency is American and the plumbing is indoors. At any given time in the USA it is estimated that more than five thousand newspeople are sneakily putting together audition tapes and another five thousand are at various post offices shipping their mothers off somewhere. While this is no doubt an exaggeration, it isn't an exaggeration by much.

Just now, watching her audition reel whip by, Chris Holland made a judgement. In her earlier days, she had definitely come on as a bimbette. Oh, nothing crass and obvious like blowing kisses at the camera or hanging an AVAILABLE FOR OCCUPY sign on her back. But little things, teeny tiny things, a fluttering eyelash here, a kind of sexy inflection there, had definitely been a part of her news presentation. And while she was not one of those feminists who wore cast iron chastity belts and threw darts at posters of Burt Reynolds, she did have enough self-respect to see what she'd been doing. Just too cute and too coy by half.

She rewound the tape, took the reel off the editing machine, put it back in its box, shut off the machine, shut out the light, and left the editing room for up front where, at this time of morning, the Channel 3 reporters gathered to get their assignments from Heinrich Himmler's illegitimate son, a fat Irishman named O'Sullivan.

O'Sullivan had been here six years, had survived three changes of management, two changes of consultant groups, an ex-wife who still believed that adultery was okay if you didn't get caught, a teenage daughter who was dating a biker she insisted on calling 'sensitive,' and a group of nine reporters who felt he was exercising a personal vendetta against each one of them.

Chris knew all these things because two nights a week she went bowling with O'Sullivan. Most of her co-workers saw this as nothing more than her sucking up to her boss, but in fact, she liked O'Sullivan and considered him one of the few men she could talk to. Behind the ketchup stained neckties, the dandruff flaked shoulders, the beard stubbled chin, and the extra thirty pounds was a man who knew about Baudelaire as well as boxing, about Degas as well as de Gaulle, and about Edward R Murrow as well as MTV. Early on—this was just after his wife had walked out on him and Chris's own main squeeze had started being unfaithful, too—they'd tried having an affair, but it had led to little more than some heavy eighth-grade-style petting, some dawn-sober admissions of loneliness and fear on both parts, and the awesome realisation that somehow, against all odds, a woman and a man had become very good platonic friends. Buddies, even pals, but not lovers. So they went bowling

29

and got beer-drunk and O'Sullivan did the best he could to treat her just like all the other reporters on his news team—shitty.

As she approached O'Sullivan's office, she heard a male voice pontificating: "I'm saying we need Joe Six-Pack. Don't get me wrong, but the psychographics of bowling are very different from the psychographics of tennis, and our advertising base damn well knows it."

This could only be Ron Pendrake, the news consultant. To confirm this, she peeked around the door and there he was inside O'Sullivan's office, Ron Pendrake himself wielding a blue Magic Marker and drawing key words on O'Sullivan's stand-up easel. Every few seconds, Pendrake would throw back a page and start a new one, always being as dramatic as possible.

Now that he was aware of her in the doorway, Pendrake did what he always did, settled his beady green eyes on her breasts, which might have been flattering under some circumstances, but Pendrake always zeroed in on your breasts to the exclusion of everything else. He still wanted his mama.

This morning, however, there was something wrong with Pendrake because right after he wrenched his eyes from her chest, he looked miserably over at O'Sullivan. And then promptly quit talking. Ron Pendrake, news consultant, never quit talking.

It was as if she'd walked in on a private conversation that had been about her.

And so she knew, of course, that something terrible had gone on here, or was about to go on, and somehow it all had something to do with her.

"Well, if it isn't the best looking woman in TV news!" Ron Pendrake said as she came into the office. That was something else he never did. Flatter you.

Oh, my God, what was happening here this morning?

Then she saw O'Sullivan's face and he took away all her doubts. He kept his head down and wouldn't look at her.

Oh, yes; oh, yes: something awful was about to happen.

"Well," said Ron Pendrake, diving for his suit jacket and his briefcase, "I just remembered that I've got to go up and see

Fenton."

He was a little guy, Pendrake, always dashing and bouncing and diving, and for some reason she'd always wanted to call him Sparky. In fact, all news consultants should be called Sparky. There was something callow and adolescent about them, as if they'd always remain the smartest kids in high school, but would never grow up beyond that.

"Well," Ron Pendrake said, managing to include both of them in the same glance. "You two have a nice day."

And so, even though his cologne was decidedly still with them, Ron Pendrake himself was not. Now, he was just quickly retreating footsteps down the hall.

She said, "So what's going on?"

"Nothing. Why?"

"I just get the feeling that something's happening."

"Why would you say that?"

He had yet to look up. He was pretending to be mightily busy looking for something in one of his desk drawers.

Finally, when he'd got all the mileage out of the drawer he could, he said, "You really look nice in that blue suit, Chris."

"How would you know? You haven't looked at me yet."

"When you came in I looked."

"Oh, I see."

He said, "Why don't you go grab us a couple cups of coffee and then sort of hang around my office awhile. I want to talk to you a little bit." He smiled. "You really do look nice in that suit. You really do, Chris."

By this time, she was trembling. Literally. And feeling a little queasy.

My God. What was going on?

Then he virtually jumped up from his desk—still not looking at her—flung an arm in the direction of the hall, and said, "Pit stop. Be right back."

"Can't you just tell—" she started to say.

But he'd already dived for the door very much in the manner of Ron Pendrake himself.

She spent the next fifteen minutes sitting like a dutiful woman in the pea green armchair he kept for visitors. In the meantime reporters, men and women alike, came and went. Those assigned to regular beat—City Hall, the police precincts, the school board—came and went without saying much. They covered the same people every day, knew pretty much what to expect, and only occasionally requested more airtime for a story they felt would be of wide public interest (airtime, the number of seconds a story is actually on the tube, is the most precious commodity a TV reporter possesses). Other reporters really needed to talk to O'Sullivan. These were the folks who needed permission to follow certain rumours down—hints of corruption or some new information about an unsolved murder or the spectre of hard drugs at a posh health spa. These required O'Sullivan's specific approval to pursue and, if pursued, had to be done so on the reporter's own time—the rest of the day being too busy with breaking stories—fires, terrible car pile-ups, missing children. On the rear wall of O'Sullivan's office was this giant sized blackboard. On this was a line for each reporter and the story he or she had been assigned to that day. Careers were made and broken on O'Sullivan's blackboard.

Some of the reporters who came and went spoke to Chris, some acknowledged her with little more than furtive nods; TV reporting being a singularly competitive enterprise, hard feelings in the newsroom were not uncommon. And it wasn't always just over who got the best story, either. A reporter named Dave Tuska, for instance, was still not speaking to Chris seven months later because Chris had requested Channel 3's neophyte camera person, Jenny Thomas. At the time, none of the other reporters had wanted Jenny and Chris was afraid that if no reporter requested her, the girl would get fired in one of the budget cuts always going on at the station. Well, Jenny proved to be the best camera person in the station—innovative, creative, fun to work with. The rest of the camera people were dull hacks by comparison. It was conventional wisdom that the most important single asset a reporter could possess was a good camera person—one who made you look good, not bad. Jenny became Chris's own camera person. So, Dave Tuska bore a grudge.

O'Sullivan finally came back. He sat down behind his desk.

"Maybe you should close the door, Chris."

"Will you quit calling me Chris?"

"Isn't that your name?"

"Not to you. To you my name's always Holland."

"Oh."

"May I have a cigarette?"

"How many does that make today?"

"One."

"Bullshit."

"Two."

"Bullshit."

"Please, Walter, I'm really nervous about this. Something's wrong and I can tell it. Otherwise you wouldn't be calling me Chris."

She went and closed the door. She came back and sat down across from him. On the desk between them was his pack of Camel filters. She pointed to the pack and he nodded. She took one and lit it and took smoke deeply and luxuriously into her chest. She could hear her lungs screaming mercy. She told them to be still.

She said, "Just say it."

"Just say what?"

He was actually, even despite the excess weight, a nice looking guy, prematurely grey hair, a noble nose, intelligent and wry blue eyes.

"Whatever's bothering you. God, Walter, you should see yourself. You look like hell."

"Thank you."

"You know what I mean. You look hangdog and afraid. You're not going to tell me my little puppy's been run over by a car, are you?"

"You don't have a little puppy."

"But that's what you look like, Walter."

He reached over and helped himself to one of his cigarettes and then he said, "You saw Pendrake?"

"Why doesn't he go over to Channel 5? They're not an empire anymore, in fact, they're a joke now. All those fat greasy salespeople and that joke of a production department. They

33

need his help. We don't."

"Ron's been doing a lot of focus groups and—" He shook his head. "Well, you know how things can happen in focus groups sometimes."

There were maybe half a dozen television consultant groups in the country. They were hired by TV stations to improve the ratings, particularly in the area of local news, which is the single biggest money maker for most local outlets. Consultants are not a beloved group. First of all, management—only too eager to have supposedly wiser heads make the decisions—gives the consultants enormous power. Many times, consultants have the authority to hire and fire both on air talent and key administrative people such as news directors. They are constantly shaping and reshaping the look and substance of news shows in order to attain higher ratings. One of their primary tools in all this is focus group testing—taking a theoretically average group of people and having them sit around looking at videotape of various on air news teams and making comments. Based on what they hear in these groups, the consultants then make sweeping recommendations to the stations about which air person is popular, and which is not. So not only do reporters have to worry about the regular TV ratings, they also have to worry about what a doctor or garbage truck driver or minister might say about them during the course of a focus group. It was widely suspected by reporters and media observers alike that these focus groups were often dishonest—you carefully select a certain group of people who will say exactly what you want them to say—but if management suspected anything, they kept their suspicions to themselves. They were too busy thanking the consultants for taking all this responsibility off their backs.

"And?" she said.

"And—" He looked at her for the first time. "And you're going to be reassigned."

"Reassigned?"

"We're starting a new segment."

"A new segment?" She realised she was repeating everything he said; she also realised she was semi-hysterical (her world

34

was about to come crashing down) but she couldn't stop herself.

"*Holland on the Town.*" He smiled but it was a sad and defeated smile. "I kind of like that, don't you?"

"What the hell is *Holland on the Town*?"

"Events."

"Events?"

"Yeah, you know, stuff that goes on in the city. It'll be on the six o'clock strip three nights a week."

"It's a community bulletin board, isn't it?"

"Huh?" he said, feigning stupidity.

"It's a goddamn community bulletin board. That's what you're talking about, isn't it, Walter?"

"Now, Chris, I wouldn't go that far. I—"

She stabbed out her cigarette. "Maybe you haven't noticed, Walter, but I'm a reporter."

"But this segment—"

"I report news, Walter. I don't report on DAR meetings or bake-offs or garden clubs."

"But, Chris, I—"

She held up her hand like a traffic cop in the middle of a busy intersection. "Don't say anything more. Please. Not right now."

So he didn't. He sat there and stared at her and looked ashamed of himself.

After a time she said, "You got me the *Holland on the Town* thing, didn't you?"

He said nothing, just stared at his folded hands riding on his stomach.

"The consultants told you that you had to fire me but you came up with this dipshit community calendar so you could save my job, didn't you?"

He still said nothing.

"I'm not going to start crying," she said.

He said, "Good."

"Look at me, Walter."

He kept his eyes down.

"Walter, goddammit, look at me."

Like a chastened little boy, he raised his gaze to meet hers.

"Now tell me the truth, Walter. You came up with the *On the*

35

Town thing, didn't you?"

He just sort of shrugged. "Well."

"You came up with it so I'd at least have some kind of job, didn't you?"

"Well," he said again.

Abruptly she leaned over the desk and kissed him on his forehead. "I really love you, Walter."

And then she sat back down and put her head down and tried very hard not to cry.

"You okay?" he said.

"Uh-huh."

"You want a Coke or something?"

"Huh-uh."

"You want another cigarette?"

She shook her head.

"Why don't you cry?" he said.

She shook her head again. She didn't want to give the bastards the satisfaction.

"I really feel bad, Holland, I really do. If I didn't have child support payments and a big suburban house I can't unload, I'd quit and tell them where to put it."

She had composed herself again. She tilted her head up and looked straight at him purposefully and said, "How come they wanted to fire me?"

"They said you were too old."

"What?"

"They said the men in the focus groups all said they wanted a younger woman in your slot."

"With bouncing breasts and a wiggling backside, no doubt?"

"No doubt."

She made a fist and then lunged for a cigarette and lit it with almost terrifying ferocity. "Those sons-of-bitches."

"Absolutely."

"What do they know about journalism, anyway?"

"Not diddly shit."

She narrowed her eyes and said, "Are you making fun of me, Walter?"

"Nope. Just sort of saying that I have this same conversation

36

every time I have to let somebody go. It's sad—the consultants don't know anything about journalism but they get to dictate to us how we should put our shows together."

"I won't do it. The *On the Town* thing."

"I know."

"I really appreciate what you were trying to do for me, but I won't do it."

"I don't blame you."

"I'm serious."

"I know."

"Just because I'm two months behind in my rent and because Gil pawned my colour TV set…" Gil was her ex-boyfriend, a would-be actor.

"He did?"

"Yeah. He needed a new suit for an audition."

"Tell him you want your money or your set right now."

"Can't."

"Why?"

"He's moved in with some new girl named Ricky."

He smiled with magnificent malice. "Gil looks like the kind of guy who'd end up with a Ricky."

She slumped in her chair again.

He said, "You all right, Holland?"

She said, "Any cut in pay?"

"In the *On the Town* thing?"

"Yeah."

"Huh-uh."

She sighed. "God, I'll have to take it, won't I?"

"If your finances are in their usual state of disrepair, yeah."

She sighed even more this time. "'And on Friday evening, ladies, don't forget our city's first all nude bake-off.'"

He laughed and added his own lewd comment.

"I'm too goddamned old, Walter? I can't believe that. Aren't I attractive anymore?"

He smiled and reached across the desk. She put her hand in his. "You're a damn good looking woman, Holland, and you know it. But these consultants—" He shook his head.

She thought back to her audition reel. She automatically

37

updated it every six months, which is what she'd been doing earlier. Now there was a good reason to box up several dubs and send them out. She'd just been demoted and was lucky she hadn't been outright fired.

"Too old?" she said again, her ego and her self esteem both reeling at once.

He grinned, looking as he always did when he grinned, like a sarcastic little kid. "Haggard, Holland. Absolutely haggard."

When Chris got back to her cubicle in the newsroom, one of the Channel 3 sales reps was standing there putting the moves on one of the young studio production women. Like most TV reps, his high opinion of himself oozed from every pore in his body. Also like most TV reps, he was chunky, not very bright, and assertive enough to make most people cringe. O'Sullivan hated TV reps. They were always coming to him and seeing if he couldn't somehow plug one of their clients on the news show somehow; or if one of their clients was involved in some bad publicity, if O'Sullivan couldn't go easy on the guy. All this was particularly galling to news directors because station general managers were invariably chosen from the ranks of reps—meaning the same stupidity, the same used car dealer ethics that kept them in money as reps had now got them ensconced in the general manager's chair.

The TV industry was jam packed with former reps who'd taken over the management reins. This said a lot about why the level of programming was so low. (O'Sullivan's favourite joke was, "Know what the three lowest forms of life are? Wife beaters, child abusers, and TV reps." He never tired of telling this particular gag.)

Chris went to her desk and tried to read the morning paper. Thanks to her tears, she almost smeared the type. Also thanks to her tears, her lower lip was trembling. She sat scrunched up tight to her desk so nobody could see her face. When somebody would walk by and say good morning, she'd mutter something that sounded like "Mmvvfffr" and hoped they wouldn't ask her to translate it.

She sat this way for fifteen minutes. Or mostly she did. Every other minute or so she'd have this little flurry of optimism and then she'd sit up straight, shoulders thrown back, and make a fist and say (to herself) *Fuck TV news consultants; they're little no dick no brain wimps anyway.* (She'd recently read one of those books that told you how to Take Charge of Your Life, and this was one of the 'Seven Dramatic Lessons' the back cover copy had promised—Lesson Three to be exact, 'Getting Pissed and Getting Even.')

And then the phone rang.

Her first inclination was not to pick up.

She'd just sound sniffly anyway.

So she let it ring.

Six, seven, eight times.

"Jesus Christ, Holland, are you fucking deaf or what?" somebody shouted over her cubicle.

Those were the dulcet tones of Mike Ramsey, Ace Reporter. He sat in the cubicle next to Chris's. He was living proof that men indeed had periods. Chris estimated that Ramsey was on the rag approximately twenty-nine days per month.

So she picked up.

"Chris Holland. Channel 3 News."

There was a slight pause, then an intelligent-sounding female voice said, "I guess I don't know how to start exactly."

"Start?"

"With my story."

"I see."

"So is it all right?"

"Ma'am?"

"If I just start in, I mean."

"Sure."

"It's about a murder."

And right then and right there, Chris forgot about all the morning's misery.

"A murder?" She was drooling.

"Several murders actually."

"Several murders?" *My God—several murders!*

"But the man they accused—he wasn't really responsible."

"He wasn't?"

There was a pause again. "I'd really like to see you in person."

"In person?"

"I couldn't make it till this evening. And even then I'm not absolutely sure about that."

"Ma'am?" Chris said.

"Yes."

"Is this all on the level?"

"Why, of course."

"You know something about the man they accused of these murders?"

"Yes," the woman said.

"Would you tell me who this man was?"

"Of course. He was my brother."

"I see."

"Do you know where the Starlight Room is?"

"In Shaffer's Mall?"

"Right."

"Sure."

"Could you meet me there at six-thirty?" the woman asked.

"Of course."

"In the lounge. We could have a drink."

"That would be nice," Chris said. Then, "Oh, wait."

"Yes?"

"How come you called me?"

The woman laughed softly, sounding almost embarrassed. "I like Channel 3 news best and I… I guess I just like your face. You don't look like a Dallas cheerleader. And that's nice."

"Believe me, there are days when I wish I did look like a Dallas cheerleader." *Like when no dick no brain TV news consultants are conducting focus groups,* she thought.

The woman was back to sounding sombre again. "Tonight then. About six-thirty."

"About six-thirty. Right."

After she hung up, Chris called over the top of her cubicle wall, "Hey, Ramsey."

"Yeah?" he shouted back. "What?"

"Thanks for telling me to answer my phone."

"Huh?"

"Never mind."

40

She sat there exultant. Several murders, she kept saying to herself over and over again, thoughts of herself as the *On the Town* girl fading fast.

Several murders.

Wasn't life grand sometimes?

2

ROB LINDSTROM—MAY 10, 1978

ROB HAD ALWAYS FELT that he would have been more popular in his college days if he'd been a Democrat. Unfortunately, he had inherited his political outlook from his father, a large, blunt Swedish immigrant who had come to these shores with nothing, and who now owned two department stores. Rob's conservatism came naturally.

Rob entered college just as the student movement of the late sixties was beginning to take over campuses. His first night in the dorm, he watched the ROTC building on the east edge of campus go up in flames. With all the smoke and the screaming and the sirens, the university resembled a war zone. Rob watched all this from his window. He was afraid to venture out.

Rob's political opinions didn't change until senior year, which was when he met Lisa. She was a dazzling blonde from New York. She was everything Rob wasn't—Catholic, sophisticated, and unafraid to try new experiences. While hardly a heavy doper, she did introduce good ol' Lutheran Rob to the pleasures of marijuana (or 'Mary Jane' as she mockingly liked to call it), New Orleans blues, dawn as seen from the dewy crest of Stratterhorn Park, oral sex (the notion of a clitoris had pretty much been an abstraction to him), and Democratic politics. Lisa's father was a congressman who had been a good friend of Adlai Stevenson's, a man who had always reminded Rob of a greatly respected child molester.

Lisa changed virtually everything about Rob. His hair got long, his grade average went from a 3.8 to a 2.1, he started wearing the same shirt two days in a row, he started seeing the humour in the Three Stooges, he began experiencing vastly

41

shifting mood changes depending on how things were going with Lisa, and he became a Democrat.

He even went to one SDS meeting with Lisa, though when he met the leader afterward he was totally put off. The leader—a fierce, bearded, crazed looking kid who carried a Bowie knife in his belt—complained that "since I joined SDS, my old man has cut my monthly allowance in half." The kid saw no humour in this. Had Lenin or Trotsky got allowances while attempting to overthrow their government? While Rob's opinion of mainstream liberalism had changed, his feelings about campus radicals hadn't. They still seemed like self indulgent children to him.

Lisa had changed one other thing about Rob: his plans for the future. His father had just assumed that after college, Rob would come back to Minneapolis and start work at one of the department stores, learning the business from the lowliest position to the most exalted. Eventually, of course, Rob's father would pass the management of the stores over to Rob.

But as graduation approached, Rob began to share Lisa's fantasy of heading for Mexico after college, and "living near the water somewhere and having lots of dope and getting away from all the hypocritical bullshit in this country. You know?"

So those were their plans anyway. But then Lisa met Michael.

Michael Blumenthal was a federal civil rights lawyer who was at the university giving a lecture to pre-law students. At this time, Lisa's plans—after returning from her eyrie in Mexico—were to become a lawyer. So she was in Michael Blumenthal's audience.

As she later told it to Rob, she just couldn't help what happened. There seemed to be an inevitability about her reaction to his dark good looks, his curious mixing of anger and compassion, and his intense desire to make the world a better place. After the lecture, she went up and introduced herself, and they became so engrossed in their conversation about his civil rights work in the South that they continued it in the student union over coffee, and then in a little bar several blocks away over beers, and finally in her apartment where, after pizza and ungodly amounts of marijuana, they climbed

42

into her rumpled bed and made love.

And three days later ran off to Missouri to elope.

She told Rob all this the day after she got back from Missouri. She had only two weeks to go till graduation and then she and Michael were moving back to New York, him working for the government and her going to Columbia.

She hoped Rob would understand, crazy as it all was. She was sure Rob would find the exact right woman for himself very soon now because there wasn't anybody sweeter or more deserving anywhere on the planet than Rob Lindstrom and she'd never forget him or all the wonderful times they'd had.

But right now she had to run. (A quick wet kiss on the cheek— the goddamn cheek—and then she was gone from his life forever.)

Just like that.

So Rob went home to his father's stores. He dealt with the 'Lisa problem' as his mother had taken to calling it by reverting to his former self (at least externally). He cut his hair, he began wearing ties and sports jackets again, he spent Sunday afternoons watching *Firing Line* with William Buckley and savouring the way Buckley thrust and parried and ultimately destroyed his liberal guests, and he dated any number of young women who were eminently right for him in most of the ways that mattered to his parents. He tried to convince himself that he had survived something that more resembled an illness than love.

His sister, Emily, was his only confidante. Only Emily knew what Rob was really going through. The killer depressions. The crying jags. The inability to eat (or at least hold anything down for long). The disinterest in sex.

He would lie for hours on his bed, going over and over his relationship with Lisa, trying to determine if he'd done anything wrong to cause her running off with Michael that way. He hated her and loved her, missed her and never wanted to see her again, lusted after her and wanted to beat her to death with his fists.

And then came the night when he took the Norpramin.

Dr Steiner, the shrink whom Emily had secretly arranged

for him to see (Rob's father seemed to believe that shrinks were part of the communist conspiracy he saw evidence of everywhere), had given Rob pills that worked as both antidepressants and sleeping pills. He was to take three of them at bedtime.

This one particular night, Rob took sixty.

Emily, out on a late date, decided to stop by his room on her way to the late night bath she liked to linger in, and when she got no response, she decided he was asleep and she'd go in and give him a little sisterly kiss.

She found him sprawled on the floor of his room and barely breathing.

Within twenty-five minutes, he was in the hospital emergency ward.

And within twenty-four hours after that, he began a three year stay at a mental hospital called Hastings House.

He killed his first woman on the night of May 11, 1978. This was the first time he escaped the mental hospital.

After a few hours' freedom, during which time he ate a good steak dinner and rented a car, he drove up into the hills where he saw a somewhat plump but pretty young woman standing in front of a somewhat battered 1968 Fairlane, the hood up, and steam pouring out of the radiator. She seemed so helpless and disconsolate that she looked positively fetching. The image of a helpless woman appealed to him enormously.

He pulled in behind where she'd parked just off the road, got out, and went over to her.

He smiled. "You look like you've got your hands full."

"I sure do." She touched surprisingly delicate fingers to her face and shook her head. "I'm supposed to be at a wedding shower in twenty minutes."

"Why don't I take a look?" he said, sounding like a doctor about to peek in at a sore throat.

He saw the problem immediately. A hole in her radiator. A rock could have put it there or kids sabotaging cars in a parking lot.

He leaned back from inside the hood. "Tell you what. Why

don't I give you a ride? There's a Standard station down the way. They can come back and tow your car in and if it's not too far out of my way, I can give you a ride to your party."

"Jeez, it's gonna need towing?"

He smiled again. "Afraid so."

She didn't say thanks for the offer of a ride; thanks for looking at my car. She was as cheap as her watch.

"So what's wrong with it?"

"Hole in your radiator probably."

Cars went by, most of them filled with teenagers prowling the night. Rock music trailed in their wake like banners fluttering in the wind.

"Jeez," she said, "why does this crap always happen to me?"

"My name's O'Rourke," he said. The odd thing was, the false name surprised him. He had no idea why he'd used it. No idea yet what he really had in mind. He put out a slender hand (he'd always hated his hands, tiny as a fourteen year old girl's, the wrists delicate no matter how long he lifted weights) and she took it.

"Paula. Stufflebeam."

"Now there's a sturdy name for you."

"Hah. Sturdy. Shitty is what you mean."

They got in the car and started driving. The radio played Andy Gibb. The girl started singing along very low and then asked if he could maybe turn up the radio a little. Even in his radio playing he was conservative. Kept it low all the time.

When the song was over, she looked at him and said, "This is a nice car."

"Thank you." He wasn't sure why but he didn't want to tell her it was rented.

"If I woulda got married last fall, I woulda had a car like this. The guy really had bucks."

"Oh?"

"But he was all fucked up, pardon my French. Nam. He had these nightmares. He scared me."

"I'm sorry for both of you."

"Well, like my mother says, there's always more fish in the sea."

45

The night was busy. Mosquitoes slapped against the windshield. Distantly he could smell the river and the hot fishy odours on the darkness. Donna Summer came on. He wondered what Lisa was doing tonight. Probably something fashionable. Her last note indicated that she had become involved in theatre and had met the neatest acting coach. He wondered if she had already betrayed her husband and if she was sleeping with this acting coach.

He knew he had to hurry. He had to get back to the hospital before he was reported missing.

Two blocks from the Standard station, he suddenly veered right, still not knowing why. A sign said WARNER PARK, TWO BLOCKS. The Beatles sang *Paperback Writer*.

"Hey," she said.

"Pardon me?"

"This ain't the way to the gas station."

"No?"

"No."

He increased his speed. He was now going forty miles per hour. He had to be careful. He could get stopped by a cop.

She looked at him. "Don't get any ideas. About me, I mean."

"Wouldn't you like to look over the city? Just sort of take a break?"

"I don't even know you."

He turned toward her. Smiled. "I'm not going to put the make on you, if that's what you're afraid of." He frowned. "I'll be honest with you."

"Yeah?"

"Yes. My girl friend—" He sighed. His words sounded painful beyond belief. "My girl friend left me for somebody else."

"That's too bad."

"So right now I could use some company, you know? Just a—friend."

"But I gotta be at that wedding shower."

"Just a few minutes is all. Just go up and look out over the city. Just a few minutes."

"Well—"

"And I won't try anything. I promise."

"You're sure?"

"I'm sure."

She sighed. "Some guy dumped me once so I know how you're feeling, the pecker." And again she sighed. "I could only spend a few minutes."

"I've got things to do myself."

"You mind if I smoke this roach I got in my purse?"

"Not at all."

"I'm not a doper or anything. I just like a little grass once in a while. It relaxes me."

"Fine."

She took out this tiny roach clip and then inserted this even tinier roach in it. He was amazed that she got it going. She took three heavy tokes on it and then leaned her head back against the seat. The Bee Gees sang *Stayin' Alive*.

"You want a toke?" she said.

"No thanks."

Her voice was kind of raspy now. "It really relaxes me."

"Yes, that's what you said."

After he parked the car, they got out and went to the edge of a grassy cliff. The night air was slow and hot, filled with fireflies and barn owls. Below them the city lay like a vast drug dream, unreal in the way it sprawled shimmering over the prairie landscape and then ended abruptly, giving way to the plains and the forest again. Next to him, Paula Stufflebeam smelled of sweat and faded perfume and sexual juices. She had a run in her stockings so bad he could see it even in the moonlit darkness and oddly enough it made him feel sorry for her. She wasn't cheap, she was poor and uneducated and there was a difference. He had to keep this in mind whenever he took to judging people from the eyrie of his privileged life.

"So who'd she dump you for?" Paula said after they'd been there a few minutes.

"A lawyer."

"A lawyer, huh? Bet he pulls down the bucks."

"No. He's a civil rights lawyer."

"You mean like black people and people like that?"

"Right."

47

"Oh." She didn't sound impressed. "Well, you know what my mother told me."

"That there're plenty of other fish in the sea?"

"Right."

He slid his arm across her shoulder and brought her closer to him. He'd never been good at making out. He'd always been afraid he was doing all the wrong things. But tonight he felt a curious self-confidence.

He brought her to him and she surprised him by coming along willingly. He felt her press up against him, the shift of her breasts beneath the polyester of her dress, the faint wisp of hair spray, and the bubblegum taste of her lipstick. Their groins were pressed together, too, and he felt a hard, breathless lust start to increase his heartbeat.

"I really don't have time to do anything," she said after pulling gently away from him.

"I know."

"But you could always call me sometime."

"I'd like that."

And he knew, then. Knew why he'd stopped for her, knew why he'd brought her here.

He leaned close as if to nuzzle her. His hands came up quickly, and found her throat with criminal ease.

"Oh, God!" she shouted there in the clearing, in the night, in the heat. "Oh, God!"

And he thought of jism and the pink lips of her pussy and of her dark moist pubic hair.

And he thought of her blood intermingled with his come.

And he pressed his hands tighter, tighter about her throat.

And the birds of this vast night watched, and a distant dog barked as if in protest, and from his pocket he took the knife he'd found in the tower, and he put it deep into her chest, brought it down, down, and as it ripped low he felt himself ejaculate, a blind moment of pleasure he'd never known before, and again he dreamed of his jism flowing with her blood, and he ripped all the more.

And then, as she fell in what seemed to be slow motion from his grasp, he thought:

48

Oh my God.

Oh. My. God.

What have I done?

And, my God, why?

Why have I done this?

And he thought of the tower and of the coiling snake inside him.

He stood as if naked on the very curve of the earth, here alone in frail starlight, and for the first time he knew there was some other reality, some more important one, than the homely truth of the every day.

She was not quite dead, still struggling and vomiting up blood, and he knew now there was time, and he took his sex in his hand and let the jism flow into the blood of her throat and chest, and he cried out to the stars like an animal betrayed.

And when he was finished, he ran. Through whipsaw undergrowth that ripped up his face and arms, running, running, the very breath of him hot and stale in his lungs, until he fell down next to a small creek where he washed from his hands and face the blood of her.

And then, helpless and unrelenting, he began to cry and knew then he was changed forever.

An hour and a half later he stood in the dust and darkness of the tower. He had not set a match to the candle tonight for he did not want to see the snake leave him. He had too many nightmares already of the snake.

And then, as if choking, he bent over and felt the cold slithering serpent begin to unwind in his belly and slide wriggling up his oesophagus and escape, hissing now, its tongue flicking, from his open mouth.

3

FROM THE CAFETERIA DOOR to the table where Marie Fane usually sat was twenty-eight steps. She knew this because she counted them every once in a while. Between the door and the table was an open space where anybody who was interested could get a clear look at her and her foot. Most of the kids in school always thought of her the same way, as 'the pretty girl who's crippled.'

They meant nothing malicious by this; it's just the way human beings remember each other, kind of like name tags—big noses or crossed eyes or skin discoloration. Most people didn't know what had caused her foot to be this way, to be angled so that she jerked a little bit every time she stepped down, only that it was a shame that a girl so fetching and quiet and dignified had to be crippled. They didn't know about the car running a kerb and smashing into her when she was five, about the four operations that came after, about the nightmares she had of kids watching her and pointing when she crossed the empty space between the doorway and the cafeteria table where she sat every day. She wasn't poor—she and her mother were reasonably well off actually—but her friends were mostly the poor kids in school. And the oddballs; oh, yes, the oddballs.

As always, she put her head down when she walked to the table. She hated it when people called her name or drew any attention to her at all. She just wanted to get to her seat and sit down and be forgotten about utterly. This was why she always carried a sack lunch that she packed every night before school. Standing in the cafeteria line just gave more people a chance to see that she was crippled.

"Hey! Beauty!"

She didn't have to wonder who it was: Tommy Powell, an obese kid who spent most of his time in comic book stores and who proved that being an outsider didn't necessarily make you sensitive to other people. Marie had asked Tommy many times not to call out to her this way but he did it anyway. Tommy had this terrible crush on her (it was probably just as painful for her as it was for him) and he could only seem to express it in the most obnoxious and childish ways.

"Hey! Beauty!" he called again.

Then he started—another typical Tommy move—singing the words to *There She Is, Miss America*, pushing out from the table and standing up in his Batman T-shirt, lime-green pants, and scuffed white Reeboks on which a variety of people had inscribed obscenities.

Lucy Carnes started tugging on his sleeve and whispering for him to sit down. Lucy knew how self conscious Marie got. Lucy had this big purple birthmark all over her left cheek so she knew all about the eyes of strangers.

The third person at the table was Richie Beck. He was a nice looking seventeen year old who had transferred this term from somewhere upstate. His appearance, his manners, and his general bearing said that he should have been with the popular kids but for some reason he'd elected to run with Tommy's group. Marie, who was interested in Rich but too shy to tell him so, suspected that he had a secret, something he was ashamed of, which was why he hung out with the group.

When she reached the table and set down her lunch sack, Tommy said, "You pack any Twinkies today?" He always tried to cadge her dessert.

She wanted to tell him how much he'd embarrassed her by singing that stupid *Miss America* song but Tommy was hopeless. Like a surprising number of kids who were socially ostracised, Tommy took his bitterness and loneliness and anger out on others.

"How're you doing?" Lucy said, smiling up at Marie and pulling her chair out for her.

"Oh, pretty good."

Lucy leaned in and said, "Sorry about Tommy."

Marie smiled, grateful for the friendship.

She sat down next to Lucy and looked closely at her friend. Lucy was beautiful. Not just pretty the way Marie was but truly and classically beautiful. With her long but perfectly formed nose, her striking blue eyes, her soft and friendly mouth, Lucy was just about ideal. Many times Marie found herself envying Lucy her looks, which only made it all the more curious when

51

Lucy told nervous little jokes about herself— 'blotch face' as she many times referred to herself. Lucy didn't seem to know how beautiful she was no matter how many times Marie told her—because of the birthmark, Lucy saw herself as a freak.

"Have to work tonight?" Lucy asked.

Marie nodded.

"I'd come over and visit you except that I have to work tonight, too." Lucy worked at a Baskin-Robbins. Many nights, she'd bring sandwiches and come over to the bookstore where Marie worked and they'd have a great time.

"Too bad," Marie said.

"Maybe next week."

Marie worked two nights a week and Saturdays at a bookstore next to the university. She liked the job but her mother worried about it. Unfortunately, despite the fact that the store was only four blocks from the university, it was located in a transitional neighbourhood, so that in addition to students and professors, you also got occasional derelicts and perverts.

"If you had any comics, I'd come over," Tommy said. "All you got there is novels."

Marie smiled at his intolerance. While most people weren't interested in middle aged men who jumped around in the somewhat goofy costumes of most comic book super heroes, Tommy saw the real squares as Marie's customers.

"Anyway, I've got some studying to do. I've got to get at least a B in trig to graduate," Tommy said.

For the first time today, Marie found herself feeling sorry for Tommy, the way his sister might, or his mother, or some weird combination of the two. While Tommy was indisputably a brain—very high SATs, for instance—he was a terrible student. He'd never learned anything remotely resembling good study habits. He spent his time with comics—some of which Marie enjoyed—and let his grades slide lower and lower, so that now he really was sweating graduation. She knew what was going on here: a counsellor had once explained the concept of self esteem to her. People like Lucy and Tommy didn't have much. A few visits to Tommy's house had told her why, too. All the time she was there studying, Tommy's mother was in the

52

bedroom of their tiny apartment, arguing violently and profanely over the phone with her boyfriend. Every once in a while, his mother's sharp voice got so loud that Tommy looked humiliated. His mother had been married four times and was planning on marrying the guy she was presently shrieking at. So instead of retreating into his schoolbooks and making way for a better future, Tommy retreated into adolescent fantasy— he sometimes talked about Batman as if he had not only met the man but also become his confidant—and let his grades slide. When Batman liked you, you didn't have to worry about not having much self esteem.

Marie was just about to tell Tommy that she would help him study for trig when Richie Beck leaned across the table and said, so quietly she couldn't even be sure he said it, "I'll come over to the store and sit with you tonight, Marie."

Lucy kicked Marie under the table and smiled. Lucy knew how much Richie's soft spoken words meant to her friend. Marie had expounded many times on how much she liked this strange but intriguing boy. Right now it was hard to tell who was more excited, Lucy or Marie.

Lucy and Marie looked at each other. Marie didn't want to do or say anything that would spoil the moment here. All she could muster was "Really?"

"Sure."

"You don't have to. I mean—"

"I know I don't have to." He averted his eyes, glanced elsewhere in the cafeteria, then looked back at her. "But I want to." He shrugged again. "Probably not a good idea for you to be in a neighbourhood like that by yourself."

"Gosh, Richie, I really appreciate it."

He leaned forward. "How're you getting over there?"

"I usually take the bus."

"Why don't I pick you up?"

She felt herself flush. "Really?"

He grinned. "Really."

"Gosh, that would be great."

"What time, then?"

"Five-thirty is when I usually leave."

53

"I'll be there at five-thirty. I'll just honk if that's all right."

"Sure. But you don't even know where I live."

Once again, it was Richie's turn to look uncomfortable. "Uh, yeah, I've, uh, driven by a few times."

"You have?"

"Yeah. On my way, uh, downtown."

Then he was up on his feet, a slender boy not a great deal taller than Marie. He wore a white button down shirt and plain Levi's jeans. He always gave the impression of quiet intelligence coupled with a kind of sadness, which was why Marie had always suspected he had some kind of secret. "I'll see you tonight," he said, and then faded away, into the sounds of rattling plates, the odours of steam table food, and the spectacle of more than thirteen hundred high school kids eating lunch at one time.

Lucy cocked her head to the left and cupped her hand behind her ear, as if hearing a distant sound. "Are those wedding bells I hear in yon castle?"

Marie punched her playfully on the arm. "All he said he'd do is give me a ride to work. No big deal."

"Right. No big deal, Marie. I can tell you're not excited."

Marie grinned. "God, I can't believe it."

"I can," Lucy said. "See, I *told* you he had a crush on you."

"Yeah, right."

"Wait till you tell your mom. She told me how you had his graduation picture on your bureau. Did you ask him for it?"

Marie shook her head. "No, I got it when I worked on the yearbook. After the printer returned everything, they were just going to throw everything away so I—"

And then she saw Tommy and realised what an impact all this must have had on him. Obviously, he'd heard everything. He was only two chairs away at the table.

Lucy followed Marie's gaze.

Tommy had his hands folded in front of him and his head hung very low. He was not moving at all. Even just watching him, you could sense his grief over Marie's happiness.

Marie said, "Don't you have that appointment in the counsellor's office?"

At first Lucy looked confused, then catching on, she nodded and said, "Say, you're right. I do."

"I'll see you in study hall at two o'clock."

"Right." Then Lucy started grinning. Obviously she was going to say something more about Richie and Marie.

But Marie shook her head and glanced again at Tommy.

Lucy nodded and said, "I'll see you at two, then."

And left.

Tommy sat unmoving for a long time. So did Marie. She made a pass through her notebook, getting ready for history next hour, and then read a few pages of *Of Mice and Men,* one of her favourite novels, and the book she was reading again for English with her favourite teacher, Mrs Lattimore. Twice, kids came up to sit down and eat lunch at their regular table but then they saw Tommy with his head down and then Marie sort off waved them on to an empty table nearby.

Finally, she got up, her leg and foot very stiff as always whenever she'd been sitting for a time, and walked down the long table and sat near Tommy.

"You feel like having a Pepsi? I thought I'd go get one." Actually, she didn't want a Pepsi and if she did go and get one, it would have been the first time in her three years at Polk. Because getting one meant walking in front of everybody for a long time, then walking all the way back to her table. Her friends were nice enough to save her the trouble by automatically getting her one whenever they went up.

He didn't raise his head. "No, thanks."

She wanted to tell him about how he dressed sometimes—say, Tommy, those comic book T-shirts you wear just emphasise your size and make you seem younger. But now that she sat here looking at him, she sensed the obstinate pride he took in his T-shirts. Wearing Batman on his chest was his way of telling people he didn't care what they thought of him. Wearing Batman on his chest was an act of defiance—he probably knew how silly it made him look, and he probably revelled in it perversely. She was no different in always wanting to hide her foot, nor was Lucy any different in the self deprecating jokes she told about the birthmark on her face. She did something

55

now she'd never done before—she reached out and touched Tommy's hand. She could feel him jerk at the touch, as if he'd been shot or electrocuted, as if he could not quite believe it.

But he didn't raise his head.

"Tommy."

He said nothing. She left her hand in place.

"Tommy."

Long pause, then: "What?"

"Do you know how much I like you?" He said nothing, kept his head down. "I consider you one of my best friends."

"Yeah. Right."

"I do."

He raised his head. She could see the tears in his eyes. "Is that what you consider Richie? A friend?"

She felt herself blush, heard herself stammer. "A different kind of friend."

"Right."

He hung his head again. He said, "Please take your hand away."

She removed her hand.

They sat there silently for a long time. Kids came and went; the kitchen help dropped plastic trays, shouted joking insults to each other, ran automatic dishwashers that roared with the force of Niagara and smelled oppressively of heat and detergent.

"Tommy."

"What?"

"Won't you look at me?"

"Why should I?"

"Because we're friends."

"No, we're not."

She sighed, waited, then: "I'm sorry if I hurt your feelings."

"I suppose you think he's cute, huh?"

Now he raised his head. "I'm sorry I said that."

They both tried to disregard the fact that he had tears in his eyes.

He put his hand on her wrist. It was a fleshy hand but a strong one, and damp with sweat. In a curious way, it felt like a baby's hand, and so the sensation of it lying on her wrist was

56

not unpleasant.

He said, "I don't like you as much as I used to, anyway."

She smiled. "Well, I like you more so I guess that evens things out."

"You don't like me more. You like me less. I can tell just by the way you look at me. About half the things I do irritate you."

She said carefully, wanting to change the subject but not be too obvious about it, "Whatever happened to Judy?"

He shrugged. "Said she didn't want to see me anymore."

"Why?"

He shrugged again, fatty shoulders beneath the Batman T-shirt. "Said I embarrassed her every time we went to the comic book store."

"How did she say you embarrassed her?"

"Oh, arguing with people and all. Like one day there was this guy in there who said that the Green Lantern was better than the Flash. So I just kind've told him his opinions sucked."

"In a real loud voice?"

"Well."

"And making your argument very personal?"

"Well. He was kind of a geek, you know?"

"We're all geeks, Tommy, our whole little group and everybody like us—don't you understand that yet?"

He stared at her. "Is Richie a geek?"

"I suppose."

"Really?"

"Why else would he sit here with us?"

"But he isn't fat and he isn't crippled and he doesn't have any birth defects and he—" He shook his head. "He doesn't look like a geek to me." He patted his massive belly. "I'm a geek."

"So am I."

"No, you're not, Marie. You always say that but—"

The bell rang, ending lunch hour, summoning the kids back to class.

She said, "When's the last time you talked to Judy?"

"Last weekend. She hung up on me."

"Why?"

"Because she said this copy she had of Wonder Woman was

57

in mint condition but it wasn't. It had a crease on the cover and the back was kind of wrinkled and—"

"And so you told her that?"

"Sure. It was just the truth."

"Sometimes you need to spare people the truth, Tommy."

"You mean lie?"

"I mean take their feelings into account. Judy's probably proud of her comic book. Then let her be proud. Don't spoil it for her."

Tommy stared at her and sighed. "I screwed up, huh?"

"Yes."

"And I should call her?"

"Yes."

"And tell her the comic book's really in mint condition when it isn't?"

"No, call her and tell her that her feelings are a lot more important than any comic book, and that you're sorry, and that you'd like to see her again."

"What if she hangs up?"

"Then wait a few days and call her again."

Tommy smiled. "You always make things sound so easy, Marie."

She touched his hand. "Things can be easy, Tommy. At least easier than we make them sometimes."

He shrugged. "Maybe so."

"Well, good luck, Tommy. I hope things go well for you with Judy."

He smiled. "I hope they go well with Richie, too." He patted her small wrist again with his big hand. "I really mean that, Marie."

"Thanks," she said.

Then it was time to walk back across the space between table and door where everybody interested could watch her walk. The nice thing about the end of the hour was the congestion. You didn't stand out in a crowd when you had people on all sides of you pushing toward the EXIT door.

When she was out of the cafeteria and heading down the long phalanx of lockers, she started thinking again of Richie, and a wildness filled her—a wildness that was one part joy and one part terror.

She had no confidence where boys were concerned. She did not want to hope for too much with Richie because she might end up getting nothing at all.

For a time, he put his head back and closed his eyes and let the apple blossom breeze through the open window balm him.

It was almost possible to forget that he was on a city bus, and that he did not know who he was, and that he was going to see—

3567 Fairlawn Terrace.

Who lived there? he wondered.

Every few minutes the bus stopped and the big doors *whooshed* open and people got on and off.

And then the bus started up again. He liked the lunge of power. It was relaxing somehow; made him feel he was being mercifully carried away from trouble.

With his eyes closed, he smelled the pieces of the day: grass and sun, warmth and wind, diesel fuel and cigarette smoke.

And the sounds: children, car horns, radios, black people, white people, Mexican people, aeroplanes, motorcycles.

The whole human jumble of it made him feel safe again, hiding once more in his own humanity.

Unlikely as it was, he slept.

When he woke, he made a tiny frightened sound.

An old lady in a faded head scarf turned to look at him with accusing blue eyes.

Drunk, and sleeping it off, her gaze said.

He sat up straight, looking desperately now at the scene surrounding the bus.

Again, he sensed that this was an area he was familiar with but his mind offered no objective proof Neat ranch houses, neither cheap nor expensive, lined the low grassy green hills on either side of the street.

I live in one of these houses.

The bus pulled over to the kerb.

The old lady, overburdened with K-Mart and Wal-Mart shopping bags, got off. She still glared at him.

The bus pulled away once more, the forward rhythm relaxing him immediately.

If only he could ride forever...

Two blocks later, he saw the street sign that read FAIRLAWN TERRACE.

He reached up and grasped the cord that would signal the driver to stop.

And then he saw the police car. It wasn't marked, of course— the police were not stupid—but it was one of those bulky dark Ford sedans whose very plainness announced it as an 'official' car and 'official' in this case meant police.

They're waiting for me.

The driver pulled over to the kerb.

He sat down again and said, self conscious because he had to speak so loudly in order to be heard, "I made a mistake. Just drive on, all right?"

Mistake? What a stupid story. I reached all the way up there and yanked on the cord. And it was a mistake?

He saw 3567 then.

It was a particularly nice ranch style, one made of both lumber and natural stone. He put his face to the bus window like a small lonely boy peering into a house.

Why was 3567 so special to him? Who lived there?

But of course he knew the answer to that one.

He lived there.

He rode the bus for the next hour and a hall. During this time he fell asleep and when he woke, he was disoriented. Not only was his name vague now; so was his purpose.

I'm on a bus. Why? Where am I going?

And then he felt the shift in his stomach.

He touched his hand to the slight swell of his belly, felt

60

something thick and round curving across the arc beneath his sternum.

He recalled something that had happened to him once as a boy.

On the back porch, autumn winds blowing dead colourful leaves scratching across the screened in windows, he saw something move in a gunny sack his father kept on the back porch for storing walnuts. He had never forgotten what happened next. He knelt down and touched the palm of his hand to the top of the gunny sack. He was sure he'd seen the sack move —and then he knew why. Beneath his hand, just under the fabric of the sack, uncoiled a fat writhing snake. He jerked back in panic. He had never been able to forget that odd sensation—the unseen reptile slithering beneath the rough material of the sack.

Just as something slithered inside his belly just now. He could feel it coil and uncoil, coil and uncoil.

The image of something inside him made him sick suddenly and he wanted to vomit. But he knew he would have to hold it as long as he was on the bus. Which was why he got off.

Fortunately, the stop at which he left the bus was a forlorn section of taverns and Laundromats and large empty fields filled with rusting deserted cars and hundreds of jagged busted pop bottles and heel-crunched beer cans.

There was an alley between two rotting taverns that seemed to be having a war of country and western jukeboxes.

He ran into the alley just as a Hank Williams, Jr., song came on and he vomited so long he was half afraid he would start seeing blood.

As he stood up, he saw that a skinny, bald guy in a dirty white apron and holding a broom in one hand was watching him.

"Only three o'clock," the bald, skinny guy said. He was obviously the owner of the tavern.

"What?" he said, pulling the back of his hand across his mouth.

"Only three o'clock. Too goddamned early to start puking."

And with that, the guy hefted his broom and went back inside.

Twenty minutes later he came to a phone booth. This was on a corner loud with semis and thick with diesel fumes. Faces were mostly black; clothes mostly bright and cheap. The people moved as if they were dragging chains behind them. Somebody had recently pissed in the phone booth. It reeked. And somebody had also smashed his head against the glass of the booth. In a circle of shattered safety glass, you could see splotches of blood and hair. A starved dog, all ribs and crazed brown eyes, stood at his feet smelling the rancid piss.

He called a phone number.

He had no idea what number it was.

A woman answered, "Hello."

He said nothing for a time.

"Hello?"

He was afraid to speak.

"It's you, isn't it?"

"I—I don't know your name."

"They said you might be confused, honey. The electroshock you've had recently and everything."

"Who are you?"

"You really don't know?"

"No."

"I'm your wife. Karen."

"Who am I?"

She paused again. "Honey, I'm afraid. For you, I mean. You can't walk around in this condition."

"A while ago I rode by in a bus... I saw a police car there."

"Two of the detectives came back."

"They're looking for me."

"Yes. But you haven't done anything really. Nobody's been hurt. They'd just like to get you back into Hastings House."

The thing in his stomach shifted again.

"I'm afraid," he said. "There's something in my stomach."

"In your stomach?"

"Yes. Some—thing. There's no other way to describe it."

"There's something in your stomach?"

"Yes. I know how that must sound but—there is."

She sighed. "Honey, can't you see that you really need to go back to Hastings House? They want to help you. They really do."

"I can't."

"But why not?"

"I'm not sure."

A pause again. "This morning Cindy heard about your escape. While I was in the bathroom, she went into the living room and turned on the set. She saw your picture."

"Cindy?"

"Our daughter. She's six."

"My God."

"She's afraid she'll never see you again. She's been crying all day."

"I'm sorry. I—I'm just so confused."

"Won't you let me help you, Richard?"

Richard. So that was his name.

"What's my last name?"

"Oh, darling."

And then she started to cry.

He couldn't stand the sound of it, her tears. He'd made her cry. And made his daughter cry. Why couldn't he help them, stop running the way she wanted him to, turn himself in?

"I'm sorry," he said again.

He hung up and left the booth, pushing the dog out on the sidewalk as he did so.

The dog barked at him.

Richard just shook his head and walked away.

4

ROB LINDSTROM—MAY 12,1989

THE THIRD MURDER was not so easy.

A) The police were looking for him and moving around in the city was dangerous. B) The confusion was getting very bad now. Sometimes he had no idea who or where he was, almost as if he were phasing in and out of a fever dream. C) The thing in his stomach was making him nauseous all the time.

In the bureau he found the same manila envelope with the same photos he had come to dread seeing. They reminded him too much of what he'd done to the two women.

Now there was a new name in the envelope.

Doreen Jackson.

He crumpled it up and threw it in the corner.

He went into the bathroom and barfed.

When he came out he went into the living room and collapsed into the chair.

Sweat beaded his forehead. His teeth were chattering. He was hot *and* cold. He couldn't decide which.

He kept clamping his hand on his stomach.

The thing inside him kept coiling and uncoiling. He slammed his fist against it.

For a moment it stopped writhing.

He lay back in the chair.

He had brought something with him from his last pass through the kitchen. Now, in the half light of night, streetlights and car lights framing the paper blinds, he raised the butcher knife up to his eyes and looked at it.

He eased the point of it down to his belly.

The thing was writhing again.

You sonofabitch. You Fucking sonofabitch, he thought.

He pressed the butcher knife against his belly.

An abortion was what he needed.

He tried to find the humour in this, in a man needing an abortion.

It would be so easy—

Just plunge the knife straight in. An abortion.

He tried. Several times.

He couldn't do it.

He started sobbing and he couldn't stop and he ended up puking instead.

Now the thing was working its way up from his stomach into his oesophagus—

Two hours later he dialled information and got the name of an outcall massage parlour.

An hour after that there was a knock on his door.

"Yes?" he said, not getting up.

"You called me. I'm from Pussycats."

"Come in."

He heard the doorknob being turned, the apartment door slowly creaking open.

She stood in silhouette. She was tall, at least six feet, and chunky. She wore hot pants and a halter and a big floppy hat. A huge purse was slung over her shoulder. She smelled of heat and sweat and cigarette smoke and sex and night and cheap wine.

"How come the light ain't on?"

"I prefer the darkness."

"I ain't into no weird shit, babe. I want you to know that up front."

"Just please come in and close the door."

"You don't turn on the light, I'm puttin' an extra five on the tab."

"Fine."

"Wear and tear on the nerves, you know?"

"Please. Just come in and close the door." So she did.

He sat in the chair and smelled her. He found her various aromas erotic.

"You want just a bj?"

"Bj?"

"Blow job."

"Oh."

"We've got a special on them tonight is why I asked."

"I see." Despite himself, he smiled. My God the world made no sense at all. Prostitution was demeaning enough; now they were selling it at discount prices.

"Can we turn on a light?"

"Not yet."

"It's kind of spooky."

"I know."

"I can see you in the chair there."

"Right."

"You want me to come over and mount you?"

"No, thanks."

65

"What kind of thing you into, then?"

"I want you to do me a favour."

"What kind of favour?"

"I'll get to that in a minute."

"Will this favour hurt me?"

"No. It'll hurt me."

"Oh," she said, sounding suddenly knowledgeable. "You're one of those guys, huh?"

He laughed. "You really do have a one track mind, don't you?"

She sounded hurt. "It's my job."

"Come over here."

"You promise not to hurt me?"

"I promise."

She came over.

"Why not set your purse down?"

She did so.

"Now kneel down here."

"I need to get paid in advance."

"Here."

He handed her a bill. "What is it?"

"A fifty."

"Really? I can't see in the dark."

"Kneel down."

"I thought you didn't want a bj."

He smiled. "Your weekend special you mean?"

He was freezing again and burning up.

She knelt down, moved herself between his legs.

She put her hands between his legs, felt his penis. He surprised himself by responding immediately.

Maybe her weekend special on bj's would be nice after all.

He took her hand, guided it up past his cock to his stomach.

"Can you feel that?"

"Your belly you mean?"

"What's in my belly."

"What's in your belly?"

"Sssh. Just leave your hand there a minute."

So she did. They didn't say anything for a time.

"God," she said, disgusted. "What is it?"

"I'm not sure."

"It's moving around inside your belly."

"I know."

"God." And she jumped up to her feet. "You better see a doctor, babe. No foolin'."

"I need you to help me."

"I can't help you, babe. Not with that. I'm sorry."

"You want to make two hundred dollars?"

"Doin' what?"

"Cutting that thing out of there."

"Are you nuts, babe?"

"All you need to do is make an incision along the top of my belly and I can reach in there and grab the thing."

"This is gettin' too much. I really need to get out of here."

She turned and started away.

He jumped up from the chair.

The butcher knife was in his hand.

He put the wooden handle of the knife against her knuckles. "Two hundred dollars. A couple of minutes work. It'll be easy. Really."

"How come you don't do it?"

"You know. I'm squeamish about cutting myself like that."

"God, this is just too weird. I'm sorry but it is."

She turned and started toward the door, stumbling around in the darkness.

Outside the night went on. Cars. Trucks. A distant train. Laughter. He wished he could be a part of it.

He thought of the envelope he'd opened earlier tonight. The one with the girl's name in it.

"Wait," he said.

"I really need to go."

"You didn't tell me your name."

"My name? What's the difference?"

"I'd just like to know."

She paused on her way to the door. Sighed.

He knew what her name was, of course.

He just wanted to hear her say it.

"Doreen Jackson."

She left.

He gave her a full minute and then he followed her.

He didn't want to kill her in the apartment.

Outside the night smelled of violets and dog shit.

She had parked down the block.

She hurried toward her rusted out ancient Mustang.

Teenagers drove by saying, "Hey, babe, you wanna fuck?"

She gave them the finger.

By now he'd caught up with her.

He realised—his feet slap-slapping against the sidewalk—
that he wore no shoes.

Just as she reached the car, he caught her and put the knife in
her back.

"You move, cunt, and I'll kill you right fucking here. You
understand?"

His voice had changed. This happened every time. He had
never before called a woman a cunt. He could not believe he
was doing this now. It was as if the man talking were somebody
else and he were merely observing the man.

He forced her to go in the passenger side of the car and he
got right in after her.

He made her drive away.

All the time he kept the knife right in her ribs.

"You fucking cunt," he kept saying. "You fucking cunt."

In the moonlight, the rock quarry was silver.

And dusty.

She started coughing immediately.

She knew, of course, why they were here. "You could just let
me go."

"Right."

"I won't tell anybody anything. I promise."

He hadn't realised, until he saw her out in the streetlight,
that she was at least partly black.

"Get out of the car."

"No, listen, mister—"

"Out."

She wouldn't go, so he pushed her.

The rock quarry was deserted, pocked with huge shadowed holes. It was like walking on the moon. The sky was black, low; the stars were innumerable and gorgeous.

He felt exhilarated in a way that he knew was madness.

He wanted to scream and come and shit and cry and laugh and murder her and heal her all at the same time.

She walked two steps ahead of him.

He kept pushing her toward the largest cavern.

When they reached the edge of it, he stabbed her in the back of the neck and then he ripped the knife out and started stabbing her along the spine.

Finally, he threw her on the ground and started stabbing her face. Once he noticed how one of her brown eyes had been caught on the point of his knife.

When he was done with her, he raised her brown bloody body as if in sacrifice and hurled her down into the utter blackness of the pit.

And then he fell to the ground, feeling the thing in him twist tight, tighter, and then begin slowly working up his oesophagus and then into his mouth and then—

He lay there, helpless, as the dark snakelike being left him, twisting, twisting, like something newly born leaving the womb.

He was cold then, colder than he'd ever been and he knew he was crying there in the silent silver dust of the quarry, and he became aware of how filthy his hands were with blood and entrails and—

Around dawn he woke up.

A tabby cat walked over to him and stood there staring and the sweet green eyes of the tabby were the first thing he saw this day.

And then he looked at his blood soaked clothes and he remembered everything. The black girl and the thing leaving him and—

He was empty; empty.

Twenty minutes later he went over to the edge of the gravel pit and looked at the broken body below. Sunlight was just starting to move across the corpse. He had ripped her clothes from her and dug out whole parts of her torso. Her arms, at such odd angles, looked as if they'd been broken in the fall.

He went to the Mustang.

Somehow he got out of there.

Twenty minutes later he found a phone booth and called his sister.

5

MARIE ALWAYS CALLED it the Agony Hour, that time of the afternoon—actually it was more like three hours —when her mother sat in front of the TV set in the living room listening to her talk shows, programs that always featured people who had been beaten by their husbands, abducted by UFOs, pursued by radiation-swollen alligators through the local sewer system, seduced by their choirmaster, unwittingly dated a transsexual for seventeen years, or traumatically lost first prize in a national nude bake-off. By turns the audience was moved to tears, laughter, the modern equivalent of hissing, and great swooping bouts of self-pity—for who in the audience hadn't (it seemed) had a husband who wore ladies' undergarments while being a practising attorney?

Marie didn't feel contempt for all the guests, of course—not the ones who'd been molested by fathers or made the quite serious decision to have his/her sex changed or found their child suddenly seized from them in a custody suit. No, these griefs were real—because she could see in the tired, swollen eyes of the people genuine sorrow. What she couldn't understand was why they went on TV. Talking about your griefs publicly cheapened and lessened them to Marie, they became spectator sport for women who feasted on sorrow the way others feasted on chocolate.

Marie and her mother had had this discussion many times over the past year. Marie would come home to their roomy and nicely decorated apartment, find her mother in tears before the TV set, and ask her mother why she liked to sit around and be sad all afternoon. All her mother would say, her voice quavering, was "Those poor people." She said this with equal compassion for babies dying of AIDS and women who had been the mistresses of politicians.

Marie's father had died when she was eleven years old. A professor, he'd left his wife and daughter comfortable on the proceeds from a large life insurance policy, which he'd dutifully kept up even in the worst of financial times. He seemed to sense that he would die young—a week before his forty-third birthday—of cancer.

After his death, Marie's mother gave up the two-storey house on the outskirts of town, and moved them into an apartment complex close to the city's largest mall and its two best schools. While Marie missed the house, she was soon enjoying herself in the vast busy city. Here, she could be anonymous, crippled to be sure, but lost in the pace and push of it all. People noticed you but they didn't notice you for long. And anyway, a mere cripple wasn't quite so freaky in a city where people wore green spiky hair and earrings in their noses and paid people to beat them.

Unfortunately, her mother didn't seem to make the transition very well. While she talked constantly of making new friends and taking advantage of all the activities swirling around her, she mostly holed up in her apartment, and went out only for mass and a few other church oriented events. Most of the time she stayed home and cleaned. In all the city there couldn't be a more spotless apartment. Furniture gleamed with wax, appliances beamed with buffing, even toilet bowls shone whitely. And somehow, in the day to day doing of these things, her mother had lost herself and her purpose in some terrible way. While she was certainly an attractive widow—a very pretty face, dark lovely hair spoiled only somewhat by the out of date pageboy style, and a trim body whose nice round breasts Marie envied from time to time—she never dated. Oh, there were men from the church, sweaty nervous widowers or lifelong bachelors, who paid furtive night calls for tea, cookies, and coffee in the front room before the great yawping electronic mouth of the TV set, but not serious men, not serious dates. So far as Marie knew, there had never been a serious man for Kathleen Marie Fane, not since the death of her husband. And so Kathleen Marie—beginning to grey now, two chins appearing where before there had been only one and the first faint brown spots of age showing on the slender hands—Kathleen Marie had her daughter and her apartment and was seemingly content with her comfortable isolation.

"Hi, Mom."

Her mother did not raise her eyes from the TV screen. "Hi." Then, "Those poor people."

"What is it today, Mom?"

"Lesbian incest victims."

"Oh."

"I didn't know there was so much of that going on."

"Neither did I."

The living room was done in Victorian furnishings, her mother having gone through an antique period not long after the death of her husband. There were some very nice pieces here, including a mahogany display cabinet with glazed doors and pagoda top and an oak framed tambour topped pedestal writing desk. Soft, pearl grey walls and beige carpeting set off the rest of the furnishings, which were an amalgam of modern set off with small, complementary period accoutrements. Whenever anybody visited Marie, the guest spent a mandatory amount of time oohing and aahing over the apartment. This wasn't the sort of place you expected to find in a modest middle class neighbourhood.

"I'm making pork chops for dinner, honey," her mother said, as Marie went to her room.

"Remember, Mom, it's a work night."

"Oh, darn." For the first time, her mother's attention left the TV set. "I'd forgotten. Honey, can't you call in sick or something?"

"Mom, they depend on me. You know that."

Marie's bookstore job had long been a point of contention at home. Hardly rich but not in dire need of money, Marie's mother saw no reason for Marie to work, especially in a used bookstore in a part of the city that was crumbling and was by most accounts dangerous.

"I thought you were going to quit," her mother said. In a lacy blouse and jeans, her dark hair pulled back with a festive pink barrette, her mother looked almost as young as she used to. Young, and quite pretty. Only the dark solemn gaze and the tight worry lines around her mouth revealed her age and her predilection to fret and stew.

Marie paused on her way back to her room. "I said I'd think about it, Mom. That's all I said. That I'd think about it."

"There was another killing near there last night. I don't know if you saw that on the news or not."

Marie smiled, hoping to lighten the mood. "Yes, but was anybody abducted by Venusians?"

"Very funny, young lady."

Marie paused in the centre of the hallway and stretched her arms out toward her mother.

Her mother took Marie's hands. "Honey, I wouldn't worry about you if I didn't love you."

"I know that, Mom."

"It's just that neighbourhood—"

"I know. But the people are so interesting, Mom. I just like it."

And that was true. The bookstore attracted all sorts of interesting people—not just the usual paperback browsers, either, but holdovers from the days of beatniks who looked through all the Jack Kerouac and Allen Ginsberg books; smart and somewhat sarcastic science professors who bought science fiction novels and made tart comments on the authors they were purchasing; and intense, lonely men and women —women she liked to think would fit into her group at school—who talked of all kinds of books (everything from mysteries to eighteenth-century romances) with great smoking passion. Despite the shabbiness of the store itself, and the somewhat frightening neighbourhood surrounding it, Marie loved her hours in the store, feeling as if she belonged there. The people who came in there took note of her foot, of course, but somehow it didn't seem to matter much to them. She strongly suspected that each of them—in his or her own way—was a geek, too.

"Anyway," Marie said. She'd been going to tell her mother later, savouring the moment when she could actually say that she had something like a date. Not exactly a date, true; but something at least not unlike a date.

"Anyway, what?" her mother said.

"Anyway, I've got a ride to and from the store tonight."

"You do?"

"I do."

"With whom?"

Marie couldn't help herself then. She grinned like a little girl opening a birthday present. "Remember I told you about Richie Beck?"

"The cute one who sits at your table every day but doesn't say much?"

"Right."

"He's going to give you a ride to and from the bookstore?"

Marie nodded. "Isn't that great?"

But instead of answering directly, her mother did something wholly unexpected, reached out and brought her daughter to her, and held her tighter than she had in years.

"I'm really happy for you," her mother said.

And Marie knew her mother was crying. That was the oddest thing of all. Her mother crying.

Marie felt her mother's warm tears on the shoulder of her cotton blouse. "Mom, are you all right?"

"I'm just happy for you."

Marie grinned again as they separated. "Mom, I'm not getting married. He's just giving me a ride."

Her mother, still crying softly, said, "But don't you see what this means?"

"What *what* means?"

"Richie. You."

"I'm afraid I don't understand."

"A boy in your life, honey. It means you won't turn out like me. Some crazed old widow lady who keeps all the toilet bowls sparkling."

In the phrase about toilet bowls, Marie heard with real sorrow that her mother did indeed know the kind of woman she'd turned into. And didn't want her daughter to turn into. Marie had never liked and loved her mother more than she did right now.

"I was just afraid that with your foot, you'd become like me," her mother said.

Then she leaned forward and gave her daughter a tearstained kiss on the cheek.

Then her mother turned and started back for the living room. "I'd better get back there, hon. Who knows? Maybe Oprah herself will get abducted this afternoon."

Now it was Marie's turn to stand there and cry softly. Crazed as her mother sometimes was, she was still the sweetest person Marie had ever known.

"What the hell're you looking so smug about?"

"Wouldn't you like to know?"

"C'mon, Holland, for Christ's sake tell me. Three hours ago you were sitting in my office crying."

"Maybe I got a phone call."

"Oh, yeah? What kind of phone call? A job offer?"

They were in the second-floor coffee room. She liked it up here because now, around five, there was never anybody up here and she could take her heels off and rub her feet and stare out the window at the silver river winding north three blocks away.

"Don't I wish," she said.

"Then if it wasn't a job offer, what kind of phone call could of made you so happy."

"Story."

"News story?"

She enjoyed keeping him in the dark. She liked seeing him sort of beg, like this big shaggy (and, all right, loveable) dog.

"Well if it's a news story phone call, don't you think you should be telling me about it?"

"Not necessarily."

"I just came up here to see how you were doing—being a pretty nice goddamned guy when you come right down to it—and now look."

"If it's anything, I'll tell you all about it."

He took his paper cup of coffee and went to the door. "Won't you even give me a hint?"

She decided to really get his motor running. "Let's just say it involves murder."

"Murder?" He sounded practically exultant. News directors always sounded practically exultant when you dropped the word 'murder.' Murders made great visuals. Great visuals.

"Several of them."

"Several of them?"

He looked as if he were going to jump on her and start strangling her until she gave him the whole story but just then a TV sales rep came in.

"Hey," the sleek rep said. "News guys up here on the second floor." He seemed stunned that such a thing could happen.

"Yeah," Chris Holland said to O'Sullivan. "Better call CBS and tell them all about it. How there are 'news guys' on the second floor."

Despite himself, O'Sullivan smiled.

And then had the good sense to leave.

Because she sure wasn't going to tell him any more. Not right now anyway.

At the door, O'Sullivan said, "Oh, yeah, I'm making some dinner tonight. Stop by."

Then, without waiting for her answer, he left.

She hadn't been in the apartment in eight years, not since the night with her brother.

She stood in the hallway now, the key she'd stolen all those years ago damp and metallic in the soft flesh of her palm.

What if Dobyns was to walk in right now?

What could she do?

How could she escape?

She eased the key into the Yale lock. Turned it gently. Looked

76

again—for the ninth time? tenth? for a sign of anybody coming or peeking out of a door.

And then she pushed at the door and went inside.

The odour was the first thing that struck her. Of dampness, of something hidden in darkness too long, unclean.

She remembered the odour vividly from the night with her brother.

She pushed the door shut behind her.

Even in the afternoon, sunlight still golden and gorgeous outside, the apartment was a place of deep shadows.

She looked around the small rooms, knowing she was afraid to move.

She forced herself to take a single step.

This is for him not for me. I've got to be brave. Anyway, I've spent all these years for this moment.

Now—

Down the hall, a door slammed shut and she jumped.

She felt terrified and ridiculous at the same time.

Her heart was loud in her ears.

Sweat like glue covered her flesh.

And then she smiled at herself, just as Rob had always smiled at her for being such a chicken. Remembering Rob's smile, the almost beatific boyishness of it, calmed her.

She took a second step. And then a third.

And then she began, traffic sounds in the background, a baby crying somewhere on the second floor, her search of the apartment.

She spent the next thirty-six minutes going through every closet and every drawer in the place, pausing only once when she had to pee.

She felt stupid, huddled just above the toilet seat (her parents had taught her too well about strange toilet seats) in an apartment she'd just broken into.

And then she was back at work.

In one drawer she found a yellowed, brittle newspaper used as lining. She lifted it out and took it over by one of the windows. She held the curtain back with one hand and studied the paper with another. May 23, 1958 was the date. She hadn't even been born then.

But she knew she didn't have time to waste looking at old newspapers and so she put it back in the drawer.

There were rings of dirt in the bathtub and in the kitchen a half eaten sandwich that two cockroaches, antennae flicking, were busy with. And in the hall closet she found an ancient, threadbare London Fog with flecks of what was probably dried blood on the sleeve.

Five minutes later she found the manila envelope.

Memories of the manila envelope Rob had showed her that night came back in jarring, upsetting images.

The girls someone had killed several decades ago —and photographed afterward—

Fingers trembling, stomach tightening, she started to slip the glossy photos from the manila envelope.

And then she heard the key in the lock. She froze, glancing around the room for someplace to hide. But the apartment was so small—

The key turning in the lock now—

The doorknob being turned—

The door being pushed inward—

The smell of the day's heat and a man's sweat—

And there, framed perfectly in the doorway, sunlight blasting behind him and turning him into little more than a silhouette, stood Richard Dobyns.

He barely hesitated.

He started to turn.

It was obvious he was going to run.

"No!" she shouted, her voice almost hysterical in the ancient shadowy room.

She had waited all these years for proof. And now her proof was running away from her.

She lunged for Dobyns, grabbing him by the sleeve.

"I want to help you. You've got to believe me," she said.

He was in the doorway, out of breath now, fear lurid in his eyes.

"Close the door, Richard, and I'll help you." She took the tone of a person trying to reassure a child or a skittish animal.

78

"You're not the police?"

"No."

He stared out the doorway with a real longing. Freedom lay that way. In this room was only a mysterious woman who claimed to want to help him but whom he deeply distrusted. She could see all this in his gaze.

"I know what happened at Hastings House," she said.

He put a shaky hand to his mouth. He licked dry lips.

"And I know about the thing in your stomach, too," she said.

"My God," he said. "Who are you?"

And then he quietly closed the door behind him and came back into the apartment.

The old black manual Royal was O'Sullivan's pride. It made him feel like a real journalist.

Would Edward R Murrow have used a wimpy word processor?

Hell no.

O'Sullivan saw the word processor as just one more symbol of journalism's decline.

In journalism school now (or 'J' school as the kids these days called it) the professors spent as much time on 'presentation' (i.e., how to put on makeup and hair spray) as they did on writing news stories.

And it showed in the kind of writing you saw on local TV. Badly structured pieces that didn't answer half the questions they raised, sometimes including—incredibly enough—the basics of the story itself.

But the makeup looked good.

And the King Kong hair spray was working hard.

So to hell with journalism.

O'Sullivan was thinking all these uncharitable thoughts because Dashing David Starrett had just handed in another totally incomprehensible tale about alleged corruption in city hall.

Not until halfway into the story did Starrett's copy tell you which city council members were allegedly involved. Not until three fourths of the way in did the copy tell you what the specific charges were. And three times in a page and a half of copy Starrett seriously violated not only the letter but the spirit of the English language.

Unfortunately for O'Sullivan, who usually ended up rewriting Dashing David's stuff, the kid was the darling of the news consultants. He booked well in focus groups because—as one grandmotherly woman supposedly told the consultant—he 'has dreamy eyes.'

Though he was not yet quite twenty-five, Dashing David would most likely get a network job within the next few years.

He had the 'presentation' part down and there was always an O'Sullivan type somewhere to do the rewriting for him.

O'Sullivan wondered if Edward R Murrow had had dreamy eyes.

Somehow O'Sullivan couldn't imagine that.

He took a break at a quarter to five.

The news would be on the air in another hour and fifteen minutes so he stood in his doorway watching the craziness.

Reporters literally tripped over each other as they stumbled toward deadlines rewriting, reediting, repolishing. There was, predictably, a flare up of egos and tempers in front of one of the small editing rooms. With nine reporters and only three rooms, the video machines needed to complete a story were at a premium. A few times punches had even been exchanged.

As he stood there, feeling properly paternal about this whole resplendent process of TV journalism, O'Sullivan started wondering about Chris again.

Had she been joking about a 'murder' tip?

Where the hell was she now?

He went back to his desk and dialled her home number.

Eight rings and no answer.

He started wondering again about the tip she claimed to have got.

If the story was true, it might just save her job as a reporter. How could even the craven consultants deny her usefulness to the staff when she unearthed the exclusive tales of butchery and slaughter so desired by the public?

He went back to his doorway and looked at his staff of kamikaze reporters.

He had to admit that even though they all used word processors, a few of them actually had the makings of good journalists. A few of them had got into the job not because of the glamour, but because they understood—corny as it sounded—the vital role journalism played in a democracy.

Holland was like that. A serious reporter.

Maybe that was why he liked her so much (and a hell of a lot more than he'd ever let on to her, being of the generation of men who believed that women could guess your true feelings through intuition or some goddamned thing like that).

So where the hell was Holland anyway?

For the first time he had the thought that maybe if the murder call was the real thing, Holland might be in a little trouble.

And that didn't make O'Sullivan feel good at all.

Even if he didn't tell her how much he cared about her (after a few brewskis, he sometimes even admitted to himself that he might even l-o-v-e her), he worried about her sometimes.

Sometimes he worried about her a lot.

6

EVERY MENTAL HOSPITAL had somebody like Gus living within its walls. He'd been at Hastings House so long —some said ever since Dwight Eisenhower had been elected president— that he didn't even have a last name anymore. He was just Gus.

At this point in his life, he was round, fish belly white, balding, and just as strange as he'd been the day his mother had first brought him here after Gus had complained too many times about the small green Martian man who kept trying to poison him. Every time the staff recommended that Gus be granted a few days at home, he would invariably do something that would make them rescind the order. One time it was sneaking into old Mrs Grummond's room and taking a dump under her pillow because she hadn't wanted to watch *Superman* in the TV room. Another time it was dressing up in Katie Dowd's slinkiest nightgown and strolling into the games room, lipstick like a rash on his mouth, and a red paper rose stuck behind his ear. Perhaps his most memorable moment at Hastings came one September day when the state inspectors arrived to check out rumours of abuse they'd heard about Hastings. Just as they reached the third floor, they heard horrifying screams coming from the opposite end of the hall. Along with Dr Bellamy himself, the inspectors ran to the source of the screams, out of breath and frightened that something terrible was going on. What they found was that Gus had commandeered the nurse's station loudspeaker microphone and was filling all the speakers with his great imitation of a guy being strangled to death, a trick he'd picked up from an episode on *Alfred Hitchcock Presents*. By this time, Hastings was a literal zoo—a human zoo—patients so horrified by the screams that they were crying and screaming themselves, and huddling in corners, and running up and down the hall, and fighting with staff nearly everywhere.

Gus later explained that he was just trying to have a little fun and was sorry that some of the patients had got so scared and that some of the staff had suffered injuries trying to calm down some of the more violent patients. But, hey, if you couldn't have a little fun in a mental hospital, where the hell *could* you have fun?

Following this last incident, Gus was made PRN, short for the Latin phrase *pro re nata*, which means 'as needed'—Gus's personal doctor had given the nurses at Hastings permission to shoot Gus up with 100 mg of Thorazine anytime they felt he needed it. As when Gus went fruitcakes on them three or four times a week, peeing in glasses of orange juice and then drinking them down, finding rats in the closets and killing them and then putting them in other patients' drawers so the vermin would turn green and fester with maggots—which meant that the nurses were damn tootin' going to keep Gus shot up every chance they got. He was just too much hassle to deal with otherwise.

While Gus sometimes suffered tardive dyskinesia, an

involuntary movement disorder suffered by many patients who had been overtreated with drugs, the nurses nonetheless kept him zoned out most of the time. He wasn't violent enough to tie down to a bed in one of the isolation rooms, but he was sure as hell violent enough to keep pacified with a needle.

When Gus was all medicated up, he walked around a lot. He didn't harm anybody, he just walked. You'd see him in the TV room and in the game room and in the visitors' room and in the hallways. Just shuffling along in his shabby pyjamas and his even shabbier robe and his flapping K-Mart house slippers. Gone was the Gus of shitting-under-people's-pillows and getting-all-dressed-up-in-drag and peeing-in-orange-juice-glasses. All that remained was this shambling, dead-eyed, slack-jawed zombie. He got so bad at these times that he had to be showered with the most helpless patients—gang showered, as they called it, hosed off like a circus animal or a car, just a row of cowering naked people like concentration camp prisoners about to be shot and thrown into a mass grave.

Yet curiously enough, it was when he was all shot up with drugs that Gus heard the voices. They came, according to Gus, from people in the tower that soared from the north-east corner of this part of the building into the black and starry sky above.

"They's not normal," Gus would tell people over and over again. "They's not normal."

And even some of the more disturbed patients—patients who heard voices of their own—would look at poor Gus and take him gently by the elbow and say, *You wanna Baby Ruth, Gus* (or) *You want some strawberry Kool-Aid, Gus?* (or) *You want me to get a nurse and have her take you back to your room, Gus?*

But he never wanted anything. He'd just go on, shuffle down the hall or out of the room or into the next room, and keep muttering "They's not normal" and looking up with childlike awe out a window where he could get a glimpse of the turreted tower.

This had been Gus's life for nearly four decades. He became an old man, one who'd seemed to give up on everything. He was not even the mad masturbator that he used to be. He now found no solace in his groin area. The drugs had made him

83

sexless. Nor did he care about visitors. The only ones he'd ever wanted to see were his own people—mother, father, aunts, uncles—and they'd passed on long ago.

He just walked around on the third floor and muttered to himself about the tower and how the people in it weren't normal. And when he'd show any signs of lucidity—any signs, in other words, that the drugs were wearing off—they'd slap him down on his bed and put the quick sharp silver needle into the right cheek of his fleshy white buttock.

This was Gus.

Other patients knew that Gus sometimes took the grille from the air conditioning duct and crawled up the dark, dusty passageway until he was on the first floor of the tower. He never had any trouble with the duct-work passage because it was pretty wide and because it was made from sheet metal that was twenty-four-gauge steel that was S-cleated for extra support and that was crimped for even more support beyond that. Gus always went after dusk because during the day, with the full staff out in force, it would be too easy to get caught entering or leaving the duct.

The grille was located at about eye level to the right of the freight elevator in a seldom-used section of the third floor.

Tonight, Gus went through his usual procedures. Once he knew nobody was around, he took a small milking stool, set it on the floor directly beneath the grille, set his clawed fingers into the grid itself, and extracted the grille from its square.

After checking one more time for sight of anybody, Gus boosted himself up and crawled into the opening. He banged his knee as he did so. A shock wave of pain moved through his entire leg and he said several curse words that he knew were wrong. He even took the Lord's name in vain and that was especially wrong.

In the pocket of his robe, he kept a flashlight. In need of fresh batteries, the beam was a dim, almost watery yellow but at least it offered a comforting glow in the gloom.

His destination was always the same. Gus liked to crawl

until he'd reached a grille identical to the one he'd just taken out. This second grille opened on to the first floor of the tower.

Now, reaching the grille, he started hearing the noises he usually did coming from somewhere high up in the shadowy top of the tower—dragging noises, as if something very heavy were being hauled with great difficulty across the floor. And the whimpering sounds. All Gus could liken them to were the sounds his puppy with cancer had made that long ago sunny afternoon. The puppy had died in Gus's lap and as it expired it made these tiny, mewling pleas. All Gus could do was hold the puppy tight and rock him back and forth the way Gus's mother did with Gus's little sister—but it had done no good. The puppy had started sweating and silver spittle spewed from its mouth and then its eyes had rolled all white with just a tiny red tracery of veins showing… and then the little dog had gone rigid in Gus's lap. Gus had cried for days after, inconsolable. He'd been convinced that the same Martians who were after him had also been after his little puppy.

He jumped down and stood in the small lobby area. The tower had only a few windows, and they were more like slats than anything. Moonlight lay silver against the slats now. Gus shone his beam around. This was like being on the ground floor of a lighthouse. All you could see in the cramped, damp darkness was a huge set of metal steps spiralling up into the blackness above.

A chittering sound made him swing his head around. In the gloom behind him, a pair of tiny red eyes watched him. A rat. One time Gus had seen a rat in here that had been as big as a cat he had once had. Gus's mind was filled with stories his mother had told him about rats—how they often snuck into houses and ate tiny babies as the infants slept in their cribs; how their fangs ran red with blood and green with poison; how they sank their fangs into your hair and started ripping your scalp apart. Or was that last one bats? Sometimes Gus got rats and bats confused.

The rat hunkered, started inexorably toward Gus.

While he wasn't as big as a cat, the grey creature with the swollen belly and the swishing spiky tail was formidable

85

nonetheless.

The rat sprang, then. Came off the floor like an animal grotesquely capable of flight. Flew directly at Gus.

But Gus was ready. He'd been through this many times here before in the mildewy darkness of the tower.

Gus expertly brought the flashlight down on the rat's head. The chittering turned into a kind of keening.

The rat slammed to the floor.

Gus brought the heel of his K-Mart slipper down on the animal's skull. He felt a pleasing pop as the rat's brains escaped the confines of its skull, spilling out through its nostrils and mouth. The animal started jerking wildly, puking and continuing to keen, and then it lay still. Dead.

"You little sonofabitch," Gus said. And smiled to himself.

He never felt more purposeful than when he'd inflicted pain on something or somebody. He couldn't tell you why he felt this way and he didn't give a damn why he felt this way. He just did.

So even squashing a rat gave Gus considerable pleasure.

He wiped the blood, hair, and flecks of bone off the head of the flashlight—he'd knocked the light out for good this time—and then looked once more at the steps.

Up at the top of them, the dragging sound was still going on.

And so was the occasional flash of amber light.

Gus had no idea what this was. During his first trips to the tower, he'd even wondered if he might not be imagining the amber light, if it might not be some kind of illusion.

But no; now almost every time he came through the vent shaft, he saw the intermittent glow coming down the stairs like a ghost just starting to take shape.

Then, as now, it would be gone.

He went over to the stairs and set one foot on the first step. He could feel his heart begin to race, his body grow sleek and pasty with sweat.

In the now claustrophobic darkness (he often told Dr Milner that he feared they would someday bury him alive), he raised his eyes to the gloom.

What made the dragging sound?

What caused the amber glow? And then he heard a new noise—a kind of snapping sound, the crack a whip makes when it meets flesh.

And he got scared.

This happened to him every time he came here. He'd just get curious about the tower—and what was up at the top—and then he'd get scared.

Because the one time he'd gone all the way to the top of the tower, Gus had seen what actually happened in the room up there.

It was just a small stone room, with a hole in the wall near the lone, mullioned window. That's where the snake came from. Or maybe it wasn't a snake exactly.

But anyway, it came coiling out of the hole, seeming to go on forever, and it angled across the floor to where the naked woman stood.

Gus couldn't keep his eyes off her.

The only woman he'd ever seen naked was his mother and he'd always felt terrible about that.

This woman was named Sally. She was from the third floor, too. She was the one with the slash marks on her wrists. Sometimes at the table she'd start sobbing and saying, I almost did it; I almost did it, *but then the muscle boys in the white uniforms would come and take her back to her room and give her the same sharp quick silver needle they always gave Gus.*

But tonight she was up here.

And in the soft moonlight through the window he could see her breasts with the big brown nipples and her tidy little thatch of pubic hair (and Gus wondered what it would be like to touch and lick her down there; exciting, he somehow knew, exciting).

And the snake, its slanted eyes throwing off an almost blinding amber light, was coiling, coiling around her leg and coiling, coiling up her body.

And she threw her head back and began touching herself between the legs and laughing and crying at the same time.

And the snake continued to coil around her body, up around her belly and then around her breasts and then angling up over her chest to where it began to feed into—

Her mouth.

She was swallowing the snake.

And as the serpent worked its way down inside her, Gus could see the amber glow begin to shine through the flesh of her belly.

The stench almost made him throw up.

The stench was horrible. All he could think of was the way dead animals left a long time in the basement always smelled.

And somehow every foot of that snake fitted into her belly, she writhed to the enormous size of it slithering down inside her. All he could think of was a scene he'd seen on TV once when a python had swallowed a small pig, the way the jaws came unhinged so the snake could swallow the animal whole.

And for a brief moment, the radiant glow came not from her belly, but her eyes—her eyes looked just the way the snake's had.

And then even that was gone.

There was just the darkness.

And then she sensed him.

She didn't even look in his direction.

But he knew she'd become aware of him.

Gus went back down the stairs through the gloom to the duct opening. He crawled inside so quickly and carelessly that he cut his hands on the edges of the sheet metal. But he kept moving, moving.

She was somewhere behind him.

He didn't want her to swallow him.

He was horrified of her swallowing him.

Two days later they found Mr Conrad in the shower. Something had dug both his eyes out and ripped off his penis so that there was just a bloody hole there.

That night they found Sally sitting up in her bed.

She was playing with Mr Conrad's limp, ragged penis.

There wasn't a trial, just a hearing, after which Sally was put on the third floor where rooms were more like cages and where you were fed through slots in the door and where no matter how hard you screamed or cried they never let you out.

A new director was appointed. Hastings House spent the next three years staging a variety of public relations events. On Christmas Eve, for instance, they had the most docile patients dress up like elves to serve dinner to two hundred orphans. There was a lot of TV coverage.

Gus was eager to tell everybody what he'd seen. Especially the part about how her eyes became just like the snake's and how she'd taken the entire snake inside her. But nobody paid much attention to him, of course.

If he wasn't talking about Sally and the serpent, then he was talking about this nice man he'd once met from Uranus. Somehow, most of Gus's words ran together. About the only other guy who'd believe him was a janitor named Telfair, whom Gus knew had also been to the tower at least a few times.

It wasn't really a date, of course, but it was a sort of *pretend* date...

From her bedroom window Marie saw Richie's car coming down the driveway and stopping at her apartment complex. Picking up her red jacket, she walked out into the living room where her mother was watching the last of the local news.

"Night, Mom," Marie said.

Her mother looked up. "Don't forget this is a school night."

"I won't."

"And—" Her mother paused, as if afraid to speak her mind. "And be careful."

"I know it's not a good neighbourhood, Mom. That's why I'm *always* careful."'

Her mother's gaze did not leave Marie's face. "I don't mean just the neighbourhood. I mean that boy, too." She hesitated again. "I don't want to see you just—disappointed over anything."

I don't want to see you get your heart broken. That's what her mother was really saying. No doubt about that.

Marie leaned over and kissed her mother tenderly on the forehead. Her mother meant well. There was no meanness or mendacity in her heart.

She went to the door, waved goodbye, and went out.

In the hall she saw Mrs Rubens. The older lady, who always wore the same sparkly rhinestone eyeglasses and the same shade of dire red lipstick, looked her over and whistled. "You must have a date tonight!"

And then it happened: a giggle. An honest-to-God giggle issuing from the otherwise mature mouth of Marie Fane. Marie couldn't believe it. She felt her cheeks burn.

Mrs Rubens, whom Marie liked very much, winked and said, "So I was right. You do have a date tonight."

"Well, not really, I guess. Or not exactly, Mrs Rubens."

"Not exactly?" Mrs Rubens smiled. "Now what could that mean?"

By now they had reached the front door. Mrs Rubens held it open for her. At such times Marie was always reminded of people's kindness. People always held doors for Marie. Given her crippled walk, they probably always would. On some paranoid occasions, she resented them. There was such a thing as being *too* kind; kind to the point of being patronising. But then she always realised that she was being unfair—that people only meant to show her that they liked her and were concerned for her.

The early evening was an explosion of wonderful aroma—everything in urgent bloom—and lovely, vital sounds.

"You have a good time tonight," Mrs Rubens said, taking her lone sack of garbage out to the big Dumpster discreetly kept on the other side of the nearest garage.

Marie walked over to the car, aware that Richie was watching her. He'd changed into a white shirt and a blue jacket. With the collar up and his dark hair piled high, he resembled a teen idol from the fifties. Especially with his slightly petulant mouth and sad dark eyes. She thought again: *Richie must have a secret otherwise he wouldn't always look so melancholy.*

The car was five years old, an Oldsmobile, the kind of vehicle that was ideal for families but that teenage boys looked a little awkward driving. It had 'Daddy's Car' stamped all over it. As if to compensate for this, Richie had the radio up loud, playing some very punky dance music.

He surprised her suddenly by bolting from the car, running around to her door, and opening it for her.

"Why thanks, Richie."

He smiled. "My pleasure."

When he got her safely ensconced, he walked around the rear of the car and got in.

So here it is, she thought. *My first actual date. Or sort-of-date, anyway.* She'd been waiting the better part of five years for this, constantly shaping and reshaping this moment to make it into the maximum thrill.

As she sat there watching him put the car in gear, watching him glance out the back window as he started moving in reverse, she wondered if she weren't at least a tad disappointed. In her fantasies, her first date had always had a gauzy unreality to it. Mere glances carried searing meaning; his few muttered words had inspired rhapsodies in her heart. Whoever it was in her dreams (and the boy changed from time to time, blond now, now dark; short sometimes, tall others) didn't look quite as young as Richie nor did he sink down in the seat quite as much as Richie, nor did he smell of excessive aftershave lotion as did Richie, nor had his voice risen an octave and a half out of sheer plain nervousness.

She strapped on her seat belt as Richie pulled out into traffic.

"You get off at nine-thirty, right?"

"Right," she said, feeling kind of sorry for him that he had to struggle to make conversation. In the cafeteria, he had always seemed so self possessed and self confident. He knew very well that she got off at nine-thirty.

"Well, maybe around nine or so I'll go get us some Dairy Queens."

"Dairy Queens? Are they open already?"

And here he looked younger than ever. Not the dark teen idol despite his calculated appearance, but rather the kid brother got up to look like the teen idol.

In that moment something came to her—something that was better than all the gauzy unreal fantasy first dates could ever offer—she liked Richie and liked him lots and thought he was really cute and clean and appealing.

"Boy, that sounds great," she said, wanting her own enthusiasm to match his.

"You like Blizzards?"

"I *love* Blizzards," she said.

He glanced over at her and grinned. "Great," he said. "Great."

Ten blocks from the bookstore you started seeing winos and homeless people. They clung to the shadows of crumbling buildings and rambled listlessly down the cracked sidewalks amid the garbage and wind-pushed litter. There were homeless dogs and cats, too, and they roamed after their human counterparts. Dirty children belonging to some of the people who lived and worked in the neighbourhood played in the gutters, too far from their parents, too close to traffic. Nobody seemed to notice or care.

Towering over all this in the near distance were the spires of the university, great Gothic structures built at the turn of the century. While the university itself had not been touched by the poverty and hopelessness and shambling violence of the streets, everything around it had been.

The Alice B Toklas Bookshop was situated in an aged two-storey brick building that sat on an alley. Across the alley was a pizza place that seemed to do business twenty-four hours a day.

Marie showed Richie where they could park in the rear—in a shadowy cove next to a Dumpster that always smelled of rotting meat from the pizza place—and then they went inside.

They walked in on a familiar scene—a customer at the cash register buying a book and Brewster giving his opinion of the book to the customer. Arnold Brewster looked like Maynard G Krebs on the old *Dobie Gillis* show. Except this was Maynard at fifty years of age. Round, bald, stoop-shouldered, he wore a wine-coloured beret, a little tuft of grey goatee on his chin, and a FUGS T-shirt. Marie wasn't even sure who the FUGS were exactly—just some kind of musical group that had prospered briefly during the hippie era.

The customer—a proper looking man, probably a professor, in a tweedy sports jacket and a white button-down shirt and a narrow dark necktie—looked as if he wanted badly to get out of here. Every time he pulled to go away, Brewster started telling him how bad a writer Sartre (the man had bought a copy of *Nausea*) really was.

Actually, Marie had met many bookstore owners who were not unlike Brewster. Maybe they weren't quite as forthcoming but they were certainly as opinionated. They ran their stores like little fiefdoms over which they were absolute masters— dispensing approval or disapproval (this author was good, this author was bad), handing out second-hand gossip (did you know that this writer was getting a divorce, that that writer was an alcoholic?), and pushing their own pets (you could tell the authors they really liked because they referred to them almost as personal friends).

As Brewster wound up his harangue ("Camus was the artist; Sartre was just a journalist"), Marie glanced over at Richie who looked both fascinated and repelled by Brewster's loud earnest diatribe.

Marie spent the last few minutes of the verbal barrage looking around the store. One thing you had to say for Brewster, he was a Zen master of organisation. Every book was very strictly categorised and God forbid you—customer or employee—put the book back in the wrong place. If he saw you do this, he'd come screaming down the aisle like a maniac and make you put the book in its proper place.

The weird thing was, Marie actually liked Brewster. He was crazed, he was obnoxious, but he loved literature and books with a true passion that was moving to see in this age of television and disco. He knew 3,453 things about Shakespeare and at least 2,978 things about Keats and this made him—by Marie's definition anyway—a holy man.

On the walls above the long aisles of books—he sold everything from the plays of Henrik Ibsen to the sleazy 'adult' westerns of Jake Foster—were drawings and photographs of the men and women he admired most—Shakespeare, of course, but also Shaw and Whitman and Hemingway and Faulkner.

When the customer left, Brewster picked up his lunch sack from underneath the register and said, "Who's this?"

"This is Richie." Then she introduced them.

"You a reader, Richie?" Brewster wanted to know, pushing his black horn-rimmed glasses back up his tiny pug nose.

"Sometimes," Richie said.

"Good," Brewster said, quite seriously. "I wouldn't want Marie here to have any friends who weren't." Then he looked back to Marie. "I cleaned it and oiled it today. Okay?"

Marie felt her cheeks burn again. "Okay."

"I know hippie-dippies like myself aren't supposed to believe in such things, but I don't want you to take any chances, all right?"

"All right."

Brewster cuffed Richie on the shoulder and said, "Nice to meet you, Richie."

"Nice to meet you."

"Talk to you tomorrow, Marie."

Then Brewster went out the back way to his car.

"You were put into Hastings House as a patient and one night while you were half asleep you felt this compulsion to go to the tower that was a part of the hospital's first building. You had to go through the air conditioning ductwork but you made it. And then upstairs in the tower—"

Emily Lindstrom then described to Richard Dobyns how he stood in the centre of the dusty tower room and watched the snake come out of the crack in the wall and how the snake then entered his body.

She then described the peculiar amber light of the snake's eyes.

He just sat across from her in the small, shadowy apartment, staring.

And then she told him about the killings.

"My brother didn't understand why he killed those women," she said gently. "And it wasn't his fault. But he didn't believe that. He just thought that the snake and the way it controlled him was—illusory."

They sat for a time in silence.

She said, "Are you thirsty?"

"No."

"Hungry?"

"No."

94

"Is there somebody you'd like me to call for you?"

"How did you know about this apartment?"

"I've spent every day since my brother's death—as you may remember, he was shot and killed by a policeman—trying to find out what happened. This apartment is part of it."

He fell into silence once more.

Traffic noise. Children being called in for dinner. A subtle drop in the temperature; the dusk chill now despite the blooming day.

She said, "I want to help you."

"You're going to the police, I suppose."

"The police won't help us. They won't believe us."

He shook his head again.

And now he did start sobbing.

He put his hand to his stomach. "I want to cut this goddamn thing out of me."

And then he just cried.

She lit a cigarette. She was down to six a day now but she couldn't quit completely. Times like these drove her to light up.

"I'm going to see a TV reporter in a little while," she said.

Slowly, he quit crying and looked up at her. "A TV reporter?"

"A woman named Chris Holland."

"How can she help?"

"I don't know if she can, but I at least want to try. She's covered a lot of murders in this city, including the ones my brother supposedly committed. She'll at least listen, I think."

"I'm afraid of tonight."

"Afraid?"

"There was a girl's name in the manila envelope."

"I saw it. Marie Fane."

He touched his stomach.

She was slowly becoming aware of the odour; the uncleanness.

"I want you to help me."

"How?" she said.

He reached in the pocket of his sport coat. "I stopped by a hock shop this afternoon. I got these."

In the shadows, he held up a pair of handcuffs.

95

"While you're gone visiting the reporter, I want you to handcuff me to the bedpost. And you take the key." He looked at her through his teary eyes. "I don't want to hurt this Fane girl. I don't want to hurt anybody at all."

She sighed. She couldn't go to the police but maybe Chris Holland could. She might at least listen to her.

"I'll be glad to help you," she said. Then, "Do you know there's some bourbon in the kitchen? Would you like a shot?"

"Yes. Please."

"I'll be right back."

While she was pouring them two drinks, he said, "You know there's an old man at Hastings House who knows all about the tower."

"There is?"

"His name's Gus."

She brought the drinks in. "Really?"

"Yes, but whenever he tells people about the tower and the snake, people just smile at him. Think he's crazy."

"I wonder how long he's known."

"Years probably. He's been there since the fifties."

"My God."

Richard Dobyns sipped his whiskey. "That's why I'm afraid to tell anybody about what's happened to me. They'll start looking at me the way they look at Gus."

"There's also a janitor named Telfair who knows about the tower." She sighed. "My brother tried to get back to Hastings House. After he killed those women, I mean. So did the other men."

"Other men?"

She nodded, sipped at her own whiskey. "Since 1891 there've been six escapees who committed murder and were then killed—either by police or by suicide. Every one of them tried to get back to the tower. One of the men committed suicide by climbing up on the turret next to the tower and jumping."

He stared at her, miserable again. "I know why those men committed suicide, believe me."

"The thing inside you," she said.

He smiled bitterly. "The devil made me do it?"

96

"Something like that, yes."

He bowed his head and ran a shaky hand through his hair. He looked up at Emily again. "I called my wife today. I couldn't explain to her, either."

"I know."

"I just wanted to see her one more time before—"

He paused. "You'll help me with the handcuffs?"

"Of course." She glanced at her wristwatch. She had to turn it so she could get the light of the dying day through the edges of the curtain. Nearly 5:45. She had to get going if she was going to be on time meeting Chris Holland.

She stood up and walked over to the chair.

This close, the odour was stomach turning.

She recalled the same smell on her brother.

His eyes had looked like Dobyns's, too. So sad; so sad.

"Come on," she said softly, taking the handcuffs from him.

She led him into the bedroom.

He sat on the soft double sized mattress, the springs squeaking beneath his weight.

She'd never held handcuffs before. Not real ones; only play ones that Rob and she used to use when they were cowboys and Indians. These cuffs were heavy and rough.

She snapped one cuff on his wrist and one cuff to the brass bedpost.

"Too tight?" she said.

"No. Fine."

"I'll be back here after I see Chris Holland."

He reached out and touched her hand. "I can't tell you what this means to me. I don't want to get—overwhelmed again and—kill anybody. You know?"

She touched his forehead gently. "I know." She smiled and touched his cheek now. "I'll be back as soon as I can."

"Would you call my wife when you come back?"

"Really?"

"Yes. It'll all sound less—insane—coming from you. Then maybe afterward I could talk to my daughter. For just a few minutes. Before we go to the police, I mean."

He was a decent and honourable man, she thought. And

97

now she wanted to cry, too.

Her brother had also been a decent and honourable man.

She left him there, handcuffed to the bed.

Chris Holland had once been picked up by a Prudential insurance salesman in a dark, chilly bar very much like this one. This was not an achievement she talked about much—especially considering the fact that afterward the insurance salesman had confessed that he didn't find the Ku Klux Klan "all bad, I mean they're just doing what they believe in." He then said that he'd kind of lied to her and that he was, in fact, ahem, *married* and was now feeling kind of shitty about going to bed with her, nothing personal you understand. And that he'd be shoving off (what was he, a goddamn sailor?). And getting home to that wife and kids. All of which left Chris feeling just great, of course, and wondering if she shouldn't give up her career, find a nice fat bald guy, and retreat to suburbia and raise some kids.

She sat in the bar now, waiting for the woman who'd called her about the murders, and realised that in the eight years since the Prudential guy her love life had not improved a whole hell of a lot. She just had lousy instincts where men were concerned. She could not seem to understand on any gut level the truth all her friends understood—that damaged men, of the type Chris liked to help put back together, inevitably dragged you down with them. Hell, even the Pru guy had had that air about him—vulnerable, hurt, lonely.

The waitress in the cute little handmaiden's costume (though Chris doubted that handmaidens had worn hot pants) brought the day's second beer, picked up her tip, and started away.

And that was when she saw the tall, very Nordic woman in the tailored grey suit standing just inside the entrance door staring at her.

The woman was sombre and beautiful and regal and, now that she was walking, quite graceful, too.

Chris had been secretly dreading that her informant would turn out to be some obviously crazed attention starved lunatic who was going to help 'solve' a murder that took place in 1903

98

or something. TV reporters were always getting calls from such folks.

But if this one was a lunatic, she was a lunatic with great breeding.

The woman came over to Chris's table and put out a long, strong dry hand. "I'm Emily Lindstrom."

"Nice to meet you, Emily. Why don't you sit down?"

So Emily Lindstrom sat down.

The first thing she did was glance around the place. The walls were all got up like the interior of a pirate's sailing vessel. On each table tiny red encased candles burned fervently. In the darkness, Frank Sinatra sang *Laura*, from the era when he still had a voice. In one corner two salesmen types, all grins and gimme-gimme eyes, were huddled over their table talking about Chris and the Lindstrom woman, obviously trying to figure out how to make their moves. Hell, Chris thought sourly, maybe they work for Prudential.

The waitress came. Emily Lindstrom ordered a small glass of dry white wine. The two salesmen were both grinning at them openly now.

"I'll get right to it if you don't mind," Emily said.

In the flickering shadows, the Lindstrom woman was even more impressive looking. There was the clarity of a young girl about her beauty, yet there was pain in her blue eyes, a pain that suggested dignity and perhaps even wisdom. If she was a crackpot, Chris thought, she sure wasn't your garden variety crackpot.

"Fine," Chris said.

"Several years ago my brother, Rob, was accused of murdering three women. When the police moved in to capture him, he was killed."

"I'm sorry."

"He didn't kill those women. Some—force had taken him over."

"I see." Chris couldn't keep the scepticism from her tone.

Emily smiled. "I'm sure you've heard stories like this many times. An innocent relative and all that."

Chris was just about to respond when she saw Emily

99

Lindstrom's upward glance.

There, right next to their table, stood the two salesmen.

"Hi, gals," the taller of the two said. "I'm Arnie."

"And I'm Cliff."

"You're the TV reporter if I'm not mistaken," Arnie said.

They both wore three-piece suits. They both wore Aqua Velva. And they both wore lounge lizard smiles.

"That would be me, yes," Chris said.

"I'd consider it an honour to buy you a drink," Arnie said. He nodded to the two unoccupied chairs gathered at the table. "You know?"

"I know, Arnie, I know. But believe it or not, this is a business meeting for me."

"Really?"

"True facts, Arnie," she said. She always had to remember that she had a public image to worry about. Even while spurning hit artists like these two bozos, she had to maintain a certain decorum. "I'm sorry but I really am busy."

Across the table, Emily Lindstrom kept her head down, her eyes almost closed, as if she were trying to will these two out of existence.

"You may not have noticed," Cliff said, "But they've got a dance floor in the back."

Emily Lindstrom's head shot up suddenly. She glared regally at Cliff. "Then why don't you and Arnie go show us how nice you look dancing together?"

Arnie lost it. "Hey, just because you're sitting here with some TV reporter doesn't give you the right to get shitty."

But Cliff, obviously the more sensible of the two, had his hand on Arnie's elbow and was gently tugging him away. "Come on, Arnie. Screw 'em."

Arnie, still angry, and a little drunker than Chris had realised, said, "Screw 'em? Hey, I wouldn't touch 'em. Either one of 'em. I don't think they're the type who go for guys—if you know what I mean."

Now Cliff's hand was more insistent on Arnie's elbow.

"You think you're some goddamn queen just because you're on the tube," Arnie said. "Well, you're no queen in my book."

Well, Chris thought uncharitably, in my book *you're* a queen.

But then the bartender was there and when he took Arnie's elbow, it was in a manner far rougher than Cliff had done.

The half filled bar was alive now with curiosity about the scene in the corner involving the TV lady and the drunk. This was a lot more interesting than most of the conversations running, as they did, to politics and baseball and routine sexual propositions.

Watching some clown making a fool of himself over a TV lady. That was pretty good.

"Sorry," the bartender said, after getting Arnie and Cliff out the front door. "I'd like you to spend the entire evening drinking on the house."

"That's nice of you," Chris said, "but not necessary. You didn't make him a jerk."

The bartender obviously appreciated her kindness. Then he took a small white pad from his back pocket. He handed her a yellow Bic along with it. "Would you mind? For my daughter, I mean. She'd get a kick out of it."

Chris had never been sure exactly why people wanted the autograph of a local TV reporter, but she was modest enough to be flattered and so she was always most agreeable about putting pen to paper.

"What's her name?"

"Eve."

"Pretty name."

So she wrote a nice little inscription to Eve, signed it, and handed the pad back. "Here you go."

"Thanks. And I wasn't kidding about the drinks being on the house. They are."

When they were alone once again, Chris said to the Lindstrom woman, "I'm really sorry."

"Actually, it's sort of fascinating. Do you go through all this very often?"

Chris smiled. "Just enough to keep me off balance."

"I'd be off balance, too."

Chris said, "But we're here to talk about you, not me."

The Lindstrom woman leaned forward. "There's a man I

101

want you to meet."

"Oh?"

"Yes. He's waiting for us at an apartment house."

"Will we leave right away?"

"No," Emily Lindstrom said. "He's going to be there for a while."

"Oh?"

"Yes. He's handcuffed to the bedpost."

And right then, Chris Holland thought: *Maybe she isn't a garden variety lunatic.*

But she sure is a lunatic of some kind.

So Chris sat there and sipped her drink and learned all about the man handcuffed to the bedpost with the giant serpent in his belly.

He wasn't sure when it happened. It just happened, too subtle to quantify in any way, some process utterly mysterious.

Handcuffed to the bed, head dangling in an almost sleepy way, an image of his daughter filling his mind (a rowboat on a scummy but not unpretty pond; lily pads the colour of frog bellies parting as the stern of the rowboat gently parted them; and Cindy's laugh; God, Cindy's laugh).

And then his head came up abruptly and he thought no more of his daughter.

He started yanking on the handcuffs.

He thought of freedom and of what he would do with that freedom.

The girl: Marie Fane.

The snake shifted in his innards now, and he felt that crazy upside down nausea again.

Marie Fane.

He was so singular of purpose now.

He had an erection but he scarcely noticed.

He thought only of working himself free.

He searched frantically for any tool or implement that would help him escape.

The only thing that looked marginally useful was a pink

plastic hairbrush on the edge of the bureau.

But what was he going to do with the hairbrush? Pry the cuffs free with it?

He was being silly.

And then he began to growl, no melodramatic transformation to hairy wolf or silken vampire, just a low vibration in his chest and larynx, like a dog at the exact moment it senses danger.

And then he began to tear more ferociously at his metal bonds, up on his feet now, and jerking at them with single-minded viciousness.

In no time at all, he was lifting the bed from the floor. It made a clattering sound as it rose, then fell; rose, then fell.

He tore himself so savagely from the bedpost that the cuff ripped deep into his wrist, hot metallic smelling blood spreading through the matted black hair on his arm.

But he hadn't snapped the cuff. That would take even more strength and he wondered if he'd ever have it.

He bit his lip so he wouldn't cry out.

The bed was already making too much noise. He couldn't afford to attract any attention. Not if he wanted to get out of here.

He knew that he had, at most, one or two chances left. Somebody was bound to call the police if he kept banging away at the bed.

He crouched down, trying to get better leverage on the bedpost.

He closed his eyes, trying to focus all his energy on the handcuffs.

Just the right amount of pressure and—

And then he felt the snake inside him shift again.

Oddly, this time there was no sense of nausea.

Indeed, if anything, he felt stronger, tougher than ever.

He bent forward a few inches, prepared himself mentally for the struggle with the bed, and then started counting backward from ten.

Ten... Nine... Eight... Seven... Six... Five...

(I've got to fucking do it this time.)

103

Four… Three… Two… One…

He jerked the handcuffs so hard that he not only lifted the entire bed off the floor but smashed it directly into the wall as well.

From upstairs, the floor erupted with pounding and a Mexican voice shouted something about *fuckin' stop it man or I'm callin' the police.*

He fell to the floor in terrible pain.

He had put so much pressure on the wrist that it now felt broken.

He got up on his haunches, holding his wrist tenderly, tears rolling down his cheeks, just rocking back and forth.

Twenty minutes went by.

He stopped crying, but his wrist didn't feel any better.

And then he was ready again.

He had to get out of here before Emily Lindstrom got back. So he prepared himself once more.

This time, almost as if for luck, he lay the palm of his free hand flat against his belly and felt the snake coil and uncoil inside.

Once again, he felt younger, stronger, tougher.

He stood up.

This time, he put his foot against the brace that ran across the bottom of the front post.

His weight would hold the bed down while he pulled. He should have thought of this before.

And then he heard her voice: Emily.

In the hallway.

Goddamn. He hadn't expected her so soon.

He turned his attention fully to the bed now. Concentrated. Foot against the brace. Painful wrist ready to be tugged on again.

Five… Four… Three…

(Emily closer now. "It's right down here.")

Two… One…

The pain was blinding.

He could scarcely stop himself from screaming.

He heard and felt rather than saw—the pain kept him blind—

104

the cuff snap away from the bedpost.

And then he was free.

If you could call it that.

Marie Fane.

She was all he could think of.

He ran to the window.

(Emily with her key in the door now, saying to somebody: "Something's wrong in there.")

And then opening the window and diving through it to the chill but grassy ground below. Free, goddammit: free.

He took off running.

He put his face down near the sink and spent the next two minutes splashing himself with cold water.

He needed to be revived, brought out of his stupor. He was having the thoughts he hated to have and he needed to do something about them.

Then somebody was there: "Walter?"

"Yeah."

"Phone. It's Holland."

"Okay. Thanks."

Before going out, O'Sullivan picked up the can of Lysol air freshener (pine scent this time around) and sprayed the one-stall john that was just off the news studio. He'd got very uptight about the aroma of his stools since management (ever the trendy ones) had turned the news studio johns unisex. He didn't mind if *men* knew he'd had Mexican food for lunch, but women were a different matter entirely.

The newsroom had virtually shut down. The early evening news over with, most reporters had scurried away to meet spouses and lovers. Ordinarily, unless there was a critical breaking news story, everybody took an hour and a half for dinner and then came back to grind out the ten o'clock edition.

A lone light flickered on the phone buttons. O'Sullivan picked up.

And spent the next fifteen minutes listening.

He knew that the Lindstrom woman who Holland described

105

was sitting right next to her so he didn't say anything sarcastic. He just said, "I'd be real leery of this story, Holland."

"We don't know where Dobyns went."

"Why don't you call the police?"

"We have."

"Have you looked for a Marie Fane in the phone book?"

"Of course."

"And nothing?"

"Nothing. There are seven Fanes. None of the six who answered were or knew of a Marie Fane."

"I wish I could help you." O'Sullivan had visions of the small Italian joint around the corner. A little table in the rear with the cliché red-and-white-checkered tablecloth in the back and a green wine bottle with candle drippings running down the neck and a small steady candle glow lighting the really sweet face of Chris Holland across from him. That's how he wanted to spend his break. Not chasing down some stupid story that more properly belonged to the *National Enquirer*.

"You can help me, Walter."

"Oh, shit. Here we go."

"There's a janitor."

"A janitor." He couldn't help being sarcastic. At least this one time.

"Yes, Walter. A janitor."

"What about him?"

"Emily talked to him on several occasions. He worked at Hastings House for forty years before he retired. He knows what's going on there. Dobyns may have contacted him. He may know something about this Marie Fane. Could you go talk to him?"

"I thought we were going to have dinner."

"We'll have dinner afterward."

"Afterward. Right."

"You want his address?"

"Whose address?"

"The janitor's address. God, Walter, you're supposed to be a news director."

"Yeah. A hungry one."

106

"Here's his name and address." So she gave it to him.

Reluctantly, he wrote it down.

"We're going to keep trying to find Marie Fane," Chris said.

"I can't believe you're buying all this."

"I'm not. Not entirely, anyway. But it's a lot more interesting than *On the Town*."

He sighed. "Yeah, I suppose that's true." He paused. "Holland, I was going to put the moves on you again tonight."

"Really?"

"Really."

"I thought we'd kind of given up on that."

"Well, no harm in trying again."

"I'd like that, Walter."

"I thought I'd buy you some pasta and a nice salad—"

"Come on, Walter. We've got work to do."

"Thanks for reminding me."

"Please go see the janitor. All right?"

"All right."

He hung up.

When he turned around and faced the deserted newsroom, he realised how lonely he felt most of the time. Cynical as he was about human nature, he needed other people around him.

Especially one person in particular named Chris Holland.

He hadn't been kidding about putting the moves on her. Who said a romance couldn't grow out of a friendship? He was already reading about just such relationships in all the magazines *(Redbook, Cosmopolitan, Good Housekeeping)* that the women were leaving in the unisex john.

He was still hoping that someday somebody would leave new copies of *Baseball Digest and Sports Illustrated* in there as well.

Resigning himself to the fact that dinner tonight was going to be at the McDonald's drive-up window, he tugged on his unlined London Fog and went out the back door to the parking lot.

She had long been a believer in premonitions, Kathleen Fane had.

One day in second grade she'd stared over at the boy across

the aisle from her—Bobby Bannock by name—and saw a strange light encircling his head. Years later, she would come to know this curious configuration of sculptured neon as an 'aura' but on that long-ago day all she knew was that the light—even though she had nothing to compare it to—bespoke something terrible that was soon to happen to Bobby Bannock.

Sister Mary Carmelita had caught her staring at Bobby and had harshly chastised Kathleen for doing so. Sister Mary Carmelita did not much approve of girls and boys interacting, even on so harmless a level as staring.

Blushing, Kathleen had sat up straight in her desk and looked at the blackboard where the nun had just finished writing the words 'Christopher Columbus.'

She did not look at Bobby the rest of the day, not even at recess when she usually sat beneath a shade tree daintily eating the crisp red autumn apple her mother always poked into the pocket of her blue buttoned sweater.

Three days later, just after school, just at the corner that so many parents complained about, Bobby was struck by a black Ford and killed. One little girl actually saw Bobby's head strike the pavement and heard his skull crack. A little boy insisted that he'd actually seen Bobby's brains ooze out through that crack.

Ever since, Kathleen had felt in some way responsible for Bobby's death. Even if he'd laughed at her—he had usually laughed at most things she'd said—she should have warned him, told him about the strange light around his head and what it portended.

She stood now at the dusk window watching the walk below. In three and a half hours, her daughter Marie would be walking up those stairs, on her way back from the bookstore and what amounted to her first date. The autumn sky—salmon pink and grey streaked with yellow now at evening—struggled to give birth to night.

Kathleen wished now that she'd handled the whole matter better.

In her defence, she thought that she might have been more receptive to the idea of a date—even admittedly an informal one—if only Marie had given her a little warning.

Kathleen shook her head.

Sometimes her life seemed to be little more than a long list of regrets.

These days she wished, for example, that she'd been more compliant with her husband where sex was concerned. He really hadn't asked for much but Kathleen had always been something of a prude and the notion of actually putting his thing in her mouth— Well, without exactly knowing why, the whole idea had always frightened her. Now she wished she'd done it, at least a few times, and at least with the pretence of enjoyment. She'd certainly enjoyed it when he'd put his mouth on her down there and—

So many regrets with Marie these days.

How badly Kathleen wanted to strike the right balance of strict but compassionate. That was the key to raising a teenager well. Strict but compassionate.

Tonight was a milestone of sorts in Marie's life. That's where the compassion should have come in. Kathleen should have shared Marie's obvious excitement for the evening.

And now there was the premonition.

It wasn't a vision. She hadn't seen any curious light around Marie's head this afternoon.

It was just a *feeling*.

A terrible, fluttering feeling in both her chest and her stomach.

Something awful was going to happen to Marie tonight.

That's where the strict came in.

She should have risked disappointing or even angering Marie and just said it—*Even though you think I'm being hysterical honey, I've just got this notion about tonight. This feeling, honey. There's no other way to explain it. I know you think your mother's crazy and old-fashioned and just trying to spoil all your fun but, honey— (And then maybe she'd tell Marie, for the first time ever, about little Bobby Bannock in second grade, and about the terrible thing that had happened to him and about the terrible sin Kathleen had committed by not warning him—)*

She continued to stare out the window.

The downtown buildings were outlined in black against a dark blue sky. Somewhere in this evening radiance was her daughter who thought she was so big and impervious but was still this little girl—

Then Kathleen smiled.

She thought of how freaky Marie considered herself. No matter how many times you told her how pretty she was or how bright or how giving or caring—

No matter what you said, Marie always considered herself a freak.

Her foot, of course. That was the culprit.

You couldn't really be pretty or bright and walk with a limp. That was what Marie thought. Believed.

So tonight would be good for her.

She hoped the boy somehow convinced Marie that she was a worthy and desirable person.

Self-esteem, Kathleen thought. Oprah and Phil and Sally Jessy and even Geraldo preached it, and so did most modern psychologists.

Self-esteem: without it you had nothing.

For a time she followed the arc of a small private plane across the very top of the sky.

Flight had always fascinated her, especially at night when the small moving lights on the wings and tail were like stars mysteriously crossing the firmament.

But then her dread premonition returned, and Kathleen forgot all about aeroplanes and stars, and thought again of Marie. Something was going to happen.

She was sure of it.

7

SEVERAL BLOCKS from the apartment building, Dobyns came running out from an alley. He was panting, staggering. He was not used to running this way.

He quickly became aware of a young mother pushing a stroller watching him.

He could imagine how he looked.

The mother shook her head in great distaste and hurried on by.

Bitch, Dobyns thought.

Smug fucking bitch.

Another block down, he found a taxi.

Guy was in there behind the wheel reading a paperback in the dim light of the overhead. Wonder the guy wasn't blind by now.

Dobyns got in the back seat. Slammed the door.

The guy put the paperback away with great reluctance, as if he were doing Dobyns here quite a favour.

"Okay," the guy said, addressing his body to the wheel.

Dobyns gave him the address.

For the first time, the cabbie took a look at Dobyns. A good one, anyway.

In the rear-view, the cabbie's eyes narrowed. Lots of cabbies got murdered these days.

A sweaty, dishevelled, panting man with crazed eyes would seem to fit the profile of Those To Be Avoided.

"You got money?" the cabbie said. "Yeah."

"Mind if I see it?"

"Why?"

The cabbie sighed. Picked up the microphone of his two-way radio. "You want me to call the fuckin' cops, pal?"

"No," Dobyns said.

"Then let's see your money."

Dobyns dug into his pants pocket and came up with a fistful of bills.

He found a twenty and handed it over to the driver.

"Sorry," the man said. "But these days you got to cover your ass."

Dobyns said nothing, sat back. "Could you turn off that light?" He wanted to be in darkness.

"The overhead?"

"Yeah."

"Bothers you, huh?"

"Yeah."

In the rear-view the cabbie offered Dobyns a small white slice of grin. "What're you, pal, some kind of vampire or something?"

The cab pulled away with the overhead light off, the cabbie's laughter trailing out the window. He seemed to find his vampire gag a major source of yuks.

In memory, the street was a perfect image from a song by Elvis early on, or Chuck Berry or Little Richard—a street where chopped and channelled '51 Mercs and '53 Oldsmobiles ferried dazzling ponytailed girls and carefully duck tailed boys up and down the avenue, where corner boys dangled Lucky Strikes from their lips and kept copies of The Amboy Dukes *in back pockets of Levi's jeans from which the belt loops had been cut away with razor blades. The sounds: glas-pak mufflers rumbling; jukeboxes thundering Fats Domino's* Ain't That a Shame *(forget the white boy bullshit Pat Boone version); police sirens cutting the night and sounding somehow cool and threatening at the same time (like a sound effect from one of the juvenile delinquent movies that always played on the double bill at the State); Italian babies screaming from tiny apartments; Irish babies screaming; black babies screaming; an argument ending with "Fuck you!" "Well fuck you too!" as one corner boy walks away from another, not really wanting to get into it (unlike movie pain, real pain hurts); and talk talk talk, wives and husbands, lovers, little kids having just gluttoned themselves on* Captain Video *and imitating the Cap'n now, and old lonely ladies saying prayers for somebody in the parish, heart attack or cancer suddenly striking. And the smells. Evening in Paris on the girls and Wildroot on the boys and cigarette smoke and Doublemint gum and smoke autumn chill and cheeseburgers with lots of thick whorls of onion and night itself, the neon of it, and the vast harrowing potential of it, too (a guy could get laid; a guy could get knifed; a guy could find God; it was great giddy fun, the vast potential of this night, and it was scary as hell too).*

What O'Sullivan wanted to know was how did you get from skinny, gangly corner boy looking good in his duck's ass and mandatory black leather jacket to now—to age-forty-three-thirty-pounds-overweight-worrier-TV-news-director?

How exactly did that happen anyway? Didn't you get to stay eighteen forever?

He stood now in the street of his youth, wondering about

this. Sometimes he had the feeling that his life—the life he'd really been meant to lead—was like a bus that was always pulling away from the corner before he could quite get aboard. So instead of being a spy or assassin or lonely cowpoke he'd ended up a news director with corns on his feet, anxiety pains in his stomach, and this dim animal notion that given the dull life he'd led, his death would be anticlimactic.

He hadn't been back in this old neighbourhood in years and if Holland hadn't conned him into it, he'd never have come back, either. Too many memories of when he'd been a reasonably cool teenager unwittingly on his way to becoming a decidedly uncool middle-ager.

O'Sullivan crossed the street toward the address he was looking for.

It had all changed.

What had once been bright was now grimy; what had once been sturdy now leaned and sagged.

Long gone were the teenagers of his time. Now there was a new language, Vietnamese, and it coiled through the dark air like a twisting yellow snake, touching the shuffling frightened old man with his shopping bag as he hurried back to his social security hovel; and the wino on his knees in the alley vomiting; and the fat Irish cop beyond rage, beyond fear any longer, sitting lonely in his squad car eating doughnuts and trying not to think about the fact that he didn't have hard ons anymore, he had soft ons.

The janitor O'Sullivan was looking for lived at the opposite end of the street above a Laundromat. As he climbed the enclosed stairs on the side of the building, O'Sullivan could hear the thrum of big industrial sized washers threatening to tear from their mountings; and he smelled the high sour stench of dirty water washing even dirtier clothes. Even this late in the evening—suppertime—you could hear the sad wail of poor little two and three-year-olds running around on the filthy linoleum floor of the Laundromat while their ADC mothers smoked endless cigarettes and gossiped about their boyfriends, especially black boyfriends whom their social workers seemed to disapprove of on general principle ("Sharon, you shouldn't

113

ought to let him wump on you like that, you know?").

The narrow passage upward smelled of fading sunlight and garbage. There was only one door at the top of the stairs and he discovered it was locked. He knocked three times before he heard something tapping on the other side of the door.

The sound was as regular and odd as a woodpecker's rapping. He wondered what it could be and—

—and then an image filled his mind.

Blind man with a cane.

Moving across a wooden floor.

Tapping.

The door opened up and there stood just such a man. Or at least O'Sullivan *thought* there stood just such a man. In the dusty gloom, he couldn't be sure.

All he could be sure of was the stench.

This apartment hadn't been cleaned since 1946 or something like that. It didn't say much for his janitorial skills.

"Are you Mr Telfair?"

"Yes."

"My name is O'Sullivan. I'm from Channel 3 news."

"Channel 3 news?"

"Yes."

"Is something wrong?"

"I'd just like to talk to you a few minutes."

"About what?"

"Well, when you were employed at Hastings House."

"Forty years."

"Forty years?"

"That's how long I worked there."

"Oh. I see. That's a long time."

"A hell of a long time." Then, at least as far as O'Sullivan could tell, Telfair turned back toward the interior of the dusty apartment.

The tapping started again.

In the darkness of the apartment, the tip of the cane against the wood tap-tapping had an eerie resonance.

O'Sullivan followed Telfair around the corner of the hallway and there lay the living room. Light from the street below painted it in various neon colours—blue-red-green; green-red-blue flashing alternately.

O'Sullivan got his first good look at the old bastard. He was blind all right, with eyes the colour of Milk of Magnesia. His head was impossibly small, like a head cannibals had shrunk, with wild strands of white hair jutting out spikelike. His slack mouth ran with silver spittle. He smelled unclean, like an animal that has been sick for a long time. The ragged white shirt he wore on his bony frame was stained as if from wounds that excreted not only blood but pus, too. He kept his knobbly hands on top of a knobbly black cane. When he turned to invite O'Sullivan to sit down, his breath almost literally knocked O'Sullivan over. The stink was incredible.

But what was most curious about Telfair was the fat animal crouching on his shoulder. At first, O'Sullivan had mistaken it for an odd-looking cat.

Now, its red eyes flaring, its teeth dripping hungrily, O'Sullivan saw it for what it was—a rat.

Telfair sat down in a ragged armchair set in front of the room's two windows. Backlit this way, Telfair was entirely in silhouette. The only detail O'Sullivan could pick out was Telfair's white useless eyes. And it was the same with the rat that sat on Telfair's shoulder watching O'Sullivan. All he could see was the rat's disturbingly red gaze.

"He bothers you, doesn't he?" Telfair said.

"I guess I just kind of buy into all the myths about rats. You know, how they carry rabies and drag babies off and stuff like that."

"You're a very intense man."

"I suppose I am." O'Sullivan sighed. In the blinking neon, he got his first good look at this room. The furniture all looked as if somebody had worked it over with a club and a knife. It was like the world's worst garage sale, boxes and sacks of junk packed tight along three of the walls, overflowing with all sorts of worthless crap, lamps that didn't glow, pop-up toasters that didn't pop up, even an old white Kelvinator refrigerator like the one the O'Sullivan family had had at home—only this one had a most peculiar door, one that hung at a comic angle by a

115

single screw. "I shouldn't have said anything about your pet. I'm sorry."

"I never have guests. I didn't even think about Charlie being on my shoulder."

"Charlie, huh?"

"When he's been bad I call him Charles."

For some reason that struck O'Sullivan as funny and he laughed out loud. Laughter sounded real weird in this dusty pauper's grave.

"Well, in seventh grade I had a milk snake named Raymond," O'Sullivan said. "He wasn't real popular around my house, either. So I guess I should understand about Charlie."

And as if to prove his master's point, red eyed Charlie climbed down from Telfair's shoulder and landed in his lap and then wriggled his head into the Oreo bag.

There was something obscene about it, the way the rat burrowed his head into the sack.

O'Sullivan could hear the munching all the way across the room where he had parked his butt on the edge of a lumpy couch with a hideous flowered slipcover over it.

"Good boy, Charlie," Telfair said, knobbly hand stroking the relentless rat. "Just remember to save a few for me."

Then, sated apparently, the rat withdrew, shaking its head as if shaking away Oreo crumbs, and then hopped back up on Telfair's shoulder.

Telfair said, "You've been talking to the Lindstrom woman, haven't you?"

"One of my reporters has."

"And she told you about the old tower."

"Yes. But I have to confess, I don't understand much about it."

Telfair chuckled with a certain satisfaction. "Nobody but me does, Mr O'Sullivan. Nobody but me does. And an old, insane patient named Gus."

Then he reached into the Oreo bag, seized another brown cookie, and popped it into his mouth.

He also, at the same time, raised his right leg off the seat of the armchair and cut a sharp, quick world record fart. "The

116

Oreos have the darndest effect on me, Mr O'Sullivan. They make me flatulent."

"Ah," O'Sullivan said. He was definitely planning to kill Holland when he saw her again.

As his teeth ground the Oreos to a fine powdery brown dust, Telfair said, "Have you ever heard of the Cloisters, Mr O'Sullivan?"

"I guess not."

"They were a splinter religious sect that roamed this state back in the 1800s. They'd been Roman Catholics until the bishop found out that they were practising black magic and then he kicked them out."

"I see." He wondered when Telfair was going to get to the UFO abductions and the out-of-body experiences.

"They also killed children. Usually runaways."

"Runaways?"

"Believe it or not, there was a teenage underground bigger than today's back in the late 1800s. And there weren't nearly as many shelters for them, either."

"Oh."

"Guess where the Cloisters put up for five years?"

"I'm afraid I don't know."

"Right where Hastings House is."

O'Sullivan could see this coming.

"Where the old tower was built was right on the burial ground."

"The authorities know about this?"

Telfair rattled his hand inside the Oreo package and snorted. His rat made a tiny chittering noise. "Authorities? They were suspicious of the Cloisters, of course, the way authorities are suspicious of any strange group, but they never really believed that the Cloisters were killing children in sacrifice."

"They never dug in the earth there?"

"Never."

"How do you know that there was a burial ground there, then?"

"I found the book."

"The book?"

117

"A sort of diary that one of the cult members kept."

"You found it?"

"Yes. Up in the tower when I was rummaging around up there." He sighed, his windpipe rattling there in the gloom. "You see, they never did use the tower, just the main building and then the other buildings they added on later. The tower was always structurally unsound. It swayed whenever there was a wind and even the smallest rain flooded the place."

"Why didn't they just tear it down?"

Telfair shrugged. "It's a nice piece of architecture. I suppose they felt that as long as nobody was in there, it wasn't hurting anything."

"So what did the diary say?"

"It told about the serpent."

"The serpent."

"Uh-huh. The huge snake that came up out of the ground one night after a certain incantation."

Now it was O'Sullivan's turn to sigh.

"You're starting to squirm, Mr O'Sullivan."

"I guess I am."

"The Cloisters sacrificed the children. That's why the serpent came. It had waited centuries for a host."

"A host?"

"Yes. The snake works its way into a human body—it shrinks down, of course—and then it takes over the intelligence and the will of that person. It makes the person go out and seek other sacrifices—children or adults, it doesn't really matter."

"I see."

Telfair laughed. "I wish you could hear yourself, Mr O'Sullivan."

"Oh?"

"You sound as if you'd like to dive out that window."

"You have to admit this is a pretty unlikely story."

"'Unlikely' is a very polite word, Mr O'Sullivan. I appreciate it."

And with that O'Sullivan got up.

He walked carefully to the window—carefully because the dusty floor was a mine trap of debris—and then he looked

118

down to the street.

He was still wondering where that teenager had gone to, the one who used to masquerade as himself. He could see the street rods again with the flames painted on the sides and the bikers all doing their self conscious Brando impressions as they wheeled their Harleys and big mother Indians to the kerb. A great sorrow overcame him then as he mourned the loss of the boy he'd been. He wanted it all to be ahead of him and it was all largely behind him and he wore neckties and had to worry about annual health check-ups and loneliness.

Yellow Vietnamese words drifted up from the street and brought him back to the present. The boy he'd been faded like a ghost.

"Over the years since Hastings House was built, Mr O'Sullivan," Telfair said, "six patients have escaped and killed people. Did you know that?"

"No, I guess I didn't."

"A man named Dobyns escaped just the other night."

"I know."

"The snake is inside him."

"How did it get there?"

"It contacted Dobyns telepathically. Dobyns started sneaking out of his room at night, going over to the tower. One night the snake appeared and got inside him."

O'Sullivan turned away from the window and came back to sit on the arm of the couch again.

"Have you talked with Dobyns?"

"No, but I don't need to. I talked to two of the other patients who escaped back in the fifties."

"And they told you about the snake."

"Yes. I felt the snake. They asked me to. They were afraid they were—crazy."

"Did you tell the administration at Hastings House?"

"I tried." Telfair laughed again. "But why would they believe me? I was just some janitor. I was lucky they didn't commit me."

"How did you meet Emily Lindstrom?"

"After her brother killed those women," Telfair said, "I called

119

her and told her everything. I even loaned her the diary."

"Obviously she listened."

Telfair stuffed his hand in the Oreo bag. This time he brought out two cookies. One he popped into his mouth. The other he held up for his pet rat to nibble on. "She listened. She didn't necessarily believe. But finally—well, finally she started looking into all this herself and then she gradually started to see that I wasn't crazy."

"My associate mentioned this apartment where all the escapees go. What's that about?"

Telfair coughed harshly, pounded himself on the chest, and said, "Shit. I quit smoking about five years ago but maybe it was already too late." As he coughed, the rat's red eyes jostled up and down on Telfair's shoulder.

Once he was composed again, Telfair said, "The first man who escaped was named Michaels. He built a small altar to the snake in one of the closets there. He killed a four-year-old girl and stripped her bones clean and put the bones in the closet. So when the snake's inside them, it always guides them there even though when they leave the hospital they usually suffer from amnesia. The third man who escaped came back to the hospital and told me all this—before he hung himself that is, the poor bastard. His name was Allard."

"You wouldn't happen to know where Dobyns is, would you?"

"Hunting."

"Hunting?"

"For a victim. You can bet on that."

"You're sure of that?"

"Absolutely. The longer the snake's in them, the more psychotic they get. Allard told me that."

"You've been to the police?"

"Several times, Mr O'Sullivan. They've got a file on me, I'm sure." He chuckled. "Filed it under 'C' for Crazy Old Bastard." He sighed. "Oh, yes, they've heard my strange tales many times."

O'Sullivan stood up. "I appreciate all this, Mr Telfair."

"Appreciate it but don't believe a word of it."

120

"I guess I'll have to think about it."

"At least you're polite. A lot of people who hear my story get pretty abusive." His hand snapped up another Oreo. "You know, ever since I retired early—about the time I was pronounced legally blind because of this retina disease—I've been telling this story to anybody who'd listen. And about the only audience I could find was this old guy who's a patient at Hastings. A guy named Gus. He actually sneaks up into the tower. He's seen the serpent. But who's going to believe him? Old bastard they keep doped up all the time—he's hardly the best witness. You see what I mean?"

Telfair got to his feet and walked over to O'Sullivan. "You want to see something cute?"

"What's that?"

"Watch." Telfair reached out and touched his pet rat on the head. "Say goodbye to the nice gentleman, Charlie."

And with that, the rat got right up on his haunches, right there on Telfair's shoulder, and started chittering crazily.

"And people say you can't train rats," Telfair said. "But what the hell do people know anyway?"

O'Sullivan took one more look at the old man's Milk of Magnesia eyes and got out of there.

While two customers were in the back in the science fiction section, Richie told Marie his secret.

Two years ago Richie and his family had lived in the state capital, where his father was a bank president. As the son of a wealthy and prominent community leader, Richie's life had been enviably simple and full. Then came the sudden bank audit and his father's even more sudden pleading of guilty to an embezzlement charge. For the previous five years, it was revealed, Richie's father had been a secret addictive gambler, first going through the family's entire small fortune, then beginning to use bank funds. Richie's entire life changed. He went from being one of his school's most popular boys to somebody people whispered about, and pointed to and smirked at. His father was sentenced to ten years in prison and the

121

family had been forced to move here to an apartment on a side of town that was barely respectable. His mother worked as a secretary in her brother's law office. How Richie and his two sisters would ever get through college was unknown at this point.

As Richie told Marie all this, she saw him suffer through embarrassment and pain. By the time he finished his story, his voice rasped with a very real agony. He was afraid for his father in prison—afraid that one of the inmates would stab him—and he was equally afraid for his mother. She was not in the best of health. The scandal had made her even weaker. And her stressful forty-hour-a-week job couldn't be doing her any good, either. Richie had taken a job at a local department store. Three nights a week and Saturdays he sold sports gear even though his interest in sports was minimal at best.

So there it was.

The secret hurt that was in his eyes but that he'd never talked about. The secret hurt that forced him to sit at the same table with the 'geeks.' She almost called him a geek—affectionately, of course—but she thought he might take it the wrong way. At least until he knew her better.

When he finished, he took a cigarette from his shirt pocket and said, "You mind?" He sounded as if he'd just finished making a long confession to a priest. He looked relieved, too.

She pointed to a sign above the door: NO SMOKING. "Brewster'd be awful mad."

"Maybe I'll step outside."

"Maybe you shouldn't smoke."

He grinned. "I figured you were the den mother type."

She grinned back. "Is that what I am?"

"No," he said, looking at her slyly, self-confidence coming back to his tone and face again. "What you are is cute. Very cute."

She felt exultant. Cute. Very cute. Maybe this first date was going to turn out just like her fantasy after all.

They were sitting on stools behind the counter with the cash register.

"Tell you what," he said.

"What?"

"Why don't I go out and have a cigarette and then go get us some Blizzards?"

"Only if you'll let me pay for my own."

"I really wish you'd let me pay for both of them." He smiled again and made a muscle with his bicep. He wasn't particularly muscular so that made his self-deprecating gesture all the sweeter to her. "That way I'd feel more macho."

"Well, if you'd feel more macho, maybe I'd better let you pay."

"Then next time you can pay."

"And will I get to be macho then?"

"You know," he said, crossing his eyes like an old vaudevillian comic, "That's a very good question."

Before she could respond, the pair from the back were at the counter. One young man—portly with long greasy hair—set down two science fiction paperbacks. The other young man—skinny and already balding even though he couldn't have been more than twenty-two or twenty-three—set down a copy of *Locus* and *Science Fiction Chronicle*.

As she checked them out—Richie still waiting around—she felt them staring at her. Occupational hazard, Brewster always told her. "You're so pretty, half the guys who come in here are going to have crushes on you. You wait and see." And so they did. While she was flattered by this kind of attention—heady stuff for a girl who usually thought of herself as some drab and crippled drudge—it also unnerved her. She didn't know how to respond.

When the two young men left, one of them pointing to a copy of an art magazine with a beautiful nude on the cover, Richie said, "Boy, you've got fans everywhere."

"They're nice guys. They come in here a lot."

"And I know why, too. To see you."

"They really like science fiction."

"They like you better."

"Strawberry."

"Huh?"

Tired of the subject of other boys—wanting to talk about

123

Richie if the subject had to be about boys at all—she said, "Strawberry. My Blizzard."

"Oh."

"You sound disappointed."

"Somehow I thought you'd be more adventurous. You know, a Blizzard with everything in it."

"Everything?"

"Sure—M&Ms and strawberries and 7-Up and—everything." He laughed. "It's the only way to live."

"Well, if you're going to go macho on me again I don't suppose I have any choice. Everything."

He was already on the way out the door. "You won't regret it. Believe me."

Then he was gone, the bell above the door tinkling, the air the sadder for his absence.

She couldn't believe how much closer she'd felt to him during the past fifteen minutes of conversation.

That was one thing her first date fantasy hadn't allowed for—real friendship to accompany the passion.

"Then do you know of a Marie Fane?"

"I think she's Kathleen's daughter. I'm not related to Kathleen but I know of her through a relative. She's like a shirt-tail cousin or something."

"How old would Marie be?"

The woman on the other end of the phone paused. "High school age or thereabouts, I'd guess."

"And her mother's name is Kathleen?"

"Yes, ma'am."

"I'll give it a try then. And thank you very much."

"Oh, you're most welcome. Like I said, we watch you on TV all the time. We like you a lot."

Chris Holland smiled. Sometimes a compliment could make you feel better than getting a new car. "Thanks again."

The woman hung up.

Chris put the phone down and said to Emily Lindstrom, "According to her there's a Kathleen Fane."

"Wonder why it isn't in the book?"

"Don't know. I'll try information."

They were still in the apartment Dobyns was using. The dead meat smell was as bad as ever.

When the wispy voiced male operator said "Information," Chris gave him the city and name she was looking for.

After half a minute, the live operator vanished and a recording took over.

"We're sorry but at the customer's request, the number is unpublished."

"Shit," Chris said, slamming the phone down. Then, "Excuse my French."

"What happened?"

"Unlisted number."

"Oh. Great. We've got to find this Marie Fane and warn her. Dobyns is on the way right now."

Chris snapped her fingers. "Cameron."

"Who?"

"Frank Cameron. He's a cop I know. He'll get the number for me."

She quickly dialled the Sixth Precinct. She wasn't used to rotary phones so the dialling was somewhat awkward.

"Detective Cameron, please."

She waited.

"Hello."

"Frank."

"Oh, God."

"You know who this is?"

"If I didn't, would I have said 'Oh, God'?"

"Good point."

He laughed. "It's something illegal, isn't it?"

"What is?"

"What you want me to do."

Cameron loved to tease her and she loved to be teased by him. He was like an older brother. A divorced man with three kids, Cameron had asked her out a few times. Great fun but no sparks alas. Fortunately both of them felt that way. Now they were just friends, just two more overworked, overstressed lonely middle class people anonymously going about the business of living and dying.

"Well, I'm not sure, actually."

"So what is it? The shift commander's called a meeting in five minutes."

"Unlisted number."

"Is that all? You mean I don't have to plant any evidence or run any drugs?"

"Not tonight."

"What's the name?"

She told him.

"Hold on a sec," he said.

"He's getting it for you?" Emily Lindstrom asked.

Chris nodded.

He came back moments later and gave her the number.

"You owe me a lunch," he said.

"McDonald's all right?"

"Sure."

"Good. That I can afford. I'll call you next week."

"Really?"

"Sure really. You helped me, didn't you?"

"Actually, it'll be nice to sit down with a woman who isn't a cop and talk. I'm not doing too well in the old dating department."

Chris laughed. "Well, I'm not doing too well in that department either, Frank, so we can commiserate."

"There you go again with those big words. Talk to you later."

After hanging up, Chris waved the number at Emily Lindstrom. "Well, here it is. Let's just hope somebody is home."

Emily crossed her fingers and held them high.

Chris dialled Kathleen Fane's number.

And waited for somebody to pick up on the other end.

Dobyns reached the street. In the pale glow of the mercury vapour lights, he stood taking polluted air deep into his lungs and getting himself ready to walk inside the bookstore.

A pimp and a hooker passed by. The pimp was obviously

126

upset with the heavily made up black woman. He had gripped her tight by the elbow and was shaking her as they moved toward a Caddy convertible.

What am I waiting for? Dobyns wondered. *I should just walk right in there and—*

Until now, he had not confronted the unspoken reason he was going into the bookstore.

The reason the knife was lashed to his leg.

The bookstore.

Inside.

Marie Fane.

Now.

He went inside.

Even from the threshold, he could see how neatly— lovingly—the store was laid out. Tidily categorised, all the books fitted perfectly into their pockets.

"May I help you?"

She was no great beauty but she was very pretty. One of those attractive, earnest looking girls boys actually seem to prefer to great beauties.

"Just looking for some old John Steinbeck novels, I guess," Dobyns said casually.

She had a nice body, the right combination of roundness and leanness.

"You'll find that to your right behind you in American literature."

He watched her carefully. He could see that his gaze upset her slightly, that she didn't know how to interpret it.

"Do you sell a lot of him?"

"Not a lot," Marie Fane said. "Mostly *The Red Pony, The Grapes of Wrath* and *Of Mice and Men*."

"That's my favourite."

"*Of Mice and Men?*"

"Right. You ever read it?"

"Yes. I loved it. Especially the ending. It was so sad."

He saw her earnestness again. The simple but almost moving way she talked about the novel. The fact that she found it so sad told him a lot about her. She was a sensitive and intelligent girl.

127

Now, she seemed even prettier to him.

"When he puts the mouse in his pocket," Dobyns said. "That's the part I always remember."

The girl nodded. "He was a great writer."

"I guess one of the novels I'm looking for is *In Dubious Battle*. You think you have that?"

"It'd be in the Steinbeck section if we did."

He'd been trying to lure her out from behind the cash register. He didn't want to grab her up front. Too near the door. Too close to somebody walking in on them. Or seeing them struggle through the glass front door.

"Thanks," he said, and walked back to the American literature section.

Richie ended up walking around the block to smoke his cigarette. Even in a run down neighbourhood such as this one, spring was meant to be enjoyed.

At first he was a little nervous—drunks and homeless people had the most baleful eyes on the planet—but soon enough he relaxed and appreciated the soft sweet breeze and the aromatic sprays of apple blossoms and dogwood that bloomed on a nearby hill.

He felt pure exhilaration. He'd never before trusted anyone enough to tell them the story about his father. For months now he'd had this secret crush on Marie but he hadn't ever expected it to lead to the kind of relationship where you talk, really talk, to somebody.

His problems hadn't gone away. There still wasn't enough money at home. His mother still looked worse and worse each day. Attending college still seemed a dimmer and dimmer hope for him. But even given all this, the fact that he'd unburdened himself with Marie made him feel as if he now had an ally. Somebody on whom he could rely.

He had a friend.

He had walked four blocks from the bookstore without even realising it. On one corner was an adult bookstore where two winos with paper bags covering their wine bottles sat hassling customers as they came out the door, apparently trying to panhandle some cash. On another corner was a Hardee's, a brilliant glowing white against the darkness and gloom of this neighbourhood. And on the third corner sat a small stone Catholic Church. He wasn't sure why, but he felt like going over there, mounting the stairs and going inside to sit in the quiet shadows and watch the votive candles flicker green and yellow and red in the darkness. Even though he wasn't sure he even believed in a personal God anymore, the prospect of sitting in church always cheered him. He'd spent many such hours following the revelations about his father.

He decided it was time to start back, pick up the Blizzards, and head for the bookstore.

He took out another cigarette and got it going. He probably wouldn't have another one for an hour or two.

When the light turned green, he crossed the street.

8

THERE WAS SOMETHING about the man. She wasn't sure what. The odd thing was that he should unnerve her when other types of customers didn't. He was well dressed, well spoken, and certainly friendly enough. At least outwardly. But while he physically resembled the majority of the university related customers, still there was something troubling about him.

The man remained in back, looking at Steinbeck novels. She opened the lid on the box and peered down at the .38. At least that's what Brewster had called the weapon. A .38. For all she knew it could have been a .45 or an .889 or some other crazy number. Small, silver, smelling now of cleaning solution and oil, the gun lay waiting for her to pick it up. Brewster had shown her several times how it worked. She would, she felt, have no trouble firing it.

She reached down. Touched it. Despite the fact that guns made her nervous and uncomfortable—and despite the fact that on the debate team she always wanted to take the pro gun registration side—feeling the gun now gave her a measure of self-confidence. She occasionally took out her father's gun at home and held it, felt the grip clutched in her palm, felt her finger on the trigger. Much as she might try to deny it, and despite her feelings about registration, holding a handgun gave her a certain self-confidence.

She looked down the aisles. Empty.

The man had disappeared. Her heart began to pound. Where had he gone?

"Hello," she said. "Hello."

On the dusty air of the old building, her voice sounded strained and very young.

"Hello. May I help you find something?"

Nothing.

Where had he gone?

Was he hiding?

Never before had she realised how many places there were to hide in the bookstore. Divided into four long, tall lanes with a full back wall packed with additional books, a person could easily hide behind one of the corners where the lanes ended.

Or could easily sneak down into the basement and wait.

"Hello," she called again.

She didn't really expect a response. None came.

Where was Richie?

God, it seemed as if he'd been gone an hour now.

How long could it take to get two Blizzards and smoke a cigarette? He shouldn't be smoking anyway. It was such a stupid, deadly habit—

"Found it."

The man had come as if from nowhere. She had been looking up and down the lanes on the east side of the store and he'd walked up from behind her.

He held in his hands a somewhat tattered Bantam paperback copy of *In Dubious Battle*.

"My lucky night, I guess," the man said. He had a very nice smile until you noticed how cold and cheerless it was. There was no warmth in his dark eyes, either.

She glanced down at the gun. Was she being dumb? What

was so menacing about this man when you came right down to it? And, to be exact, she'd felt this same sort of panic working on her before in the store—some of her mother's paranoia rubbing off on her.

She took his ten-dollar bill and set it on the corner of the register, the way Brewster had shown her, to make change.

She had just got the register open when she heard him moving.

When she looked up again, he was gone.

Quickly, her eyes scanned the lanes. No sight of him—but of course she couldn't see all the lanes. She heard a clicking sound and turned around. Saw him.

At the door.

Snapping the safety lock in place.

Pulling down the white shade with the red word CLOSED on it.

"What're you doing?" she said.

"You know what I'm doing."

"This isn't funny."

"It isn't meant to be funny."

"You go unlock that door or I'll call the police."

An old fashioned black phone sat on the counter. He walked over to it. He lifted the receiver and handed it to her. "Be my guest."

"I've got a friend who's coming back. He'll know something's wrong."

"I'm not going to hurt you, you know."

"I wasn't lying about my friend. His name's Richie."

"All I want is for us to have a nice time."

"Please."

He walked around the counter.

Just when she thought she might leap free from him, he snatched her wrist in his hand. He was very strong. And very quick.

"Ow," she said.

"See, you're making me do this."

"No, I'm not. Please."

"You help me out and I'll help you out."

131

She was afraid to guess what he meant by that.

In disbelief, she watched him unzip his trousers. In moments, his penis was in his hand. It was longer and harder than she'd ever imagined a penis could be.

He guided her hand down to it.

"No!" she said.

He slapped her with such stunning force that she literally lost her senses—all she was aware of was darkness and coldness rushing up her sinuses and up into her head. A darkness and coldness she equated with death.

Only as she began to compose herself was she aware that he'd torn her blouse and bra away from her chest. Her small but full breasts were exposed to the drab light and drafts of the aged bookstore.

He pulled her to him. She was aware of his penis rubbing up against her own sex and of the scent of him—sharp and sweaty now, filled with desire and danger.

He got his fingers on her own zipper, got her fly open, and then crammed his hand inside her panties, finding her dry sex immediately.

"You'd better relax, honey. You don't want to be dry when I get inside you."

She tried to slap him, but it was no use. She could not find an angle from which a slap would hurt him. He had her pressed tightly to him.

With brutal force, he tore her jeans away from her hips and threw her back against the counter. He got her legs spread apart and tried to get up inside her.

This time she managed to slap him on the back of the head.

If he felt the blow, he gave no clue. Instead, he tried for a second time to get up inside her, the head of his penis brushing the lips of her vagina.

When she screamed, he brought his hand up as if by magic and struck her with terrible fury across the mouth.

She felt blood fill the inside of her mouth immediately. She knew she would not scream anymore. She was too afraid of getting hit again.

Where was Richie?

A cigarette and a quick trip to the Dairy Queen couldn't possibly have—

"Now you listen, you little cunt. I want to enjoy you. Do you understand me?"

He had his face pushed right up against hers. His features were huge, grotesque. "I want to get inside you and have a good time. If you try to stop me, I'll kill you."

And then he reached down as if he were going to pick up something from the floor—there was the sound of something being unclasped—and then a small butcher knife filled his hand.

He brought the gleaming blade not to her face, not to her throat, but to her left breast.

"You know what this knife could do to that?" The tip of the blade tweaked her pink nipple. "You want to find out what it could do to that?" She heard herself whimpering, pleading: "No, no." "Then you do what I tell you, you understand? You do what I tell you or I'm going to take you apart piece by piece." He seized her breast with such force that she felt her knees buckle. "And I'm going to start with your nice little tit here. All right?"

Something like a scream started up her throat and through the bubbling blood in her mouth but the back of his hand smashed across her lips once again, killing the sound utterly.

"Now let's have some fun," he said.

The woman ahead of him in line wore tight white stretch pants. She must have been at least one hundred pounds overweight. Easily. She ordered three Buster Bars, two Dillies, a ninety-five-cent cone, and two large Blizzards. She wore no wedding ring and she had no kids with her. Richie had the depressing feeling that maybe all the goodies were just for her. He was depressed because he had an aunt like that. Ever since her husband—an Amway distributor who called everybody 'Chief' and 'Ace'—had left her, all she seemed capable of was pigging out. She'd even had surgery to waylay her incredible eating binges. But so far anyway it was no use. She still ate like a Roman legion.

The woman's goodies fitted into three big white bags. She

kept her eyes down as she left the fluorescent haven of the DQ to return to the dark and mean streets surrounding the place. Her skin-tight pants and a cherry coloured tank top only emphasised her enormous size. That's why her eyes were downcast, of course. Shame that others could see her addiction and feel superior to her because of it. Maybe even hate her a little. Watching her—seeing others stare at her—Richie felt sorry for her. He could tell you all about being stared at and whispered about.

He stepped up to the window and gave the cute young girl in the chocolate spattered white uniform his order.

Marie managed to bring her knee straight up between the man's legs and catch him squarely in the groin. He went tumbling backward, his arms flailing out, the knife skittering across the ancient linoleum floor.

Her first impulse was to leap for the door, get it open, and run out to the sidewalk.

Sobbing, she started running around the counter. Running as best she could, anyway, with her crippled foot. Behind her, she heard a noise. She wasn't sure what it was but she wasn't going to stop to find out either.

She had just put her hand out to the safety lock when he clamped his arm on her shoulder and spun her around.

"You shouldn't have done that, bitch."

This time he slapped her so hard she was lifted half a foot off the floor and slammed into the counter, the back of her head cracking against the telephone.

He came at her again, raking the fingers of one hand into her tender sex, and grabbing her neck with the other hand.

He jerked her to him and started kissing her.

His tongue was hot and wet and foul in her mouth. She could hear him groaning with pleasure and feel his penis rubbing against her vagina.

She bit his tongue so hard she could taste blood. This time it wasn't hers, it was his.

He was in such pain that he picked her up like a lawn chair

134

and hurled her into a wire display rack of paperbacks.

She felt the wire biting into her naked back as her weight brought the whole display down. She saw a blur of colourful paperback covers flying past her eyes as the books flew in various directions.

"You fucking cunt," he said.

She could see the blood she'd drawn. His whole mouth was ugly with soaking red blood.

He bent down and grabbed the knife by the hilt.

Chest heaving, wiping off the blood with the back of his hand, he came over to stand above her.

She tried to scramble backward but there was no place to go. She was flush up against the head of a lane. It was at least two feet wide and six feet tall.

He stood over her, his genitals still exposed, blood oozing from his mouth, the knife held ready in his right hand.

"I wasn't going to kill you, cunt. At least not right away. But now I've changed my mind."

He reached down and grabbed a handful of her hair and snapped her to her feet.

"Mrs Kathleen Fane?"

"Yes."

"Mrs Fane. This is Chris Holland from Channel 3 News."

"Oh. Yes."

"I'm trying to reach a Marie Fane."

"Marie. Why she's my daughter."

"Do you know where I can reach her?"

"I—suppose. But can you tell me why you need to talk to her?"

"There really isn't time now, Mrs Fane. You'll just have to trust me."

"Well, she works in a bookstore."

"Do you know the name of it?"

"The Alice B Toklas Bookstore. It's over in the university district."

"And she's there now?"

135

"She should be."

"Thank you very much, Mrs Fane."

"But—"

Knowing she was scaring the hell out of the woman, Chris hung up. She didn't always like the things she had to do as a reporter.

She looked through the phone book, found the Alice B Toklas Bookstore, and dialled.

The phone rang ten times.

"Shit," Chris said. This time she didn't say pardon my French.

"What's wrong?"

"No answer at the bookstore where Marie is supposed to be working tonight." She hung up and started dialling again immediately.

"Who're you calling?" Emily Lindstrom asked.

"O'Sullivan. He's got a car phone and he should be able to—"

And then there he was.

"Walter?"

"Just the person I want to talk to, Holland. Do you know he has a pet rat that rides around on his shoulder?"

"Things are more serious than that. Do you know where the Alice B Toklas Bookstore is?"

"Sure. Over by the university. It's where I get my copy of the *New York Review of Books* every week."

"I need to meet you there as soon as possible. All right?"

"This is all pretty crazy shit, Holland. I hope you know that by now."

"Maybe not as crazy as you think, Walter," she said, and hung up.

This time, Marie managed to duck the slap the man aimed right at her mouth.

He had pushed her flat back against the chest-high counter again, and Marie tried to think of some way to reach the gun Brewster had left under the cash register for her.

The man waved the knife closer, closer to her chest.

136

He lunged.

Marie jumped sideways two steps.

The knife went deep into the varnished wood of the counter. The man made a grunting sound, almost as if he'd been wounded.

Marie moved backward now. She knew she could never reach the door and get it open before he grabbed her again so she tried to position herself for jumping behind the counter. If she could work her way leftward, she knew she could dive beneath the cash register and get the .38.

The man jerked the knife out of the wood and turned to face her again.

"You think you're going to make it out of this all right. But you're not. Take my word for it. You're not."

Marie said nothing, just kept moving so he couldn't easily grab her, and kept glancing at the opening on the side of the counter. Two steps led to the counter platform and the cash register.

By now, the man had pulled his clothes on again. Except for his crooked tie, he looked pretty much as he had when he'd first come in here.

He kept circling, circling, muttering angrily to himself.

The knife kept snicking at the air, snicking.

Then Marie heard the knock.

At first—her mind spinning with fears of her own death and with what seemed to be her doomed attempt to reach the gun—she wasn't even sure if it was knocking.

Maybe it was just some extraneous sound from the sidewalk or street.

"Marie!"

Several knocks fell against the door now.

She clearly recognised Richie's voice.

Her gaze began flitting to the door. If she could let Richie in…

But she made a mistake by watching the door too long.

She gave the man just enough time to jump across the four feet separating them and grab her around the neck.

In moments she felt his sweaty face breathing hot foul

breath against the side of her face, the blade of the butcher knife held tight against her throat.

"You're going to walk over to that door and let him in," he said. "Do you understand?"

She nodded.

"You're not going to scream. You're not going to kick me. You're not going to do anything except let him in and then stand back. You got it?"

Again, she nodded.

He shoved her with his hips, keeping the edge of the blade exactly against her carotid artery. One slice and—

She felt so many things as he pushed her toward the door— terror, confusion, panic. She even felt guilty. If only she'd cried out, warned Richie away.

Now she'd drag him into this and God only knew what—

"Open it," the man whispered harshly in her ear.

This time when he shoved her, she felt his swollen erection against her buttock.

My God, even in the midst of all this, he was still sexually aroused.

The thought of this stunned and sickened her.

She reached out and tripped the hold that would undo the lock.

The lock opened like a shot.

The door crept open half an inch or so.

Diesel fumes and the chilling night air rushed through the tiny crack.

"Marie?"

She could hear the fear and indecision in Richie's voice, hear the questions he had to be asking himself: Should he come in? Should he run for help? By now, he had to know that something was wrong in here, terribly wrong.

The door creaked open.

A section of Richie's head angled around the edge of the wooden frame.

"Marie—" he started to say. And then he saw her there, took in the man who had the knife at her throat.

Something terrible started to form in his throat, some

138

sympathetic wail of protest.

But before Richie could get much of the sound out, the man said, "Get in here, punk."

Richie's first instinct was obviously to run. You could see him start to withdraw in the doorway, wriggle himself free, and run for help.

The man said, "If you don't get in here right now, I'm going to kill her on the spot. You understand?"

Marie could see the colour fading fast from Richie's face. She could also see that he was just starting to take serious note of her virtual nudity. While she'd been able to pull her jeans up around her waist, she hadn't had the opportunity to snap them shut. Her panties torn by the man, she knew that dark pubic hair blossomed in the V of her open fly.

Richie came inside. "Don't hurt her. Please. All right?"

"Lock the door and come over here."

Richie came over. Stood two feet away.

The man said, "Anybody else know you're in here?"

Richie shook his head, glanced at Marie. She saw both fear and sympathy in his eyes.

"Then you're going to be the only witness, kid."

And with that, the man began to pull the knife across Marie's throat.

There was no pain. That was the first thing she noticed. She knew she'd been cut but still there was no pain. Not yet anyway.

She was wriggling against the man's grasp when she saw Richie hurl himself across the empty floor between them.

Richie let out a sound that was both bravado and nerves, some ancient war noise that humans had learned long ago from some lower species.

Richie hit them so hard that all three of them were knocked to the floor. He scrambled to his feet immediately, grabbing Marie's hand and helping her get upright, too.

On the floor, the man was crawling toward the knife that had once again been knocked from his grasp.

"Call the police!" Richie said to Marie.

Frantically, she shook her head. "He tore the wires out from

139

the wall."

The man grabbed the knife, jumped to his feet, spun around, and faced Richie.

"You little sonofabitch," the man said.

He seemed even more insane now than he had earlier. Obviously he'd assumed that Marie would be all his, to do with as he chose. But Richie had spoiled those plans and the man was enraged.

"Richie, watch out!" Marie cried as the man started circling Richie, much as he had Marie herself.

Richie looked about desperately. Whatever courage had come to him in the first moments of seeing Marie in the man's grasp was now given to caution and anxiety.

Marie realised that there was only one way she could help Richie. Reach the door and run out to the sidewalk and start screaming for help.

But as she started for the door, she saw a nightmare take shape.

The man jumped on Richie, slamming him to the floor. In seconds he had the knife at Richie's throat and had torn a deep gash from one side of the throat to the other.

Richie made a horrible gasping sound—almost as if he wanted to vomit—and the man once again pulled the knife all the way back across Richie's throat.

Blood began to flood the floor.

Richie's eyes showed pleading and panic. He looked like a small child in the throes of death.

Marie knew she was screaming but it sounded as if somebody else were making the sound.

The man was bending over Richie like some feasting animal and then abruptly he was on his feet.

Marie was running.

She had no idea where.

She was just running.

Running.

Through the door. Out onto the sidewalk. Screaming, screaming. Out into the street.

Headlights and blaring horns. Shouted obscenities.

Collapsing into the middle of the street itself. Brakes screeching. The stomach-turning sound of one car slamming into the rear end of another car. More blaring horns. More shouted obscenities. *Richie lying bleeding to death back there on the floor and the man—*

Richie; Richie…

He didn't get the bitch. He'd come here to get the cunt—fuck her till she cried out—then slash her throat.

Instead he cut up some goddamned punk who must have been her boyfriend or something.

He saw her go for the door and he went after her.

He knew his whole hand was bloody, that the knife blade was running, dripping with blood.

He also saw—peripherally—that there were people on the sidewalk watching him as he lunged into the street after her.

He didn't care.

The only thing that brought him back to his senses was the noise of cars slamming on brakes and horns shouting at each other like wounded animals.

He didn't follow her into the street.

Hell, she was probably going to get killed out there.

Taking stock of his circumstances—wild looking man with a bloody knife in his hand, neighbourhood yokels starting to shout for help now, terrified of him —he decided the only thing he could do at this point was get in his car and get out of here.

Somewhere a police siren exploded.

Not far away.

He pushed past two simpering old ladies and ran to the side of the bookstore.

All he could think of was the tower and safety.

He ran.

9

BY THE TIME Chris, Emily Lindstrom, and O'Sullivan reached the crime scene, squad cars had cordoned off the entire street. Grim looking uniformed cops—men and women alike—stood next to their squad cars waving long silver flashlights and rerouting traffic. Car passengers seemed equally divided between those who were irritated at being sent two blocks out of their way, and those who were irritated because they couldn't get a closer glimpse of all the trouble.

O'Sullivan took a big PRESS card (black letters on white cardboard for easy reading), set it up behind his steering wheel, and pulled up to one of the uniformed cops.

"I'm O'Sullivan from Channel 3."

The cop—a trim black man—leaned in and said, "There isn't much room in there with the ambulance. Why don't you pull over by that tree there."

"Thanks."

The cop nodded and went back to his job.

After they'd parked and got out, Chris looked at the display past the yellow police tape. The old buildings of the neighbourhood were awash in the splashing red and blue lights of the emergency vehicles. On the other side of the barricades the police had set up stood at least twenty cops, some in uniform, most in suits.

There wasn't a smile to be seen anywhere. Reporters from TV stations were busy with mobile lights and cameras trying to get interviews with officers who clearly had no intention of saying anything at this point. It was too early to know what had gone on here. Ordinary citizens stood on the edge of the perimeter. Most of them looked shocked. Death is always hard to accept but sudden violent death is even tougher—it reminds everybody of how fragile life truly is. One moment you can be walking down the street happy and content, the next you can be on the sidewalk bleeding to death from a stab wound or a gunshot. And no amount of prestige or wealth can save you from the unexpected, either.

Then Chris saw the teenage girl the police were leading out

of the bookstore. Chris's heart broke for her. Not only was the girl in shock, but even from ten yards away you could hear the low, moaning animal noise that violent death prompts from those forced to witness it.

The girl was drenched with blood and now, as she held her hands to her face as the TV lights bore in on her, her lovely, soft face became streaked with blood, too.

It was then that Chris noticed the girl's limp. She wondered if this was the result of the murder that had taken place inside the bookstore.

"Jesus," O'Sullivan said when he saw the girl trapped in the glare of the lights.

Then before Chris knew what he was doing, O'Sullivan vaulted a barricade—he might be thirty pounds overweight but he was surprisingly nimble—and ran over in front of the lights. He started waving his arms and blocking the girl with his body so the police could more easily help her into the waiting squad car.

Chris smiled, thinking that this was just the kind of move that proved he was first a human being and second a reporter. Much as she liked some reporters, she didn't find many of them all that admirable as human beings.

Once the girl was in the car and speeding safely away, O'Sullivan turned reporter again. The Channel 3 team—two camera people and the station's reigning hunk who didn't look any smarter than usual—came trotting breathlessly up to their boss, awaiting his commands.

Rather than stand around, Chris decided to start soaking up some colour. Even if she'd been demoted to daily calendar lady, she still recognised a good—if bleak—story when she saw one.

She spent the next ten minutes familiarising herself with the scene in general. She wondered what the motive for the killing had been. Robbery seemed unlikely. Certainly the Alice B Toklas Bookstore wouldn't have contained enough money to justify such slaughter. (Though, of course, if the killer was a junkie, he might well have murdered these people for a few dollars.) And from what she was gathering, a young white middle class boy had been murdered inside.

A few people in the crowd recognised her and pointed and smiled. You might not get much money as a local TV reporter but you got about all the fame you could handle. Grocery store, record shop, movie theatre—it didn't matter—wherever you went your public awaited you. Of course, not everyone loved you. She'd been spit at, given the finger to, and cursed out loud. And this was all during her off-duty hours.

The crime scene was laid out, as usual, to keep the maximum number of people out and let the minimum number of people inside the yellow crime scene tape. Two uniformed officers stood logging official people in and out, writing down what they were wearing so that if later there were questions about fibres or blood or latent fingerprints, they'd know if any of these belonged to police personnel. She'd seen some crime scenes that had been limited to two or three people, police identification officers—who did diagrams and snapped photos and gathered all sorts of evidence—and one person from the coroner's office. All the activity was directed by a police commander on the scene (and many times not even the commander was let inside the yellow tape) and a commander back at the precinct. The object was to survey and catalogue the crime scene and get out before anybody had a chance to disturb or disrupt evidence. Understandably, uniformed police officers kept not only Chris but all the other reporters away as well.

This was the front of the store. She decided to try her luck in the alley, where the investigation was limited to one side of the pavement.

Two white coated men from the Medical Examiner's office stood by a wall examining a great stain of blood. The men recognised her and nodded as she walked past. Probably they didn't yet know she was now the daily calendar lady. They probably still thought she was a crack reporter. They probably didn't know how old she was, either. Too old to be anything but a calendar lady. But that was self-pity and that was one thing she always tried to spare herself. She had her health, her good if not brilliant mind, her good if not gorgeous looks, and there were one hell of a lot of people on this planet who had one whole lot less. She considered self-pity the most unbecoming

144

of all feelings and whenever she felt herself slipping into it she bit her lip till she drew blood.

She drew blood right now.

She walked past the light in the centre of the alley, into the chill gloom near the misty light at the opposite end.

The place reeked of garbage and other filth. Near a light pole she could see the carcass of a cat that had been eaten up by some kind of scavenger. Most of the belly was gone. Its front paws and jaw were frozen in a position of extreme terror and pain. She loved cats. The poor little thing.

When Chris got back to the front of the bookstore, she found that the reporters had doubled, perhaps tripled in number. Uniformed police officers held them at bay ten feet on the other side of the yellow tape. The number of onlookers had increased, too. There was a carnival atmosphere now. Among the gloomy faces you saw a smile or two. Know-it-alls in the crowd pointed things out to newly arrived spectators. The slaying had gone from a numbing, depressing experience to one of novelty and even thrills. By now it wasn't a human experience—a life with a history and loved ones—but rather just one more titillation for the tube.

She found O'Sullivan barking at his reporters, ordering them to try to outflank the officers so they could get a better shot of the store interior. His moment of humanity—seeing that the teenage girl was protected from the wolf pack of reporters— had passed and he was once again his familiar self, a news director in a competitive TV market very worried about ratings and determined to get some kind of edge on his foes at the other stations.

So now, instead of walking up to the crime scene commander, she bypassed him and went over to O'Sullivan.

She had to wait until he was finished intimidating his troops.

He turned to her and said, "Channel 6 is going to beat the hell out of us on this story. They're up to something. I know it." O'Sullivan always said this. Then he narrowed his eyes and said, "Where's Lindstrom?"

"On the other side of the barricade."

Some of the people in the crowd had recognised her. They

were pointing and waving. She waved back. Anything except face O'Sullivan's scrutiny.

"Where you going after this?"

"Emily wants to talk to the Fane girl."

"You think you can get in to see her?"

She crossed her fingers. "Hope so." Then she gave him a most unprofessional kiss on the cheek and left.

Five blocks from the bookstore, Richard Dobyns was hiding in the deep shadows of a five-storey all-night parking garage. He was on the third floor.

Crouched in a corner of the place, he was slowly becoming aware of smells: leaky motor oil, fading cigarette smoke, his own sticky sweat, and the chill breeze off the nearby river smelling of fish and pollutants.

He was slowly becoming aware of sights, too: the way the perfectly waxed hood of a new Lincoln shone in the starlight through the open wall, the stars themselves inscrutable and imperious, and closer by the concrete floor slanting down into shadows. There were only a few cars left on this floor. The place looked deserted and lonely in the dim and dirty overhead light. Occasionally, from down below, he could hear footsteps and cars starting up, and then a laugh or two.

He wanted to be one of them. One of those everyday normal people getting into an everyday normal car going home to an everyday normal wife and kids. All his life he'd wanted to be everyday and normal yet he never had been quite—not in high school where he'd been the nerdy editor of the school newspaper or in college where he'd been the nerdy editor of the literary. He'd always felt the outsider, walking around with a nervous insincere smile on his face, and knowing a sorrow even he couldn't quite define.

Well, given what he'd done in the past twenty-four hours, now he was the ultimate outsider—

He tried to keep images of the teenage boy from his mind. My God, he'd—

His breath still came in spasms.

Leaning back against the rough concrete wall, he felt his chest and belly heave as breath ripped upward through his lungs.

And then he felt the thing inside him shift.

Not a major shift, just a small one as if adjusting position.

He put his hand to his stomach.

And felt it.

Moving now; twisting.

He put his head back against the concrete wall again and closed his eyes. A shadow cut his face perfectly in two. He'd gone unshaven and his beard was a stubbly black. His dark hair was wildly messed up. And now a single silver tear slid down the curve of his cheek. It rolled to his dry lips and settled there feeling hot and tasting salty. He did not open his eyes or move his head for long minutes.

Our Father who art in heaven—

And then he heard the voices.

Man and woman.

Young, probably about his age.

Coming toward him.

His eyes came open. He looked momentarily as if he were coming out of a very deep trance. The dark eyes flicked left, right—

Coming toward him.

"Come on, admit it. You thought she was cute."

"Well—"

"It's all right, David. I won't get jealous. She's a movie star, not somebody you can call up for a date."

The man chuckled. "Right, you won't get jealous. Remember the night I told you I thought Demi Moore was so good looking?"

Now the woman laughed. "You just happened to catch me on an off night."

"Sure," the man said. "An off night."

They walked a few steps in silence then, and there was no doubt where they were heading. The Lincoln with Dobyns hiding on the other side.

If he waited till they came around to his side, they would be

147

at an advantage, standing over him—

He had to move now—

He sprang up off the concrete floor to his feet, running around the rear end of the Lincoln right toward them. The door leading downstairs was perhaps thirty yards behind them.

This was the only thing he could do.

When they saw him appear, like some berserk jack-in-the-box abruptly popping up, they both screamed.

The man was brave. He pulled the woman to him protectively.

Dobyns ran right past them, his footsteps echoing *flap-flap-flap* in the empty parking garage, all the way to the door, then faster *flap-flap-flap* as he took the stairs down to the ground floor two at a time.

Three blocks away, in an area that was mostly shadowy warehouses long left deserted, he found a phone booth glowing in the blackness.

He fed change into the phone and then dialled a certain number with trembling fingers.

"Hello."

Right away, she said, "Please, Richard. Please just turn yourself over."

"I take it the phone is tapped."

"Richard, please, the police have assured me that—"

He laughed. "I'll bet they've assured you of a lot of things, haven't they?"

"Richard, I—"

"I'm sorry, honey. I can't turn myself over. I—can't. There's no other way to explain it."

"But—"

"I need you to do me a favour."

"Richard, there's a detective standing—"

"I know there's a detective there. I just need to talk to Cindy a minute. Just put her on the phone. Please do that for me."

There was a long pause on the other end. Then a little girl's voice, more sombre than he'd ever heard it, said, "Hi, Daddy."

"Hi, pumpkin."

"There are policemen here."

"I know, honey."

"They want you to talk to them. They promised Mommy that they won't hurt you."

"I know, sweetie. But it's you I want to talk to. I—" But how could he explain to anybody—even to himself—the terrible darkness that overcame him when the thing inside wanted him to kill? "Do you know how much I love you?"

"Yes, Daddy. And I love you."

"That's what you've got to remember, pumpkin. How much we love each other. Okay, sweetheart?"

"All right, Daddy."

"Now I've got to go. I'm sorry but I do."

Cindy started crying. "I love you, Daddy; I love you, Daddy." He could hear the terror in her voice and hated himself for putting it there.

His wife took the phone. "Richard—"

"Take care of Cindy, honey. You'll both make it through this somehow, darling, I know you will."

And then he hung up and faced black night again.

It was time to return to the tower.

Once they got rolling in the car again, Emily Lindstrom spoke. She'd been quiet for nearly twenty minutes.

"It's always different from on TV, isn't it?"

"What is?"

"Oh, just the—reality of it," Emily Lindstrom said. "Even when you see the body bags, you don't smell the blood and the faeces and you don't see the eyes of the youngsters standing around and gawking."

"No, you don't."

Emily sighed, put her head back. "Tonight brought everything back. The way it was with Rob, I mean."

"I'm sorry."

"You shouldn't be sorry. You're the best friend I've had since this whole thing started years ago." She looked over at Chris and smiled. "Even if you don't believe it."

Chris braked for a red light. Full night was here now. You

could tell how raw the wind was by the way the young spring trees bent and swayed, and the way storm windows rattled on the aged houses of this neighbourhood. "Who said I didn't believe you?"

"Then you do?"

"Well," Chris said.

Emily smiled again. "I don't blame you. A cult buries the bones of murdered children somewhere and a hundred years later a serpent—"

"By the way, what's the difference between 'snake' and 'serpent'?"

"Technically, none," Emily said, "but you're changing the subject."

"I am, aren't I?" Chris said, and pulled away from the stoplight.

They drove another five minutes in silence. The homes got bigger, cleaner. The electric lights in the gloom looked inviting. Chris wanted to be inside one of those places, feet tucked under her on the couch, a good movie on HBO and a bowl of popcorn on her lap.

"There's even an incantation."

"Oh?" Chris said.

"Yes. If you say the words at the right time, you can force the serpent to leave the person's body."

Chris shuddered. "I don't think I'd want to be around to see that. Would you?"

Emily stared out the window at the blowing darkness. "Have a chance to destroy the thing that destroyed my brother's life? Oh, I'd want to be around, Chris, believe me."

They now reached a long strip of fast-food places. The night sky was aglow with neon red and yellow and green and purple. Teenagers in shiny cars drove up and down the strip, followed occasionally by a police squad car.

"I was right, wasn't I?"

"About me believing you?"

"Yes," Emily said.

"May I reserve judgement?"

"Sure. You may do anything you please."

150

"I like you."

"And I like you."

"And I want to believe you."

"And I want you to believe me, too."

"But I need time to see how things go. Can you blame me?"

"No," Emily said, and looked out the dark window again. "No, I can't blame you."

"We'll be there in a little bit," Chris said, changing the subject again.

"At Marie's?"

"Yes. I just hope her mother will let us see her."

Emily said, "So do I. And I hope Marie saw that Dobyns was under some kind of trance when he killed that boy." She bit her lip. "The police wouldn't even listen to me when I tried to tell them about Rob."

Chris could see how the stress was getting to Emily now. Emily looked older suddenly in the dashboard light, and no longer so poised or self confident.

"Do you think we could stop at Denny's for a cup of coffee?" Emily said.

"Sure."

"I—guess I need some coffee right now."

There was a Denny's two blocks ahead.

Her first impression was, *This is not my daughter. This is someone else's daughter. There has been a mistake. A terrible mistake.*

Kathleen Fane watched as two uniformed policemen led the Marie impostor up the carpeted steps to the second-floor landing of the apartment house. They moved the girl very carefully, very slowly, as if she were a piece of extraordinarily precious sculpture that might break at any moment.

Even from several feet away, Kathleen could see the blood that was splattered all over her daughter. She had seen people involved in car accidents who hadn't looked so bloody. The scene at the bookstore must have been horrible beyond description.

Marie's eyes were the worst part. 'Shock' was the clinical

word. But it came nowhere near describing the deadness of the once-beautiful blue gaze. Mother and daughter alike had regarded Marie's eyes as her most attractive feature but now they were terrifying.

As Kathleen walked out in the hall toward her daughter and the policemen, she hoped to see at least some faint flicker of recognition in Marie's eyes. But nothing; nothing. The girl didn't even look up when Kathleen reached out and took her arm.

Kathleen tried not to cry—she knew this was a difficult time for the police officers as well as for Marie and herself—but she could not hold back completely, silver tears formed in the corners of her eyes.

"Good evening, ma'am," the stouter of the two officers said.

"Thank you so much. Thank you so much," Kathleen said, taking Marie from them. The girl's limp was still decidedly pronounced. In fact, her mother wondered if it wasn't worse now. Then, "When I asked about the boy they said they weren't positive that he was— Is he—?" She tried twice to say the word 'dead.' Neither time would her tongue and lips quite form the word.

The taller of the two officers—the slender one—nodded. It was easy to see the grief in his eyes. Obviously police officers were no more exempt from urban horrors than anyone else. The officer told Kathleen about taking Marie to the hospital, about the doctor's examination of the cut on her neck, and of her state in general.

Kathleen took in a breath sharply, thinking of the poor boy's mother. It made so little sense. You send your kids off for what's supposed to be a night of light work and lots of fun and a few hours later, one of them is dead and the other has totally withdrawn from reality.

"Shouldn't she be at the hospital?" Kathleen said, just before taking Marie inside.

"The doctor said she'll be all right tonight but that you should call your family doctor in the morning. He gave her some medication." The officer handed Kathleen a small brown plastic bottle.

"Thank you, officers," Kathleen said.

She took her daughter inside. There were three locks—a dead bolt and two chain locks—but ordinarily she only used one of them. She used to laugh about how paranoid the previous occupant of this apartment must have been. But tonight, without any hesitation, she used all three locks. And she knew that she would for the rest of her life.

The couch made into a comfortable double bed. Kathleen plumped it up even further with two layers of blankets and a nice clean peppermint-striped sheet with matching pillowcases. She then put two heavy comforters on the bed. Then she helped her daughter lie down.

Earlier, Kathleen had given Marie a long, hot shower. She'd even washed Marie's hair and blow-dried it. As a final touch, trying for anything that would get the girl to speak, she sprayed on some of the expensive perfume Marie had given her for Christmas. In her best sheer white nightgown, in her best dark blue robe and matching corduroy slippers, Marie looked very pretty.

Once her daughter was on the couch with the covers pulled up over her, Kathleen went to the kitchen and fixed them a snack, leftover slices of white turkey meat with light daubs of yellow mustard on rye bread, a big dill pickle each, a scattering of chips and two glasses of skim milk turned into the pauper's malted milk with the help of Kraft Chocolate Malt.

She set the two plates on the coffee table in front of the couch and then sat down. "Now you eat what you want, hon. Or nothing at all. It's up to you."

Everything was fine now except for Marie's eyes. They hadn't changed. They still stared off at some horrible private vision.

Kathleen picked up her sandwich. Maybe if she ate, Marie would do likewise. She took a bite from the sandwich, swallowed it, and raised a chip to her mouth. She smiled at her daughter. "I know I'm supposed to be on a diet, hon. No need to remind me."

Marie said nothing. Still stared down at the bed in which she sat.

After two more bites, Kathleen said, "Know what I think I'm going to do? Call Dr Mason. Tell him everything that's going on

153

and see what he's got to say." She smiled and leaned over and kissed her lovely daughter on the cheek. Marie sat there statue still. If she was aware of her mother's presence, she gave no hint at all.

Kathleen got up and went over to the alcove between living room and dining room. There, in the corner, was a leather chair and light for reading, and next to it on a small table filled with books was a phone.

She found Dr Mason's number with her other emergency numbers in the back of the telephone book. She didn't get Dr Mason, of course, she got a somewhat crabby sounding young woman who seemed displeased that anybody would call Dr Mason at this time of night. Reluctantly, the young woman took the message and said that she'd have Dr Mason call back. Kathleen wanted to say something catty—she always curbed her tongue when people insulted her; simply accepted their unkindnesses—but she decided this would be the worst time of all to be self-assertive. What if Marie heard her? An atmosphere of tension and argument would be all the girl would need at a time like this.

Kathleen went back and finished her sandwich. Marie said nothing. Stared.

Once, Marie made a noise. Kathleen almost leapt out of her chair. Was Marie about to talk? No. Marie settled down again, this time even closing her eyes, as if she were drifting off to sleep.

When the phone rang, Kathleen jumped from her chair and strode across the room with only a few steps.

She caught the receiver on the third ring. "Hello."

No sound. A presence—you could tell somebody was on the other end of the line—breathing. Listening. But not talking.

"Hello," Kathleen said.

The breathing again. The listening.

"Who is this please?"

She almost laughed at her politeness. Here it was the worst night of her life—her daughter could easily have become the victim of a senseless slaughter—and she was saying please and thank you.

154

"If you don't say something, I'm going to hang up."

"Not. Done."

A male voice said these two words.

"I beg your pardon?"

"Not. Done."

"I don't know what you're talking about."

"Marie."

"Yes? What about Marie?" She could hear the panic in her voice.

"Not. Done."

Then the male caller hung up.

It was clear enough what he'd been getting at.

His work with Marie was not done yet. The work that had started back in the bookstore.

Now Kathleen hung up.

She immediately dialled 911 for the police.

After he hung up, Dobyns leaned forward in the phone booth and pressed his forehead against the glass.

He could see his reflection.

He stared at it the way he would the face of a stranger who, for some reason, looked familiar.

He would not hurt the girl anymore. He would go back to Hastings House and sneak into the tower and rid himself of the being that rode inside his stomach. He would let nobody stop him; nobody.

He stumbled from the phone booth, alternately cold and hot, alternately euphoric and depressed. He was sorry he had called the Fane woman. The thing inside him had taken control again—

He still remembered Marie Fane's eyes in the bookstore.

She could have been his own daughter a few years later—

He staggered through the shadows.

Back to Hastings House and the tower.

Somehow he would rid himself of—

But just then nausea worked its way up from his stomach into his throat and he knew the thing was moving again, demonstrating its dominance.

He kept stumbling forward—

155

O'Sullivan had started out as a newspaperman back in the glorious days of Watergate. That era had been one of the few in American history when journalists were esteemed and exalted by their fellow citizens, even if they had worn flowered ties and wide lapels and sideburns that reached to their jawlines.

O'Sullivan had been glad to take advantage of all this glory, even if he was little more than a glorified copy boy. Night after night he'd stood drinking white wine in the fashionable singles bars of those days declaiming on the subject of the journalist's responsibility to the democracy. Anybody who had even an inkling of what he was talking about thought he sounded pretty silly and full of himself, but to miniskirted insurance company secretaries (bored with guys who hit on them with little more than a few gags lifted from *The Mary Tyler Moore Show*), O'Sullivan sounded pretty good, especially after the young women had had more than their share of drinks.

A few years later, going nowhere as a reporter on the paper, O'Sullivan had some drinks with Channel 3's then news director and decided what the hell, to try it as a TV guy. Understand now, O'Sullivan had been thirty pounds lighter in those days, and most of his Irish dark hair was intact, and he still had a warm feeling for most people that came across as a kind of ingenuous charm. In other words, he worked pretty well on the tube. He was appealing if not downright handsome, he had a nice 'gonadic' voice (as one of the more eloquent news consultants once described it), and he found that he sort of liked the limitations of the form—cramming everything you could into a minute or a minute-and-a-half report. On the paper you might have two or three thousand words to tell your story; on the tube you had a max of three hundred.

He rarely thought of these things anymore except when he went over to the newspaper. Even late at night, when there were mostly just kids working, O'Sullivan got The Stare.

The Stare is something that newspaper journalists always visit on television journalists. It transmits, in effect, the notion that TV people aren't really reporters after all and that they couldn't report a parking meter violation with any accuracy or style.

O'Sullivan stood on the edge of the newsroom now, letting the six or seven folks who had the graveyard shift aim The Stare at him.

O'Sullivan missed the *clackety-clack* of the typewriter days. Now everything was word processors and they didn't make any respectable journalistic noises at all.

At this time of night, the vast room with its teletypes and desks, its paste-up boards and overloaded photo desks, was quiet and dark. Now that they'd had their fun flinging The Stare at him, the reporters went back to their work on the phones and their computer screens.

They knew him from his occasional appearances on TV but he didn't know them. There was a whole new generation at work here and not a friendly face among them. Who could he get to let him into the computer morgue?

From behind him then came a thunderous flushing noise from one of the johns. A few moments later the tune of *Eleanor Rigby* was whistled on the air and a tall, gaunt man bald on top but with shoulder length hair in back came strolling out from the men's room. Despite his white shirt and conservative necktie, his little granny-glasses and his PEACE NOW button on the pocket of his shirt said that he still wished the era of Flower Power were upon us. He was obviously O'Sullivan's age or thereabouts but there was something youthful about him, too, some vitality and wryness that too many meetings with too many TV consultants had drained from O'Sullivan.

"Hey, O'Sullivan."

"Hey, Rooney."

"You must be slumming."

O'Sullivan grinned. "You're right. I am."

"Still going out with Chris Holland?"

"Sometimes."

"I envy you that."

"What's wrong with your wife? Last time I looked, she was a pretty nice woman."

"Dumped me."

157

"I'm sorry."

"Yeah, so am I actually." For a moment pain tightened Rooney's gaze and then he said, "Whatever happened to that beer you were going to buy me last year when I let you go through our morgue?"

"How about adding it to the other beer I'm going to buy you for letting me use the morgue tonight?"

Rooney smiled. "TV has made you a ruthless, cynical sonofabitch, hasn't it."

O'Sullivan patted his stomach. "No, TV has made me a chunk-o who picks up a Snickers every time he has an anxiety attack."

"Why don't you come back to the newspaper? They don't pay us enough to afford Snickers."

"Maybe that's a good idea."

Rooney clapped him on the back. "Actually, it's good to see you, O'Sullivan. You're not half as big an asshole as most people think."

Laughing, O'Sullivan followed Rooney down the hall to the computer morgue. Rooney opened the door, pointed to the coffee-pot in the corner of the big room that was laid out with computers much like viewers in the microfilm room of a library. Here was where the newspaper stored decades of information on thousands of local subjects.

"You got to leave a quarter for each cup of coffee, though," Rooney said. "You remember Marge? The little black woman who runs this room?"

"I remember Marge all right."

"She runs a tight ship. She'll hunt you down to the ends of the earth if you take a cup of coffee without leaving a quarter for it."

"Don't worry. I will. She scares the hell out of me."

Rooney smiled and left, closing the door behind him.

Hastings House was built just before the turn of the century. In the photos from that time, the place looked about a tenth the size of its present form. A couple of stiff looking gents in top hats and long Edwardian coats could be seen, in one photo, turning over shovelfuls of dirt to get the project started—and

158

then a year later standing in the same top hats and long Edwardian coats on the steps of the new building.

In the background, the tower was clear and impressive in the winter sunlight. Constructed of native stone, with a kind of turreted top, it rose against the sky with medieval grace, though the stories from the time quickly noted that the tower could not be used because of faulty construction.

In 1912 patient escapes tied to murders began. The first such incident involved a man named Fogarty. He had managed to walk away from the facility and had, several hours later, accosted a woman in her home. After raping her, he took a knife and began what the paper vaguely described as 'a series of mutilations.' She was found dead, at suppertime, by her two youngest children who had been 'down the road playing.' He had also been suspected of killing a four-year-old girl, but her body was never found.

Reading this, O'Sullivan sighed. Most people like to look back on past times with a patronising nostalgia. People were so much simpler then, they like to think. And life was so much easier, a Currier and Ives world of humble, pleasant people leading humble, pleasant lives. Well, to cure that nonsense, just sit down and read through some old newspapers as O'Sullivan was doing tonight. The Currier and Ives nonsense gets quickly buried. People then were just as petty, mean, and scared as they are now.

After twenty minutes, O'Sullivan went over and dropped a quarter into the change by the coffee-pot. It was like dropping money in the votive candle slot. Not unlike God, Marge demanded her due.

Then O'Sullivan got down to real work. And odd as it sounded, some of the things the Lindstrom woman said didn't sound half as crazy as they had over the phone earlier tonight. Not half as crazy at all.

By the time he was finished, O'Sullivan had deposited more than a dollar in the change box, and emptied his bladder three times.

During her fifth cup of coffee, Emily Lindstrom said, "Sometimes I wonder if it's just my vanity."

"Your vanity?"

"Ummm. With Rob. You know, the family honour and all that. Just not wanting people to think my brother's a killer."

"I'm sure it's more than that."

Emily sighed and looked around Denny's. A nearby sporting event must have let out within the past half-hour because the restaurant had suddenly filled up with what looked like father-and-son night.

Emily sipped her coffee and said, "After we talk to Marie Fane, I want to try and find Dobyns."

"Oh?"

"I told you about the incantation."

"Yes."

"I want to see if it works."

Chris's gaze dropped to her own coffee.

"I appreciate you not smiling."

"Why would I smile?"

"Incantation. It's not a word you hear very often in modern day society."

"I suppose not."

Emily leaned forward with more urgency than she intended. "There really was a cult, Chris. And there really is a serpent. As unlikely as it sounds."

Chris wasn't exactly sure what to say but then the sweaty, overworked waitress leaned in and gave Chris the bill and saved her from saying anything at all.

Five minutes later they were out in the parking lot. The nice spring night was suddenly as cold as early November.

Abbott was saying to Costello, "They ain't gonna cook our goose. They're gonna cook somethin' else." And then he pointed to his rather formidable posterior.

They were standing outside this big metal pot that was boiling over as a group of natives (Africans, supposedly, and cannibals to boot) were licking their chops at the prospect of eating up two white boys dumb enough to give them trouble.

The movie was *Africa Screams* and it was made long after Bud and Lou were hot and that was pretty obvious because of all the cheap sets and nowhere actors. Kathleen Fane had seen this movie when she was about Marie's age, a time of her life she was resolutely sentimental about (how shiny and fine most things are remembered or anticipated) and God knew she needed something to put up against the horrors of tonight, of her dear sweet precious daughter Marie who'd nearly been murdered a few hours ago.

Murdered. My God! What must that boy's family be going through right now?

The Chief now goosed Lou with a spear.

Lou looked into the big boiling pot and made a face.

Kathleen giggled.

It wasn't all that funny, of course—Bud and Lou were sort of like Jerry Lewis, once you got past fifteen they kind of lost their magic—but the face he made was so clean and childish and wholesome, so redolent of her innocence, that she giggled out loud.

And then immediately felt guilty.

What if she woke Marie up?

Kathleen was in the small room they used as a combination sewing room and den. There was a nice big bookcase filled with all the Doubleday Book Club editions she'd taken over the years (Book of the Month Club and Literary Guild were too expensive) and a wall full of photos of when there'd been three of them. Now, she got up and went to the door and looked out into the living room, at the frosty moonlight that fell through the window onto the couch. Marie was still asleep. Kathleen sighed gratefully.

She went back into the den and turned the sound even lower, pulling the rocking chair even closer to the screen.

As she settled back into the movie, she started thinking again about the anonymous caller. She was glad she'd called 911. Talking to the police officer had made her feel reassured. When she told him what had happened to Marie tonight, he got very sympathetic (even over the phone he had a bedside manner

161

that many doctors would envy) and said that it was better to be safe than sorry (which actually sounded kind of cute coming from him, a manly cop) and that he'd have a car immediately begin cruising past her house and checking for anything untoward. That was the word he'd used. Untoward. It was a nice, strong word and helped reassure her even more.

Lou now started making his famous chittering noises (he only chattered when he was afraid) and shaking his head NO! when the Chief suggested he step into the pot and become the dinner for all these hungry natives.

She set her head back, feeling the blanket she'd knitted cosy and warm against her spine.

Everything had changed tonight. What Marie had witnessed would alter her in some irrevocable way forever. Every other event in her life would be measured—good or bad—against this one.

Thinking this, Kathleen felt a mother's fury pounding through her bloodstream.

She wanted to take the man who'd done this and—

The phone rang, startling her.

For a moment she had to gather herself. It was like coming up through water, the sunlight and sounds almost harsh on the senses.

She'd been so engrossed in imagining what she'd like to do to the man that—

The phone rang again. The fourth time.

She rose from the rocker and went to answer it.

"Hello," she said.

A pause. A hesitation.

My God it was the same caller who'd earlier—

"Mrs Fane?"

"Yes."

"It's me. Sergeant Milford. You called me earlier."

A sigh so profound she felt her knees weaken. "Oh, hello, Sergeant."

"I just wanted to check and see how things are going."

"He hasn't called back."

"Good. We're going to have a patrol car posted outside the

162

apartment house the rest of the night."

"Thank you. I appreciate that."

"How's your daughter?"

"Sleeping."

"That's the best medicine. For right now, anyway."

"I suppose that's right." She hesitated. "Is it natural for me to be angry at a time like this?"

"Very natural."

"I've never felt like this before."

"I've got kids, too. I can't imagine what I'd be like."

"I always thought I was against the death penalty. But that was just because murder had never touched me personally. After tonight—"

"People can get their minds changed about a lot of things, sometimes." He coughed. "If you'd like, I could try you again in a half hour or so."

"Oh, that's all right. I'll probably be asleep by then. But I really do appreciate your interest."

"Take care of yourself, Mrs Fane. I'll check in with you tomorrow."

"Thank you, Sergeant."

She hung up and went back to her rocker. The call had the same effect on her as a glass of warm milk. She was very sleepy.

She had just settled into the last part of Bud and Lou's unlikely adventure when her daughter screamed.

10

IT TOOK KATHLEEN FANE ten minutes to calm Marie. The screaming that had summoned mother to daughter was enough to awaken neighbours. Kathleen wanted to walk through the corridors apologising to everybody. A very properly raised middle aged woman, she felt that the worst thing a human being could do was make a scene. But then, holding a trembling Marie in her arms, she decided she was being silly. There wasn't a single thing to apologise for—not given the circumstances.

They sat in the living room, on the rocker, Marie in her

mother's lap as if she were a small child. The only sound was that of the rocker squeaking comfortably back and forth. Kathleen held her daughter tightly, and every few minutes pressed a handkerchief to the girl's forehead. Marie was sticky with sweat.

"I'm afraid he'll get me, Mom," Marie said.

Kathleen felt momentary relief when Marie spoke. She'd secretly feared that Marie's shock was so deep, the girl wouldn't speak for a long time. Kathleen was a worrier—neurotic was the more precise word—and she tended to extrapolate the worst possible outcome of every problem.

"They've probably caught him already."

Kathleen knew instantly it had been the wrong thing to say. False hopes that would only make the situation worse.

"You mean they *have* caught him?"

"Not yet. Not right this minute. But soon—I'm sure they will, honey."

Marie stared up at her mother. She did not seem the least self-conscious about sitting in the chair with Kathleen, which pleased Kathleen greatly. Sometimes she wished she had a time machine and could go back to the days when their family had numbered three. Back when a pre-car-accident Marie had been a small, happy child of four, concerned mostly with pretty butterflies and old Woody Woodpecker cartoons on TV (she'd always liked to imitate Woody's laugh).

"You should have seen him," Marie said. "In the store—and in my nightmare. That's why I was screaming when you came in here."

"I assumed that was why, darling."

"His eyes—" She swallowed hard and shook her head. "I can't describe them." She looked at the bed. And smiled. Kathleen couldn't believe it. "Are your legs asleep yet, Mom?"

"My legs?"

"Having your sixteen-year-old daughter on your lap can't be real comfortable."

"It's a pleasure."

Marie leaned forward and kissed her mother tenderly on the cheek. "It's a pleasure for me, too, Mom. You've done so much for me."

Kathleen hugged her daughter to her and started rocking again gently.

"You sure I'm not killing you?" Marie laughed.

"Well, if you are, then it's a very pleasurable death."

But Marie stood up anyway. "I'd like to lie down, I think." Kathleen saw how pale and shaky Marie had suddenly become. For months, maybe years after, Marie would be subject to seismic shocks like this.

Kathleen helped Marie to the couch. Marie lay down. Kathleen drew the covers up to Marie's chest and turned up the electric blanket a notch. Then she felt something small and hard on the mattress next to Marie. "What's this, hon?"

For a moment Marie seemed embarrassed. "Oh, nothing, Mom, just—"

But by now Kathleen had already pulled the object from beneath the covers.

"I remembered where you kept it," Marie said, her voice almost plaintive. "With Daddy's other things."

What Kathleen held was a .38 revolver with walnut grips that her late husband had used for target practice. A gentle man, he'd never been one for hunting, for taking the lives of fellow creatures even if they were lower on the so-called intelligence scale. But he had been a fanatical target shooter, several times winning various state meets.

"Is it—loaded?" Kathleen said.

"Yes."

"You knew how to do it?"

"From a show I watched on PBS. I watched it because of things you told me about Daddy. I thought it was a show he might have liked. You know?"

"Oh, honey," Kathleen said, and took her daughter's hand. Kathleen felt again that sharp sense of loss that had been hers ever since the death of her husband. And she could see now that Marie still felt it, too. "Are you sure you feel comfortable with this?"

"A lot more comfortable with it than without it, Mom."

Kathleen looked down at the weapon, traced her fingers

over the blued steel and the chambers for bullets. How could she deny her daughter the sense of security the .38 obviously gave her? "You sure you want to sleep with it under the covers? Maybe it could go off and—"

Marie leaned up and kissed her. For a fleeting moment the girl's face was clear of all pain and something like a smile played on her mouth. "Mom, it'll be all right. I'm sure I won't have to use it. But it'll make me feel a lot better, all right?" She nodded toward the den where the TV played bright and low in the shadows across the room. "Why don't we watch David Letterman?"

"I didn't think you liked David Letterman."

Marie laughed. There was an undertone of bitterness in the laugh, as if all evidence of youth had suddenly gone from her. "Tonight David Letterman sounds wonderful, Mom."

Kathleen nodded. She switched on the TV in the living room and then went to turn off the one in the den.

They had been watching the show ten minutes when the phone rang.

Kathleen got up too quickly to get it. She hoped Marie didn't notice the anxious way she'd half leapt to the phone.

"Hello."

"Mrs Fane. This is Sergeant Knowles. I'm downstairs at the door."

"Oh. Yes, Sergeant."

"There are two people here who'd like to talk to Marie."

"I'm afraid that's impossible, Sergeant. Marie is resting."

"They said they wouldn't need more than a few minutes."

"I'm afraid not."

"Who is it, Mom?" Marie said.

"Excuse me a moment, Sergeant."

"Yes, ma'am."

Kathleen cupped the phone. "Two people are here to see you."

"Who?"

"I didn't ask. You don't want company now." Marie shrugged.

"Why don't you ask who it is?" Into the receiver, Kathleen said, "Who is it, Sergeant?"

"Chris Holland from Channel 3 news and a friend of hers."

Kathleen told Marie who it was.

Marie said, "Why don't we see them, Mom?"

"But why?"

"I'm feeling better right now, Mom. It'd be okay for a few minutes."

"You sure?"

Marie nodded.

Into the receiver, Kathleen said, "Why don't you send them up, Sergeant. But tell them they can stay only a few minutes."

"All right, Mrs Fane."

"And thank you. I feel much better knowing you're down there."

"Just doing my job, ma'am."

Kathleen hung up.

"I like her," Marie said.

"Who?"

"Chris Holland. On Channel 3."

"I'm not sure which one she is."

"You like her, too. You've told me you do."

Kathleen came over and looked at her tired, drained daughter. "I still don't know why this couldn't have waited till tomorrow or something."

"I'll tell her everything that happened to me. Then I can tell the other reporters that I've already told Channel 3. Then maybe they won't bother me so much."

Marie put out her hand and Kathleen took it, holding it tenderly.

"I'm not sure what I'm up to, Mom. Everything's just kind of crazy right now. I figure why not see Chris Holland. You know?"

Kathleen smiled. "Well, honey, anytime you want them to leave, you just tell me."

Marie managed a smile, too. "My mom the bouncer."

Then the two women were at the door. They came in and made pleasant hellos and then proceeded to ask many strange questions, particularly the beautiful but distraught woman who was tagging along with Chris Holland.

It was when the Lindstrom woman asked if Marie had noticed

167

the killer's stomach—any movement inside the killer's stomach—that Kathleen began to doubt in a serious way if the woman was sane.

When you came right down to it, Security Chief Andy Todd sort of liked Jeff Claiborne, even if the male nurse was gay. Jeff liked all the things any normal young man would—baseball, politics, the tyre sales Goodyear was always having—and never once expressed the least interest in anything such as ballet, longhair music, or sculpture. Jeff had even expressed an interest in getting involved in some 'security action' sometime. Andy just figured that maybe Jeff hadn't met the right young woman yet and when he did he'd probably slide on the ol' condom and start screwing his brains out. In the meantime, Andy had to suffer Jeff's subtle allusions to his roommate Ric, as if the R-i-c didn't tell you all you needed to know. Anyway, Jeff always worked in some reference to Ric in their conversations and every time he did Andy got tight. Real tight. It was a crime against nature and for Jeff's own sake Andy wanted to punch Ric's face in and then tell him to go join the Marines and leave Jeff alone.

All these thoughts had been brought up earlier tonight when the two men had taken their late coffee break together. One of the security guards had come down with flu so Andy was spelling him and there was no way he was going to put in an eighteen-hour day without plenty of breaks. So, anyway, shaggy-haired Jeff had eaten his apple while ample-bellied Andy had snarfed down his Twinkie (he figured it was okay to cheat on his blood pressure as long as his wife didn't find out). Things had been going fine, the two men talking about the Cubs (or the Cubbies as Andy always called them) and World War II (while Andy had never been in the armed forces, he did have the entire Time-Life World War II collection) and the tractor pull that would be going on out at the fair this summer. Everything was going fine. No mention of R-i-c.

And then Andy noticed the earring.

It wasn't a big earring.

No bigger than a pigeon turd, as a matter of fact.

But it was an earring.

And it was riding plain and bold in Jeff's right earlobe.

And the whole thing just frosted the shit right out of Andy.

"Whoa," Andy said.

"Huh?"

"What's that?"

"What's what?"

"In your ear?"

At least the little bastard had sense enough to blush. "Oh, Ric gave it to me for my birthday."

"Ric did, huh?"

"Yeah."

"You ever think maybe it was time for Ric to sort of move out and find his own place and leave you alone?"

"He's a nice guy."

Andy stared at him, the way he would at his own son. "I think you're a fine young man, Jeff."

He could see how nervous this all made Jeff.

"I appreciate that, Andy."

"But that doesn't mean I approve of everything you do. You understand what I'm trying to say?"

And Jeff, embarrassed and uneasy, dropped his gaze. "I understand, Andy."

"You don't want folks to start makin' fun of you, do you?"

Jeff just sort of vaguely shook his head.

"Once they see that earring, that's just what they're gonna start doin', I'm afraid."

"You wouldn't make fun of me, would you, Andy?"

Andy could feel the young man's pain and suddenly Andy felt for shit and wished he hadn't brought it up in the first place. Maybe it was the kid's own business and maybe Andy should just keep his mouth shut.

And it was then the phone rang and Andy leapt to it with a gratitude that was impossible to contain.

Gratitude till he heard who it was. Frank Dvorak. The same front gate guard who had let Dobyns escape.

"Yes, Frank, what is it?" Andy knew that he should have been over his mad by now, but he wasn't. Couldn't get over it.

169

"I thought I should tell you somethin'."

"What?"

"There's somebody down by the garage. Can't make out who it is. Maybe Dobyns."

"Can't you go check?"

"I'm waiting for a call."

Andy sighed: *Can't leave the gate. Waiting for his goddamn girl friend again.* "You want me to check it out?"

"If you wouldn't mind."

Goddamn Dvorak wanted to be petted like a dog.

"Okay," Andy said. He hung up and turned to Jeff. "You're always saying your job gets dull. You want to try mine for a while?" Maybe being a security guy would make a man out of Jeff yet.

"Really?" Jeff said.

"Really."

"Great!" Jeff said. He polished off the last of the diet Pepsi, got up from the wobbly plastic table, took his empty food wrappers over to the communal garbage can, and then joined Andy on his way to the elevator that would take him to the basement parking garage adjacent to the tower.

Two and a half minutes later, the elevator door rolled open and yellow light spilled into the dark garage, touching on the fenders and grills of the hospital vehicles. The concrete garage smelled of dampness and car oil.

When the elevator door closed, Andy snapped on his flashlight, leading the way through the gloom. "You still glad you came?"

Jeff laughed. "Sure. Am I supposed to be scared or something?"

"It's pretty dark down here."

"I'll be fine, Andy. Honest." There was a laugh in his voice.

When they reached the middle of the garage, Andy stopped and shone his light down a wide row of vehicles that was four deep. Somebody could easily be hiding between the cars.

Andy drew his Magnum.

"Stay right by me," Andy said.

"You really think Dobyns came back here?"

"Guess we'll have to ask him if we run into him, huh?"

"Guess so."

They took a few more steps and then Andy heard the noise. He crouched down in front of a panel truck, waving for Jeff to crouch down, too.

Andy killed his light.

The moon lay a thin veneer of cold silver over half the garage. All the vehicles looked like slumbering animals inside the vast cage of wire mesh that ran across the back windows of the big garage.

"You wait here," Andy said.

"How come?"

"For Christ's sake, Jeff, just do what I say."

Andy still wasn't sure what he'd heard. His first inclination was to say that it was a car door squeaking open and shut.

Whoever it was—and Jeff had a good point, why *would* Dobyns come back to the hospital?—may have just climbed into a vehicle to hide.

Andy spent the next five minutes walking up and down the dark aisles between cars and trucks. His rubber soles squawked loudly against the damp concrete floor and his light seemed to grow fainter, particularly as the beam was lost in the shadowy confines of a back seat.

Several times he paused to listen but all he heard were the sounds of the night and of his own breathing. He was getting a little old for this kind of thing. His weight and his bad heart didn't exactly make him an ideal guy for this sort of thing. He wondered how Jeff was doing, if the kid was spooked by now. But Jeff had more balls than Andy had given him credit for.

Then Andy found the station wagon with one of the side doors open. The wagons got taken home a lot and used by some of the more prominent staffers as temporary second or third cars.

Andy came even with the station wagon and began playing his light around inside. Back seat was empty, as was the cargo area in back. Couple issues of *Time* magazine and a brown paper

171

bag filled with empty cans of Diet-Rite cola, apparently on their way back to the supermarket.

Finished with the driver's side of the wagon, Andy decided to go around and check the left side. That's what they taught you to do in security school, anyway. Check both right and left; check both up and down. Because you never know.

Stuffed into the well between front seat and firewall, he found the body, or at least what was left of a security guard named Petry.

Andy had missed this the first time because he hadn't bothered to shine his light on the front floor.

Now, he stood cursing himself for his incompetence and staring down at the ugliest sight he'd ever seen.

Petry's throat had been cut so that his entire raincoat was soaked with blood. His eyes had rolled back so that now only the whites stared up at Andy. The security guard shivered. My God, this would give him nightmares for years. Petry's arm was extended in such a way that it looked as if he were grasping for a lifeline. His arm and hand blended in with the dark dashboard and seat covers because they were soaked with his own blood.

Then Andy heard the cry.

For the first time since he'd come down to the garage, he felt real fear, something Andy didn't readily admit to. He thought of himself as a competent, rational human being who could meet virtually any challenge life put in his path, and meet it with optimism and courage.

But now there was a sickening feeling in the pit of his stomach and an embarrassing twitch in his gunhand. He kept thinking of Petry's white eyes and red bloody face. It made Andy feel as if he were ten years old and in bad need of his father's reassuring voice. The old man was fourteen years dead now (heart attack, the way he'd wanted to go anyway) and there wasn't a day Andy didn't think about him.

Andy hoped the old man was with him right now. Somehow. Somewhere.

"Jeff?" Andy called out, shining his light into the cavelike darkness of the huge, echoing garage. "Jeff, are you all right?"

172

But there was no response.

Andy moved, inch by nervous inch, to the back of the garage.

And then he saw the elevator door roll open. The elevator car was a yellow rectangle in utter blackness.

A man got on and turned around to face Andy. At first Andy was under the impression that this was Jeff. He even relaxed a little. It was Jeff and Jeff was fine and everything was going to be all right, despite the way Andy had found Petry.

Andy, cognisant of the extra rolls of weight on his belly, hips, and thighs—and certainly cognisant of his high blood pressure—started running toward the yellow rectangle.

"Jeff! Wait for me!" Andy shouted in the echoing gloom.

But then as he drew closer—breath searing through his chest now, his head a little dizzy—he saw that the man standing in the elevator car was not Jeff at all.

It was Dobyns.

The elevator door rattled shut.

Andy was left alone in the darkness.

And then his left foot kicked against something. Andy angled the flashlight beam down on Jeff's face.

Laid out on the floor, Jeff looked like a corpse in a morgue awaiting his turn under the autopsy knife.

Dobyns had done pretty much the same things to Jeff that he'd done to Petry. Throat slashed, defence cuts all over the hands and arms from where Jeff had been trying to defend himself, blood and pus and excrement pooled around Jeff's hips. The kid smelled pretty bad.

Then Andy's beam lingered a moment on Jeff s ear, on the silly goddamn little earring that his friend Ric had given him. And Andy felt like shit. Who was he to make judgements on how other people lived? He was just this silly fucking middle aged fat man who was still playing at cops and robbers. Hell, he'd never even been in the armed forces.

"So long, kid," Andy said softly, there in the gloom of the garage.

It was then that he became aware of the elevator door opening again, of the yellow rectangle glowing like a hole in the ebon wall of night.

Dobyns stood in the door of the elevator car.

What the hell was he doing? What the hell did he want?

Andy killed his flashlight.

Stood there breathing so heavy and so ragged he was getting scared. *The old man just pitching over one night on the back porch, dead.* With a family medical history like that, it sure could happen to Andy easy enough.

Andy had to be careful.

His heart was just as much a threat to him as Dobyns.

Andy put his head down, seeing the vague outline of Jeff s body on the floor. Andy wanted to be respectful, not brush against the corpse. He took small, precise steps, moving around the body, then starting to walk away from it, toward the elevator door.

By now his gun hand was twitching badly and the Magnum was as heavy as a bag of cement.

He raised his head again to glance ahead to the elevator car.

Still there. Still open. A glowing yellow hole.

But there was one thing wrong. Badly wrong.

Dobyns was no longer in the elevator car.

He had come out here to the garage.

Given what he'd already done to Petry and Jeff, could there be any doubt what fate he had in mind for Andy?

It was then that the pain, like a piece of jagged summer lightning, crossed Andy's chest right to left and forced him to slump against the wall.

My God, he was having a heart attack.

And a sociopathic butcher named Dobyns was somewhere nearby with a knife.

And getting closer.

In the damp darkness of the garage.

Andy could hear Dobyns breathing every once in a while; hear his foot scraping, scraping against the concrete floor.

Getting closer.

Andy rubbed the area just above his sternum, where the pain had last been. The tightness in his chest was beginning to disperse, and the dizziness was gradually leaving his head.

Andy narrowed his eyes, scanning the gloom surrounding

him. He felt as if he were a tiny life raft adrift on a chill, fog-bound ocean with no possible hope of rescue.

He wanted to run to the elevator, but he was afraid that the exertion would cause a heart attack.

Or he could run out of the garage through the doors at the other end.

But somewhere behind him lurked Dobyns. Waiting.

The scraping sound again.

Dobyns moving.

Andy started to crouch next to the car and that was when he saw the keys in the ignition of the Dodge. Or thought he saw them.

Andy was filled—with the happiness of a biblical prophet discovering the light and the way and the truth—with a wonderful idea.

What if he got in the car real fast-like, locked the door, turned on the ignition, and then drove out of there?

Dobyns couldn't do a damn thing about it.

Except get out of the way.

Andy would be safe. And he could go to a nearby hospital and have them put him on an EEG and see if there'd been any heart damage or not.

Of course the tricky part would be getting inside the car.

In this kind of darkness, the dome light would go on like a bank of night lights at Wrigley Field.

Then he realised he was being ridiculous. He had a Magnum; Dobyns had only a knife. And Dobyns, however murderous he might be, was no superhuman monster. He would pay proper respect to a Magnum.

Still crouching, Andy put his hand on the door handle, then paused, listening for Dobyns.

Outside the hospital's fences, he could hear traffic. Thrum of tyre on pavement; honk of irritated driver.

He eased open the car door.

Wishing he weighed fifty pounds less, he heaved himself up into the seat.

The first thing he did was close the door. The second thing he did was lock the door. The third thing he did was start the engine. Or tried to.

Nothing happened. Not a single fucking thing. Oh, a little clicking noise, if you wanted to get technical. The tiny clicking noise made by the key as it tripped the lock. But other than that—nothing.

Then he vaguely remembered Schmitty, the man who took care of all the hospital vehicles, telling him that some new cars needed batteries and that he was going to take out all the old batteries and trade them in for new ones.

That's why Andy heard nothing except the clicking when he twisted the key.

My God. No battery.

Sonofabitch.

He felt this great urge to cry. To put his head against the steering wheel and just start sobbing. Like a helpless little boy.

But then he realised that he was safe.

He could sit here all night and Dobyns couldn't touch him. The car doors were locked. He had his Magnum. Dobyns couldn't possibly harm him. No way.

Then he saw the headlights come on to his right, the great glowing eyes of an unimaginable monster.

The headlights belonged to the large truck the hospital used to scrape off the drives in winter and carry heavy loads the rest of the year.

Now, the driver of the truck stepped on the gas while the gearshift was in neutral. The truck roared like a beast that wanted to be fed.

The truck roared one more time, and then leapt forward.

Andy, mesmerised, was blinded by the headlights as they shot closer, closer. The driver had thoughtfully set them on high beam so they'd be sure to be dazzling.

The driver? Dobyns, of course.

The first assault caught Andy's car right in the passenger door. There was a great, echoing crash of shattering glass and twisting metal and Andy's screams.

Andy was knocked clear across the front seat, his head slammed into the window on the passenger's side.

The pain came instantly back to his chest. This time it started running up and down his right arm, too. He wanted to move, scramble out of the car, but he felt confusion and panic and could not concentrate enough to—

The second assault caught the front fender on the driver's side and was delivered with such shattering force that Andy's car was spun halfway around and ended up facing the opposite direction.

Smashed glass tinkled to the concrete, echoing, and Andy's screams were now sobs and pleas for help.

The truck pulled back, tyres squealing, gears grinding, for one last assault.

Andy saw this coming. He put both his hands squarely against the dashboard...

Holy Mary, Mother of God, pray for us sinners now and at the hour of our—

The truck backed all the way to the garage door. It was going to come at Andy from behind.

And then Andy looked down at the Magnum on the seat next to him.

Of course My Lord.

He'd been so frightened, so disoriented, so worried about heart attack that he'd completely forgotten his own best defence.

Quickly he unlatched the seat belt, turned around so that he was facing the rear of the car, and set the Magnum on top of the seat.

He aimed directly at the windshield of the truck. *You sonofabitch Dobyns. You psycho sonofabitch.* Andy was ready.

And Dobyns was more than happy to oblige.

This time the truck's tyres created so much smoke, the rear end of the truck appeared to be on fire as it came piling toward Andy.

Andy opened fire.

It was like target practice on the range.

Even above the screaming tyres, you could hear the Magnum explode, each time Andy's hand and arm jerked back with the recoil.

Indeed it was like target practice.

The closer the truck got, its huge yellow eyes searching

mercilessly inside Andy's car, the oftener Andy pulled the trigger.

By the time of the great crash, by the time the truck pushed Andy all the way to the back of the garage and smashed him into the rear wall… by that time, Andy was out of ammunition.

Nothing would have helped Andy in this situation. Not even a seat belt.

When the car met the wall, Andy was thrown upward into the skyliner. To him, it felt as if the impact broke his head apart in three ragged pieces. Then the impact hurled him forward against the dashboard, the edge of which came against the centre of his spinal column with the force of a well-delivered karate blow. Even as he continued to tumble through the air, Andy could feel his legs go dead and he thought of a terrible word: 'paralysed.'

Then he drifted into blessed unconsciousness.

What he saw next gave him a curious peace. From somewhere high overhead—some unimaginable distance, really—he looked down on the scene in the garage. The smashed up car. The roaring truck. Dobyns racing from the truck now, bloody knife in hand.

And then Andy saw himself. He looked terrible. Covered with his own blood, and at least as smashed and broken as the car he was in.

Then Dobyns was in the car, checking out the body named Andy to see if it was still alive. When Dobyns found a pulse, he took his knife and slashed both of Andy's wrists so that blood flowed freely.

Then Dobyns took his knife and cut Andy's throat. He was very good at it by now, Dobyns was quite efficient. Just one downward cutting slash dragged across the Adam's apple, and the job was done.

Andy watched all this with a growing feeling of peace and security. He was glad that the body named Andy was unconscious because otherwise he'd be panic stricken beyond imagining. Gagging, trying to stop his throat from bleeding— No, the body named Andy had no understanding of the peace that awaited it. But the Andy that watched it all knew it well.

When Dobyns had cut Andy's throat, the fat man had sprayed

blood all over himself and Dobyns.

Now, withdrawing from the car, Dobyns wiped blood from his eyes and mouth.

He ran back to the elevator again. It would take him to the floor nearest the tower.

11

"DID YOU NOTICE anything about his stomach, Marie?"

"His stomach?"

"Yes. Anything—strange?"

"No, I'm sorry. I guess not." Marie hesitated. "But there was a weird smell."

"Oh?" Emily Lindstrom said. "Can you describe it?"

Marie shrugged. "Well, I guess I don't know what to say except that it was—it smelled like rotten meat or something."

Chris Holland and Emily Lindstrom had been in the Fane apartment for fifteen minutes now. While Marie had looked and sounded remarkably good, Chris now saw that the girl was still in the throes of shock. Soon, she would come in direct contact with her feelings about the slaying tonight and then—

Right now, the girl was instinctively using this interview as a way of avoiding her feelings. Chris had seen this following many traffic accidents, how badly injured people suddenly developed this great need to talk—this was just another manifestation of their shock—before they came crashing down.

"Please think back to his stomach," Emily was saying.

Too intense, Chris thought. *I've got to get her to ease off the girl or Marie will break for sure.*

Kathleen Fane was starting to watch Emily, too. The beautiful blond woman sounded as if she too were on the verge of snapping.

Chris said, "Did he say anything to you while this was all happening?"

Marie's cheeks flushed. "Dirty words."

"I'm sorry."

"The same dirty words over and over again."

179

"And then he just grabbed Richie?"

"Yes. And—"

And Chris (so worried about Emily's insensitivity) saw that she'd asked exactly the wrong question at exactly the wrong time.

The question forced the girl to confront the images of her friend's murder again.

With no warning whatsoever, she began crying very softly, and then sobbing so hard that her entire body shook.

Her mother was up from her chair in moments, and then sitting next to the girl and holding her with great tenderness.

"Please," Kathleen Fane said, "I think it's time you both leave."

While there was no malice in the woman's tone, there was certainly steel. This was not a request; it was an absolute command.

"I'm sorry if I made you mad back there."

"You got pretty intense."

"I just had to know about his stomach."

"I got the message."

"I'm sorry."

"I was just concerned about Marie."

Emily Lindstrom's voice softened. "The poor girl. She'll probably never really get over it."

Chris was headed back to the station. The harsh wind was blowing litter across the lighted drive of a service station. At a 7-Eleven people were getting knocked around by the same wind as they tried to run to their cars. For a moment Chris felt snug and warm inside her car, even if it was rocking slightly with every other gust.

And that was when, over the rock station that Chris was playing low in the background, they first heard about the killings at Hastings House.

"Two, perhaps as many as three employees of the mental facility have been killed tonight. This is all the information we have right now. But please stay tuned. We'll be updating this story every few minutes."

"To repeat—"

Emily snapped off the radio. "He went back to the hospital."

"But why? I thought he was trying to escape."

"There's only one reason I can think of."

"What's that?"

Emily Lindstrom said, "He wants to get into the tower."

For the second time tonight, O'Sullivan saw a section of the city turned into a kind of hell by the lights of emergency vehicles.

Hastings House had always had a quiet dignity for O'Sullivan—if you ever went crazy, this was clearly the place for them to take you—but tonight the dignity was being trampled by cops and reporters and onlookers roaming around the grounds, and by patients standing in heavily barred windows.

From the way the officials were running around, it was clear that they had no idea where Dobyns was.

Near the rear, at the entrance to the underground parking garage, an ambulance attendant was just closing the back doors on his boxy vehicle, three bodies having been set inside five minutes ago.

"Hey, O'Sullivan."

A cop named Schultz came up. In his grey suit and fashionably greasy hair (what was with everybody wanting to look like Jerry Lewis all of a sudden?), Schultz looked to be on the same diet O'Sullivan was —pancakes and malts.

"Nice gut you've got there," Schultz said, beating him to it.

"Yeah, like I didn't notice yours or anything," O'Sullivan said.

"So I've put on a few pounds."

"A few. Right."

"I quit smoking anyway."

"I don't even have that excuse," O'Sullivan said.

The four redbrick buildings that made up the new section of Hastings House had always reminded O'Sullivan of the small liberal arts college he'd gone to, spending four and a half years of wasted time pleading with WASP princesses for just a glimpse of the treasure between their legs.

"The way I get it," Schultz said, "the guy who stiffed the three staffers in the garage is the same guy who escaped from here the other night. Why the hell would he want to come back here?"

O'Sullivan shrugged. "You think he's still here?"

"Probably. There are a lot of places to hide."

"Why wouldn't he run away?"

"The police shrink thinks he probably came back here to turn himself in but then one of the guards spooked him so he killed these three guys."

O'Sullivan felt no temptation whatsoever to mention anything about cults or serpents that slithered inside the human body.

Schultz would never let him forget it.

"You still going out with Candy?" O'Sullivan said.

"Huh-uh."

"How come?"

"Let's just say that Candy wasn't exactly the most faithful woman I've ever known."

"I hear you. That's how my first wife was. I'm just glad she was hittin' on all these guys before AIDS showed up."

Somebody shouted Schultz's name. Then he was gone and O'Sullivan was thinking of what Schultz had said about Dobyns: He was probably still around here somewhere.

For the first time that evening O'Sullivan raised his eyes to the black sky that was streaked with misty moonlight and racing grey clouds.

The tower appeared medieval and almost majestic against the night sky.

As they pulled into the parking lot of Hastings House, Emily said, "I'm going up to the tower."

"What?"

"It's the only way I can convince him to turn himself over."

"But he'll kill you."

182

"No, he won't."

Chris shook her head. "I don't know how you can be so sure of that."

"The incantation."

Chris pulled the car into a parking space and shut off the engine. Before her, the grounds of Hastings House flashed with lights from the various emergency vehicles. Uniformed men and women with bullhorns and flashlights ran around the grounds. In one corner stood four men wearing flak jackets and holding rifles. This was obviously a SWAT team.

Their leader was talking with somebody over a walkie-talkie. The men looked very military.

"Then let me go with you," Chris said.

"No," Emily said. "I don't want you to risk your life for me." She looked at Chris with her luminous eyes and sombre beautiful face. "I need to do this for my brother, Chris, I really do."

"So you get up there and then what?"

"I ask him to come with me."

"And if he refuses?"

"He won't refuse. He's desperate. It's worth a try."

"It's so dangerous."

"If I can get him to come with me, it will save a lot of lives. The police may think they'll have an easy time of capturing him, but they won't."

Chris nodded to the SWAT team standing on the shadowy grounds in front of them. "What if they already know he's in the tower?"

"They don't. As far as they know, nobody has ever used the tower. They think it's strictly for decorative purposes."

"Emily—"

But as Chris spoke, Emily's hand was already on the door handle, pressing downward.

"I'm scared for you, Emily," Chris said.

"Don't be," Emily said. "Be happy for me. This is what I've been waiting for ever since my brother escaped from here that night."

Chris took her hand. "Just be careful."

Emily smiled her sad smile. "You be careful, too." And then

183

she started out of the car.

"Wait a minute," Chris said.

"What?"

"I didn't think of this before. How're you going to get up into the tower?"

"My brother told me the route."

"You're sure he's up there?"

Emily smiled again. "Positive." She patted Chris's hand. "Now I've really got to be going."

Dobyns's hands and arms were soaked with blood as he ran up the winding stairs leading to the tower.

In any structure that has been closed to light and warmth as long as the tower had, a dankness sets in. In Dobyns's case, this meant that his sinuses erupted.

As he felt his way up the wall, wishing he could see better, wishing he did not still hear the sounds of the security men as they'd died, he began sneezing violently.

Maybe I need to buy a little Dristan tonight, he thought. *Stop in at my favourite neighbourhood pharmacy and have them fix me up.*

Deep within his bowels, the snake moved, turning, shifting.

Below him now, somewhere at the bottom of the stairs, he heard the wooden partition covering the window being pushed back. The window was how he got in and out of the tower. Who else knew how to slide the partition back and forth?

His eyes searched the darkness below, uselessly.

He stood absolutely still, listening.

Footsteps scraped across the sandy floor leading to the staircase that wound to the very top of the tower.

Somebody was coming for him.

He formed a mental image of policemen in dark uniforms and flak jackets. Guns ready. Coming up the steps.

But no; for some reason he knew that this person coming after him was not a police officer at all.

Someone else. Someone with a different mission entirely.

And he chose then—just at this very moment in the cold shifting dusty shadows of the tower—to sneeze.

The footsteps below stopped.

Despite all the external noise seeping into the place—two-way radios on emergency vehicles; cops shouting back and forth; a distant siren—something like silence imposed itself on the tower now.

He waited, wondering who was below.

He touched his stomach. Beneath his hairy belly, he could feel the snake writhing.

He started climbing the steps, higher, higher now, clear to the tower.

Below him, the other footsteps began again, too.

Soon enough, he would meet this person.

Marie felt unclean. Usually, as in gym class, she liked the sensation of sweating, of cleaning her body of impurities. But tonight sweating felt different, pasty and dirty as she rolled around on the couchbed, sleeping fitfully. Earlier, she'd dreamed of the killer in the bookstore, the man coming closer, closer, and Marie grasping a gun and—

The apartment was dark except for a night-light in the bathroom. Not even a television could be heard on this floor of the apartment house. No, there were just the incidental sounds that all houses made during the night—the furnace, the plumbing, windows rattling faintly in the wind.

She had been to the bathroom, peeing, every fifteen minutes since her mother had gone to bed. Marie always peed when she was anxious. She couldn't sleep. Each time she closed her eyes, she saw the face of the killer. Each time she closed her eyes, she saw him in the bookstore, the knife in his hand, slashing Richie's throat—

In the bathroom she flushed the toilet, washed her hands, and walked back to the living room. She considered turning on the television but decided it might wake her mother. And, in certain ways, her mother needed the sleep worse than she did. She had long known that, in general, she was a stronger person than her mother and had, ever since she was a young girl, felt protective toward Kathleen. Thinking of her mother now, she

185

smiled. She was a 'good egg' (the same phrase Kathleen always used describing people she liked), lonely, frightened, fragile... and a good egg.

Marie walked over to the front window, parted the curtains a half inch, and looked down at the apartment building's parking lot.

There, directly beneath the mercury vapour light that swayed in the wind, sat a black-and-white police car.

Marie felt instantly safe.

With the back door locked, there was only one way the killer could get in—the front door—and any such attempt would immediately be stopped by the policeman sitting out there now.

Marie spent the next few minutes looking around the neighbourhood from her eyrie. She liked late nights like this when all the houses were snug asleep and the trees blew in the wind and the moon rode the sky just the way it had for millions of years. There was a mysteriousness to the night that Marie loved. Somehow night was her friend and day her enemy— she could hide in the night, not be crippled, not be afraid, just be Marie, nobody pointing or whispering. Yes, night was her friend—

Then she thought about the events at the bookstore and had to amend that.

Most times, night was her friend.

Tonight being a terrible, bloody exception.

Suddenly, as her eyes scanned the neighbourhood, the dark houses, the deep shadows, she realised that night was now her enemy.

Because the killer was out there. Somewhere. Hiding.

Her gaze dropped to the police car again. If she squinted hard, she could make out the figure of a police officer sitting on the driver's side behind the steering wheel. From here, she could not tell where he was looking, or what he was doing.

It was enough to know he was there.

She closed the curtains and went back to the rumpled bedclothes on the couch. The sheets were damp, cold damp, from her drying sweat.

Beneath the covers she saw the shape of the gun. She leaned down and touched it.

In its way, her father's gun was just as reassuring as the police officer in the parking lot.

Like her mother, Marie frequently communicated with her father, even carrying on long conversations with him. And she knew the words weren't imaginary, either. She believed in another realm of existence, an eternal realm of existence, and if your faith was true enough and deep enough, then you learned how to communicate with the people in that realm.

She jumped when she heard the creaking noise on the fire escape.

Without thinking, her hand wriggled down inside the covers and retrieved the gun. It felt bulky but comforting in her hand.

The fire escape.

That's how he'd get up here.

He would first of all have checked the parking lot and seen the police officer and then begun to search for alternative ways into the Fane apartment.

And the fire escape was a very logical way.

Clutching the gun to her breasts, Marie moved soundlessly across the carpet to the window that looked down on the backyard. The iron fire escape ran at an angle across this wall.

Marie moved up to the curtains, teased them open with one trembling finger.

God, she wished she weren't so afraid.

Even with her father's gun, she was shaking and dry mouthed.

She looked down at the fire escape that zigzagged down two floors to the ground.

There he was!

Climbing up the steps!

Coming right toward her!

And then she laughed at herself. Out loud.

She'd always had the ability to frighten herself. When she was a little girl, she'd kept her parents running into her room all night long, because she could not disabuse herself of the notion that terrible monsters lurked beneath her bed and in the closet. Her parents would turn on the lights and show her that nothing, absolutely nothing, was there, but as soon as the lights went off and they left, she got scared again because she knew the monsters were back.

And so tonight, gazing down at the fire escape, she'd briefly imagined she'd seen the killer there.

Knife in hand.

Skulking—what a fine word that was, skulking—up the steps to kill her.

She listened to the wind and watched moonlight trapped in the spring trees make patterns against the wall where the fire escape ran.

The fire escape was empty.

She'd only been imagining him there.

She laughed out loud at herself again.

"You scared me."

At the words, Marie spun around, terrified, holding the gun out from her as if ready to fire.

Her mother stood ten feet away, stunned that her daughter would be pointing the gun at her.

"Honey, please put that down. It scares me."

Marie glanced from the gun to her mother. "I'm sorry," she said.

She walked across to the couch and set the gun next to her pillow.

Her mother came over and embraced her. "Are you all right?"

"I just couldn't sleep," Marie said. She mussed her mother's hair and then let her go. "I couldn't sleep. I kept waking up and having nightmares about the—the man at the store. But look."

She walked with her mother over to the window.

Marie pulled back the curtain as if she were displaying a gift and said, "There's a police car right out there."

Kathleen squeezed Marie's hand. "That should make you feel safer."

"It does."

Marie saw her mother in profile as Kathleen stared down at

the police car. There were times when she realised that her mother was getting old, times when she realised—had no choice but to realise—that her mother wouldn't live forever. Now, as always when she had this thought, a heavy sorrow burdened Marie and she wanted to grab her mother and hold her and tell her a million things that, unfortunately, humans had no way of telling each other. 'I love you' had to suffice yet 'I love you' was nothing more than code for a thousand feelings, and nuances of feeling, that could never be expressed.

Her mother turned to Marie and looked startled by the girl's expression. "You okay, hon?"

"I'm fine."

"You look so sad."

Marie lied quickly. "I was just thinking about Dad. You know how I get."

Kathleen gave Marie another hug. "Well, you know he's here with us, don't you, honey?"

"I sure do." Marie smiled. "I talked to him tonight."

"Would you like a sandwich?"

"No, thanks, Mom."

"Glass of milk, then?"

"No, thanks." Marie yawned and stretched. "I'm pretty tired. Those pills I took make me feel weak. I just wish I could sleep."

"Glass of warm milk and a good book always puts me to sleep."

Marie smiled. "For a fragile little woman, you've got a will of iron. Has anybody ever told you that?"

"Everybody I've ever known over two days. I think it's their way of telling me I'm pushy."

Marie smiled. "Will of iron sounds better than pushy."

Kathleen laughed. "I think you're right. Will of iron sounds much better, in fact." She took Marie's elbow and pointed her in the direction of the couch. "Now why don't you go over there and pick up your book and I'll bring you in a glass of warm milk."

Marie knew that about all she could do at this point was comply.

The moment she slid beneath the covers, exhaustion began

189

creeping up her legs, spreading into her arms and shoulders.

In the kitchen her mother sounded happily busy. There seemed to be no time that Kathleen was happier than when she was being Marie's mother—domestic, fretful, tirelessly energetic. The woman obviously regarded motherhood as some kind of religious calling.

Marie reached up, clipped on the table lamp, and picked up her book. Her mother was right. Warm milk, a few pages of the Irwin Shaw paperback she'd been working on for a week, and she'd be asleep for sure. And hopefully, this time she'd stay asleep.

Her mother came into the room like a maiden in a parade, bearing the glass of warm milk on a saucer with an air of great ceremony.

"Would you like some toast?"

"No, Mother. And you don't need to fix me a three-course meal. Why don't you set the milk down, kiss me good night, and go in and get some sleep. You look exhausted."

Her mother seemed surprised. "But, honey, mothers are *supposed* to look exhausted."

"I suppose it says that in the Mother's Handbook."

Kathleen picked up the joke. "Yes, it does. Right on page sixty-three."

Kathleen leaned down, kissed Marie tenderly on the forehead, and then said good night.

"You can always come in and sleep with me," Kathleen said from the top of the hallway. She gathered her robe about her and nodded good night.

"I think I'm a bit old for that, Mother. Anyway, I found out that the boogeyman doesn't actually exist."

But after her mother had gone to bed, after the lonely wind began rattling the windows again, Marie thought of what she'd said about the boogeyman not existing.

But she'd been wrong, of course.

He did exist after all.

And Marie had seen him earlier tonight in the bookstore.

12

FOR A LONG and terrible moment, Emily Lindstrom felt that she was losing her sight. After pushing past the partition covering the tower's downstairs window, she had climbed up over the sill and dropped down into the shifting dusty darkness of the ground floor.

Everything was fine, then. She could hear Dobyns on the steps somewhere above her. All these years of searching, of investigating, and now the time was drawing near...

But then she had started climbing the steps and it was then she became—for the first time in her years of trying to find the truth for the sake of her brother and her family—afraid.

She wasn't even sure why she so suddenly felt her chest gripped with terror and why her legs felt so wobbly and why her body was sheathed in an invisible sticky body bag of sweat...

But she continued higher, higher.

Every seventh step in the darkness, her shoes grating against the sandy surface of the steps, the staircase wound tightly around just like a—snake.

There was no light whatsoever at this point. The staircase was narrow and confining as a coffin.

Higher, higher.

The words of the incantation began to fill her mind and silently touch her lips.

What if, when she confronted him, she got scared and forgot the incantation?

What then?

Higher, higher.

At one point she stumbled and reached out a quick hand to save her from striking her face against the edge of a step.

The grainy surface of the concrete cut deeply into her hand and she grimaced, the pain playing into her and making her feel even more vulnerable now that she was frightened.

But she continued to climb.

Nothing could deter her now; nothing.

Dobyns stood in the tower's lone room, waiting.

The floor was littered with bones of various kinds, both human and animal. There had been many sacrifices up here over the years, especially back in the days when a few members of the original cult were still alive.

Dobyns could feel the snake within him pressing against the curve of his belly.

The snake, too, was excited. Waiting.

By the time she reached the final step, she was completely out of breath. She put a hand against the rough stone wall and simply held on, letting her breath rip through her lungs and chest in deep, shuddering spasms.

Before her was the dark shape of a small door. Inside, she knew, Dobyns waited for her.

In just a minute or so—

She put her hand out to the door—

—reached the knob and turned it—

—and pushed the door inward and—

There was just enough light to see Dobyns standing in the centre of the tiny, circular room.

His eyes appeared to be closed. His hands were at his side. Faintly, she could hear him breathing, as if the dust and dampness of this place had disturbed his lungs.

She stepped into the room.

And saw his eyes fly open.

The pupils were a glowing amber colour.

He spoke in a voice that could not possibly be his own, low and raspy and guttural. "Have you come to give me your pussy, Miss Lindstrom?"

My God he—

"Or perhaps you want to suck my cock."

There in the darkness, the glow of his eyes held with a terrible power she could not break.

She walked closer to him. "I came to help you."

And he laughed, the sound of it as obscene as his words.

She put out a tentative hand, wanting to touch him and see

192

if the rest of him was as inhuman as his eyes.

And then she saw the struggle taking place in his stomach and chest.

The serpent was beginning to work its way up inside his chest. So violent was this shifting, this climbing, that Dobyns began to sway with its rhythms.

"I *can* help you," she said.

"The same way you helped your brother?"

"No, please, you've got to believe me. I know words that can—"

And just then the snake inside him threw Dobyns back against the wall and for a moment the man's voice was his own. "Help me, Miss Lindstrom! Please! Help me!"

As Dobyns stood writhing against the wall, his entire body shaking and shimmying as the snake struggled upward inside him, she walked closer—

—and then closer still—

—and began to speak the incantation she'd found in the old diary kept by one of the cult members who'd tried to free herself of the snake's domain.

And so Emily Lindstrom began. "In the name of the Divine Saviour, I command that the evil beast within you—"

And then it burst free, the serpent inside Dobyns.

Dobyns's eyes went dark, as if he had been suddenly blinded, the amber glowing eyes belonging to the head of the huge snake that now burst free of Dobyns's mouth.

Emily continued the incantation. She knew it was the only way.

The snake, about two feet of its body uncoiling from the man's mouth, snapped its head wildly back and forth like a heat sensing device seeking a target.

"I command that the evil beast within you—" Emily Lindstrom went on.

And then the great uncoiling snake, eyes glowing an even deeper amber now, struck with a ferocity Emily could not believe.

It struck her face, more specifically her mouth, sinking its two angled teeth deep into the flesh of her tongue.

193

And then it began to snap its head back and forth again, ripping her tongue out from its roots as it did so.

She screamed as she saw her own tongue torn free from her mouth, the snake holding it bloody in its teeth, and finally flinging it across the room against the wall.

Emily fell to the floor, uselessly covering her mouth with her long, lovely hands. She was trying to stop the blood that poured from her mouth now. But of course it was no use.

The snake began to go back inside Dobyns. And eventually the dead dark eyes of the man filled once more with the shining amber light and the snake coiled again around his intestines.

He left the sobbing, hysterical woman on the floor and quickly ran down the steps deeper, deeper into the darkness of the tower.

He had one more thing to do tonight.

His mind was filled with Marie Fane's melancholy, pretty face.

O'Sullivan said, taking her hard by the wrist, "You've got to tell them, Holland. And right now."

"But her brother. She's—"

"To hell with her brother. Dobyns is a very dangerous man. If you really think he's up there—"

"Shit," Chris said. "You're right. As usual."

They were standing in the middle of it, all the craziness, the big emergency vehicles that looked like giant electronic bugs.

The cop people and the Hastings House people and the press people and the just-plain-gawkers people running back and forth between various buildings of the institution and the driveway that was packed with official cars.

After Emily Lindstrom had walked over to the tower, Chris had found O'Sullivan and asked him about his interview with the retired janitor. O'Sullivan had rolled his nice blue Irish eyes and told her about the pet rat the guy carried around on his shoulder and the way he shared his Oreos with the rat and how Oreos made him fart.

"Oreos make him fart?" she'd said.

194

"That's what I'm telling ya, Holland. The guy's a fucking fruitcake."

"So you didn't believe his story about the cult and all that?"

And he'd looked at her directly—accusingly, actually—with those nice Irish blue eyes and said, "You mean to tell me you do believe him? The Lindstrom woman is one thing but this guy—"

"Well," she'd said, "Not exactly believe him but then not exactly not believe him, either, if you know what I mean."

So now, standing beside her with red and blue lights lashing across the brick buildings, and a fine cold mist starting to come down, and the people moving in every direction—all this going on, O'Sullivan said, "You've got to find the cops and tell them."

"I'm sorry, O'Sullivan. I wasn't thinking very straight, was I?"

"No, you weren't. Now go find the fucking cops."

"The fucking cops," she said. "I'll go find them."

And that's just what she did.

"Hi," she said to Detective Staley, a chunky guy who still wore Wildroot (she wanted to point out to him sometime that he'd shown great wisdom in keeping his hair greasy right through the sixties and seventies and eighties, seeming to know instinctively that the look would be back in the nineties).

"Hi," he said. He was watching the last body bag and shaking his head. "I'm kinda busy, Chrissie." He always called her that. He'd told her he had a daughter that name.

"I know you're looking for Dobyns, Hal."

"No shit, we're looking for Dobyns. You should see what he did to those three guys in the garage down there." He shook his head again.

"I think I know where he is."

And right then Detective Hal Staley did a double take that Shemp would have been proud of. "You know where Dobyns is?"

"Yeah," she said, sorry now she hadn't told him ten minutes ago. "Yeah, I do."

She went back to O'Sullivan who was shouting instructions to two young reporters who'd clearly got their PhDs in hair spray.

195

"So you tell 'em?"

"So I told them," she said.

She pointed to two uniformed cops pushing the big searchlight rightward, toward the tower.

"They're going to go looking for him," she said.

O'Sullivan smiled at her. "I don't know whether to give you a kiss or pat you on the ass."

She smiled back. "Later on, why don't you try a little of both?" Goddamn, could she get corny about this guy, she thought.

And then, moments after the searchlight splashed across the top of the stone medieval tower, somebody shouted, "Look, there's a woman in the window."

Chris turned to see and immediately got her first good look at Emily Lindstrom up there in the lonely tower window, the same kind probably that Rapunzel used to let her hair down.

And Chris screamed because this wasn't the Emily Lindstrom she knew at all.

Not with blood pouring out of her mouth and her hands fluttering wildly about her blood-splashed hair.

"Oh, God," Chris said, "Oh, God."

5

ON THE WAY to Marie Fane's, Dobyns several times saw police cruisers. One in particular, parked at a kerb, the patrolman obviously bored and looking for some action, studied Dobyns carefully. Dobyns felt the man's eyes on him, trying to find anything that could justify turning on the red light and pulling Dobyns over. Dobyns sat perfectly still at the stoplight, foot on the brake, hands held low on the steering wheel so the patrolman couldn't see the blood. There had been no time to clean himself.

The light changed to green.

Dobyns pulled slowly away, his stomach knotting, sweat glazing his face. His right leg was twitching.

He just wanted to kill Marie Fane and then he didn't care what happened to him.

He watched the patrol car in his rear-view mirror.

The patrolman sat up straight suddenly, as if he might clip on the headlights and come after Dobyns.

Dobyns's stomach was in such misery, he was afraid he might vomit.

A gentle curve in the road, and the patrol car was out of sight. For the next two blocks, Dobyns continued to glance anxiously in his rear-view but the patrol car was nowhere to be seen.

After three blocks Dobyns quit glancing backward entirely and concentrated on his driving.

The night was black and suddenly wet. Fat silver drops of rain splashed against his windshield. On either side of the street the spring trees bent under a hard, steady wind. An electric DX sign supported on a tall, thin pole looked as if it might be knocked off its base under the onslaught.

Dobyns passed through three distinctly different types of neighbourhood—a working class neighbourhood of small, orderly houses; a mixed ghetto where blacks and Mexicans lived out an armed and very tenuous truce; and a small boutique shopping district that did its best to resemble a Midwestern Rodeo Drive.

Then he was into the hilly, woodsy area known as the Highlands and it was here he found the redbrick apartment complex where the Fanes lived.

Dobyns parked a block away, on a dark side street. When he got out of the car, he took his jacket, shrugged into it, and the knife, which he stuck in his belt. Wind and rain invigorated him and he was appreciative of it. The car ride had made him dozy. He felt single minded, tough again.

He touched the wooden handle of the knife, almost for luck.

He had no trouble spotting the police patrol car.

It sat almost directly beneath a mercury vapour light. Surrounded by older, drab vehicles, the patrol car shone like a beacon.

Dobyns paused at the edge of the parking lot, moving behind the corner of a garage so he could gather himself and decide

197

what to do.

His heart hammered and even given the rain, his face felt oily with sweat. He sensed great danger, enormous risk. He was enjoying himself.

His first thought was to sneak up on the patrol car and kill the patrolman when he was unaware. But would he really be unaware? Sneaking up on a trained, alert police officer would not be easy. And more, it would probably not work.

Abruptly, and making no attempt whatsoever to be hidden from view, Dobyns strolled boldly out into the parking lot. Unless the police officer was asleep, the man would spot Dobyns right away.

Dobyns started weaving.

Doing a drunk impression was difficult. The tendency was to overdo it and not be believable.

Dobyns effected a small, swaying rhythm, almost like a rumba. And every fourth step or so, he came down very hard, as if he'd tripped and were about to pitch forward.

He was halfway into the parking lot, wind and rain slapping his face, when he saw the dome light go on inside the patrol car.

A tall, chunky officer in a dark uniform got out of the car, closing the door behind him. He wore a green rain jacket.

Dobyns pretended not to see him, just continued his weaving, hesitant way across the parking lot.

The officer reached him in no time, a looming, imposing figure who smelled of aftershave and cigarettes.

"Good evening, sir," the officer said. He was the new breed, better educated, better trained. Even intercepting a drunk, he was polite and by-the-book. "I'd like to ask you where you're going."

Dobyns stopped. Aware of the blood, he kept his hands shoved into his jacket pockets. He managed to get a single syllable out: "Home."

"Mind telling me where home is?"

Dobyns, continuing his drunk performance, rolled his head on his neck and sort of pointed with his nose to the apartment complex next to this one. "Down there."

"Would you like me to walk with you, sir?" the officer said.

198

Dobyns almost smiled. The cop was making it so easy. Sure Dobyns would like him to walk with him. Out of the light, into the shadows.

Dobyns, as if he were so drunk he hadn't even heard any of the exchange, started walking again.

The officer, sighing, fell into step beside him.

Then Dobyns made a stupid mistake. He forgot about keeping his hands in his pockets. He brought his right hand up to his face to wipe away rain.

The cop, who had been watching Dobyns carefully, spotted the bloody hand immediately.

"I'd like you to stop here, sir."

The officer's tone had changed. He had gone from helpful public servant to suspicious policeman.

Dobyns kept walking, as if he hadn't heard. He'd realised his mistake, of course, and was terrified that he would now not be able to get to Marie Fane.

"Sir, I'd like you to stop," the officer repeated. His voice had an edge now.

In moments, Dobyns knew, the man would be going for his service revolver.

Dobyns did two things simultaneously: he lunged for the cop and he jerked the knife free from his belt.

The officer, who had obviously not expected this abrupt change of behaviour, started to crouch and pull out his weapon but by then it was too late.

Dobyns put the knife deep into the officer's chest.

And then for good measure, as the officer was starting to fall backward, Dobyns ripped the knife out and plunged it into the man's forehead.

Before the man could scream, Dobyns kicked him skilfully in the throat.

The officer pitched over backward, sprawling in the parking lot shadows as if he'd been crucified.

Blood now discoloured the front of his green rain jacket. He made tiny bubbling sounds and then tiny whimpering sounds and then, as Dobyns stood there watching him in the wind and the rain, the police officer made no sounds at all.

Dobyns raised his head, eyes scanning the dark apartment house before him.

Soon now, Marie, he thought. *Soon now.*

He dragged the policeman's body over under a nearby parked car so that nobody could see it, and then he set to work exchanging clothes with the dead officer.

Marie's eyes came open to darkness. Soaked in sweat, unable to completely separate herself from the nightmare but unable to quite recall it either, she lay on the couch listening to the cold wind screech branches across the windows and rain pelt the roof.

He was in the apartment house.

When she had this thought, she sat straight up, her eyes searching the shadows of the living room, her ears animal— alert to the myriad of late-night sounds.

He was in the apartment house.

Pushing back the covers, she put her good foot and then her crippled foot to the floor, grabbing her robe as she did so. Belting her robe, she moved to the window that overlooked the parking lot and the patrol car below.

The wind was strong enough that the black-and-white police car was being buffeted about. She narrowed her eyes for a glimpse of the officer inside the car. For some reason, she could not make out the man behind the wheel. Was it just her eyesight?

She scanned the rest of the parking lot. It still looked eerie and cold in the faint purple mercury vapour light. The cars filling it looked lonely and solitary, as if they'd been abandoned rather than simply parked.

Her gaze returned to the police car.

Was the officer out of his car and patrolling the grounds? For a moment she allowed herself this high good hope— yes, that was it, he was out of his car and checking the doors and ground floor windows, making certain that everything was all right. And when he was done, he'd be back in his car and Marie would be able to see him and everything would be fine. Just fine.

He was in the apartment house.

Letting the curtain fall back in place, Marie turned around and looked at the hallway. Dark. Silent. As was her mother's room. It sounded as if her mother had finally got to sleep. She certainly didn't want to wake her on the basis of some paranoid notion that the killer had somehow got past the policeman and was now in the house.

But somehow, no amount of rational thinking could rid her mind of the thought that the killer was nearby.

She went back to the bed and picked up the gun that was snuggled beneath the covers. She held the weapon tight to her chest, speaking silently to her father as she did so. *Be with me, Dad. See that Mom and I are all right and that the killer doesn't get in here. Pray for us, Dad.*

It was then she heard the rasping of something being inserted into the doorknob.

The sound of the tumbling locks was very loud. And then he was there, a silhouette against the yellow light in the hallway. The butcher knife was dark and long in his right hand.

Stumbling over an ottoman, she plunged for the phone, wishing now she'd turned on the light as soon as she'd left the couch.

She had to crawl to reach the stand on which the phone rested.

Behind her, the killer quietly closed the door and came into the living room.

He said nothing. Just kept walking slowly, purposefully, closer, closer.

At last her hand found the cold receiver and lifted it to her ear.

And heard—nothing.

And then she heard him laugh: "You stupid little bitch. I cut the wires."

His laugh grew so loud and so hideous, she had to clamp her hand over her ears.

"Honey, honey!" her mother said.

Her mother seemed very far away. Miles away. Her voice very faint. Gradually, the way her mother was shaking her began to affect Marie.

"You were only dreaming, Marie. Please wake up."

Dreaming. Nightmare. The police car empty. The killer jimmying the lock. Coming in. The phone lines cut. The killer coming closer, closer—

Marie's eyes opened, finally. The living room was bathed in the soft glow of the table lamp.

In her blue robe, her mother looked both familiar and pretty. And reassuring. "Are you all right now, honey?"

Marie nodded. "It was a pretty bad dream."

"I know, hon."

"He came in and—"

Her mother took Marie gently by the shoulders and said, "It's over, hon. Why don't we talk about something else?"

Marie nodded. "You're probably right. I think I'll go wash my face and maybe brush my teeth." Marie was an inveterate brusher. She liked the clean cool taste of toothpaste.

"And being lazy," her mother said, "I'll wait right here."

Marie smiled at the notion of her mother being lazy, and padded into the bathroom.

She sat briefly on the chill toilet seat, peeing, and then stood over the sink. She ran hot water until it steamed and then took a fresh washcloth and let it soak in the hot water. Marie liked to apply a hot cloth to her face like a compress. Afterward, her flesh always tingled and felt alive.

Finished with the washcloth, the nightmare finally receding, she opened up the medicine cabinet, took down her toothbrush and toothpaste, and set to work developing a foamy cleansing solvent for her teeth. She was careful to brush properly to get the maximum benefits from her work.

Done brushing, she ran water over the teeth of her brush, put brush and paste back in the medicine cabinet, and then returned to the living room.

A policeman stood next to the couch. He smiled at her and said, "Good evening."

She recognised him at once for who he really was. Even in the uniform, even wearing a hat, it was clear he was the killer she'd seen earlier tonight in the bookstore. "Your mother was nice enough to let me in." He smiled again. "Women are always suckers for uniforms."

"Where is my mother?" she said.

"She's in the bedroom."

"What have you done with her?"

He stared at her. "Calm down."

"I want to go see her."

"You're really starting to lose it."

She turned, and started hobbling down the hallway to her mother's bedroom. Her crippled foot slowed her down considerably.

She heard and felt him right behind her.

Her mother was on the bed. Her clothes had been ripped off her. Her small breasts and tiny thatch of pubic hair gave her a vulnerable look that broke Marie's heart. The gag in her mother's mouth kept her from saying anything. She watched Marie come into the room.

"Did he hurt you?" Marie asked her mother.

Kathleen shook her head. Her face was pale, her eyes frightened.

"Untie her," Marie said.

He slapped her hard directly across the mouth. Marie soon tasted blood in her mouth.

On the bed, her mother made sounds of protest lost in the gag as she rocked uselessly back and forth, straining at the cloth in her mouth.

"You've got a very nice mother; very co-operative," the killer said. "But we've seen enough of her for now. I want to go back to the living room."

Marie started to complain again but her mother shook her head. Comply, the gesture said. Go along, the gesture said.

Marie stared back at the killer. "You're going to kill us, aren't you?"

"I don't want to talk right now," the man said.

He grabbed Marie's shoulder and pushed her toward the

door. "C'mon, now." Then he wound her hair round his hand and put the knife to her throat. "And don't try to scream or anything foolish. Do you understand?"

Behind her, Marie heard her mother cry something plaintive behind the gag.

He pushed Marie out into the hall.

When she was halfway toward the living room, he reached for the back of her nightgown and tore it in a single violent motion.

Marie didn't have time to grab it before the two halves of the gown fell away from her entirely. She reacted instinctively by covering her breasts with her hands.

He shoved her into the living room.

He kept staring at her breasts. She could not entirely hide them behind her hands.

At knifepoint, he forced her across the room to the couch. He said nothing. He smelled of sweat and blood. His eyes were crazed. His breath made her nauseous.

He pushed her down on the couch and then dropped down himself and straddled her.

She could feel his sizeable erection pushing against her vagina.

"You're a virgin, aren't you?"

She said nothing. Beneath her shoulder, she could feel the shape of her father's gun.

There had to be some way to reach it—

He pushed his hips tighter into her. "You are, aren't you?"

"Yes," she whispered.

He smiled. "Good."

He reached down to the warmth between her legs.

His knuckles brushed against her softness.

"Do you like how that feels?"

"No," she said.

"No?" he said. "Maybe not right now. But when I'm inside you, you will. I promise you."

Again her shoulder rubbed the gun. She had to distract him some way.

He brought the point of the knife blade to her throat. "Do

knives scare you?"

"Yes."

"I kind've thought they would."

"You could run. I couldn't stop you. You could get away before the police come."

His face was huge in her eyes. He had yellow, slightly crooked teeth and he needed a shave and blood spattered his nose and cheeks and he smelled oily and filthy. Now his mouth opened wide as a cavern and he laughed. "Oh, you're real concerned for my welfare, aren't you? That's just what you'd like to see, isn't it? Me get away." He laughed again, the sound rolling around the dark cave of his open mouth.

He put some pressure on the knife.

She felt the tip of it cut her skin. She felt a tiny drop of blood roll down her neck.

"I'm going to lay this knife right next to me while I'm fucking you. And if you make any noise at all, I'm going to kill you right on the spot. You understand?"

He took his knuckles again and traced them across the shape of her vagina.

"You'll want to get wet, otherwise it's going to hurt a lot." He grinned with yellow teeth. "I'm sorry there isn't time for foreplay."

It was then she brought her knee straight up between his legs and had the satisfaction of feeling her knee collide with his testicles.

He let out an almost amazing groan of pain. He jerked up off her momentarily, just enough so she could roll over on her stomach and touch the shape of the gun with her fingers.

He collapsed on her back, ripping out a handful of hair as he did so. "You cunt; you're going to pay for that."

She wanted to cry but she felt so many emotions—terror, pain, rage, uselessness—that she could do nothing but lie there.

And let her fingers gently touch the gun.

He got another handful of hair and started pulling again. Steadily, so the pain would be constant.

"You try that again, and I'll kill your mother first. You understand me, cunt?"

205

She nodded, sobbed.

His groping hand found her buttock. Began gliding gently over its curve. Then he started squeezing so hard it hurt.

"Maybe I'll do you back door. Maybe that's the way you'll like it," he said.

He had an erection again. He pushed it between the mounds of her buttocks.

Her hand started to tighten on the handle of the gun.

His hand shot out, grabbed hers. "What the hell you think you're doing?"

My God. Has he found the gun? If I don't have the gun then there's no hope—

"You put your hand down here when I need it."

He twisted her entire arm, yanking her hand behind her back. He set her fingers on his erection. He had somehow managed to unzip himself.

Her fingers recoiled at the touch but when he jerked on her arm, making it feel as if he'd snap it in two, she had no choice but to let him guide her hand back to him.

"You and I are going to be friends," he said as he stroked her hand up and down the shaft of his erection. "Very good friends."

Abruptly he let go of her arm and pushed himself down between her legs, his penis brushing against her vagina for the first time.

"You make any noise, cunt, and I'll kill your mother first. You hear me?"

Unable to speak, she only nodded.

"Good. Then we'll get along fine."

He jammed himself up inside her.

Her entire insides caught fire with a pain that brought swimming darkness to her eyes and a dying cry to her throat.

Any sound, and he'll kill Mom.

He started moving around inside her, finding his rhythm, taking his pleasure.

She was still completely dry. Each thrust only made her feel the drier. Each thrust only made her clench her fists and bite down on her tongue the harder.

"Oh, God, cunt, you really feel good."

The tremulous sounds of his domination were almost as bad as the actual feel of him inside.

His strokes got longer now. His breathing was obscenely loud.

She knew he'd be finished in moments. And then he'd kill her. He had no other reason to keep her alive.

She had to move now.

Sliding her hand under the blanket, she wriggled her fingers like snakes up the couch until she felt the handle of the gun.

His hand clamped her wrist!

So he'd found out about the gun after all. So now there was no hope whatsoever.

But it had only been a move of passion, his grabbing her arm. He was thrusting faster and deeper; faster and deeper. Despite herself, she was getting wet down there.

Faster and deeper.

She grabbed it then and pulled it quickly into her chest, hidden away from his sight. The gun felt huge and wonderful in her palm.

When he came, he bit her so hard on the neck that he drew blood. She started to whimper—apparently he was afraid she was going to scream—and he picked up the knife and pushed it hard against the back of her neck.

"Don't say a fucking word, bitch. Not a fucking word."

She would have to do it quickly, she knew. He was much faster and stronger. There was a good chance he would see the gun before she had time to use it, and take it from her.

He withdrew from her and started to stand up. She could hear the couch springs squeak from the pressure of his knees.

She could hear his trousers rustle as he began to pull them up.

And then she rolled over and pushed the gun up, holding it tight in both hands.

His face reflected both astonishment and fear.

The first place she shot him was in the groin.

She shot his penis off. Limp, it dropped off like a piece of brittle statuary. Blood began pouring from the hole in his crotch. For good measure, she put another bullet in the bloody cleft the first bullet had left behind.

The second place she shot him was in the chest.

By this time, however, he had tapped into his rage so he was coming for her.

She scrambled backward off the couch, getting tangled up in the blankets and screaming.

He reached down and slapped her so hard that she didn't have time to get a shot off.

He grabbed the gun from her and tossed it behind him on the living room floor.

Then he picked up his knife from the couch, leaned down and grabbed her hair, and pulled her face up to his.

"I'm going to enjoy this, cunt. I'm really going to enjoy this."

Please, Dad. Please pray for me. Please help me.

Even with the gun, she had not killed him. And now he was going to kill her.

He put the cold, clean edge of the knife against her jugular and was about to draw it across her throat when the gunfire broke out.

At first, Marie had no idea what was happening.

But as the killer's knife fell from her throat, and as the killer began to pitch forward dead as the bullets slammed into his back, she saw standing there the best friend she'd ever had, her mother.

Even in the frenzy and horror of this moment, Marie took time to note wryly that Kathleen, after escaping her bonds, had first done the proper thing. She'd put on a robe before coming out into the living room and saving her daughter's life.

By now neighbours were in the hallway, thundering with words and excited exclamations.

Kathleen, composing herself, setting the empty gun on the coffee table as if she'd just finished a perfunctory round of target practice, went to the door.

Marie found her own robe and rose dazedly to her feet. The killer was sprawled face down across the couch. The peppermint stripes of the sheets were soaked red with his blood.

His face was turned in profile and he shocked her by speaking. He reached out a hand and touched her robe,

208

streaking blood down the light blue cotton.

His face angled up toward hers. He had changed somehow—the rage was gone and in his eyes there was the sense of a different man.

He said, "I don't know what they'll do to you. Your name was on the wall. You were supposed to die. They'll punish you for this."

And then his face fell again to the couch, and he died.

Marie, shuddering, wondered what he'd meant. *I don't know what they'll do to you. Your name was on the wall. You were supposed to die. They'll punish you for this.*

But then neighbours were pouring through the door. And sirens were exploding on the night nearby. And best of all her mother, Kathleen, was hugging her.

The long night had ended at last.

Two Months Later

SHE HARDLY EVER left her room. The others frightened her. She was not sure why but she did not trust them.

So long into the night she stood at the window, watching, watching, not sure for what, just knowing that at some point she would understand the compulsion to stand here until her legs grew sore and tired.

And then one night it happened and for long weeks afterward, she wondered if it hadn't all been a dream.

But no, she knew better than that. It hadn't been a dream. She had indeed visited the tower that stood at midnight in the silver rain like a beckoning finger.

For a time, she was troubled and of course they gave her shots with long silver needles, and her doctors cooed and whispered and reassured, but she did not tell them of course. Not about the hole in the tower where the serpent had slithered free, nor the way the serpent had come across the floor to her and—

She just accepted their shots and slept their sleep and mouthed their words...

...and then one day at last she went home.

Four Months Later

AS USUAL, MARIE fixed dinner and brought it into the living room where her mother sat in her pink robe and her pink fuzzy slippers. She really was a very good looking middle aged woman.

"Program started yet?" Marie said, taking one of those long, crippled steps that she would never get used to.

"Not yet, hon."

"Good. I want to see it."

Her mother looked at her curiously. "You're sure, hon? I mean, you're sure you feel up to it?"

Marie sighed, then shrugged. "Uh, I guess so. If it gets too much I'll—I'll just go in my room and read."

Marie sat down on the couch next to her mother and watched TV. There was a station break and a dogfood commercial and a tampon commercial and a Pepsi commercial and then a familiar face and voice filled the screen.

"Good evening. This is Chris Holland of Channel 3 News." Then the camera shot widened out and in the night behind her you could see Hastings House, including the tower. "Six months ago, a man escaped from this mental hospital and went on a murderous rampage in this city that lasted thirty-six hours and claimed five lives. In the past, other people who stayed in this hospital also became murderers. There is a rumour this happened because of the strange powers to be found in the tower you're looking at now.

"Are there any truths to these allegations? Exactly what's in the tower anyway? And is it true that a hundred years ago a very powerful and sinister cult buried the bones of the children it murdered in the ground where the tower now stands?"

"Some people familiar with these cases insist that the descendants of the cult still operate in this city, helping possessed individuals find their prey and kill them to satisfy a dark god that takes the form of a serpent."

The camera pushed in now for a close-up of Chris's face.

211

"I've spent the last six months doing an intensive investigation of my own into all these questions. In fact, I should be a little bit grateful to the whole thing. The Dobyns murders saved my job. And even got me a modest promotion."

She shook her head fetchingly. "But I'm not here to talk about myself. I'm here to talk about nineteen murders that have taken place in this city over the past one hundred years. Murders that may not be as commonplace as once seemed."

And with that, they were into another commercial.

The TV show lasted sixty minutes and during it the trouble in Kathleen's stomach began again.

Ever since her stay at Hastings House and her strange dreams of visiting the tower late one night, she had felt a curious pressure in her belly. Just lately there was movement down there, too, as if something were moving around inside.

She wished she'd never gone to stay at Hastings House. But following the night when Richard Dobyns raped and nearly killed Marie right here in the apartment, Kathleen had gone into a depression so deep that no amount of outpatient counselling seemed to help. So the psychologist she saw recommended a brief stay in Hastings House. Marie had visited her every day. That was the only thing that had made Kathleen's stay tolerable.

"I really like her, don't you?"

"Hmm? I'm sorry, hon. I guess my mind was drifting off."

"Chris Holland. Don't you think she's doing a good job?" Marie said.

"Oh, yes, hon. A very good job."

And just then, Kathleen felt it again, the sensation of something heavy in her stomach shifting position.

What could it be?

Four Nights Later

IN THE ALLEY, behind the tavern, you could hear it all, the cursing and the laughter, the sudden bursts of excitement over the game on the television and the equally sudden anger as chairs were thrown back and men started throwing punches at each other. It was this way every night—month in, month out; year in, year out. The only things that changed were the country and western tunes on the jukebox and even they had a certain dead sameness in melody and lyrics alike.

The woman waited in the alley. The night wind chafed her face and legs. Sundown, a quick brilliant red and gold, had died like a guttering fire along the horizon and now there was only darkness and the cold steady chill of the wind.

She had been here, in the shadows of a large, ancient garage directly across from the back door of the tavern, for twenty minutes.

Certainly the man would come along soon enough.

And just then the door opened to a rush of music and laughter and the stink of beer and cigarette smoke and then he was there.

He was probably in his early thirties, chunky, balding, sort of cute in a chipmunk kind of way, dressed in a heavily lined zipper jacket, faded blue jeans and work boots, and dangling a steel lunch pail from the thick fingers of his right hand.

He stood in the wind, teetering as if he were so drunk he would pitch over on his side, finishing his cigarette and looking up the alley to the parking lot. He was driving, of course. American roads were filled with people at least as drunk as he was.

It was a narrow little alley, almost a cul-de-sac, and so when she took three steps out of the shadows of the garage, he saw her at once.

He took his cigarette from his lips and flicked it to the ground. "You look like you're lost, lady."

It was easy enough to see on his suddenly smiling face that he was quite appreciative of her good looks, even if she was ten years older than him.

She shrugged. "Just kind of lonely, I guess."

The only real light in the alley was the soft blue neon reading TAVERN above the back door. You could see he was trying to get a better look at her but that there wasn't enough light.

"You with somebody inside?" he said. He was still weaving a bit but lust had given him an edge now. At least he didn't look as if he were going to fall over any longer.

"No. I'm alone."

She let her words sink in.

"Now that's a real shame."

For the first time, she smiled. She had a good smile and she knew it.

He got excited and put his hand out to take her shoulder. "I got a car."

"You got somewhere in mind to go?"

"Uh, sure." She could tell by his hesitation that he was married. He was trying to make some quick plans. "This other little tavern I know. You can get real cosy in the back."

He pulled her closer now, just the way she wanted him to.

She brought the straight razor up from her coat, flicked open the blade, and slashed it quick and deep across his throat.

He was so disoriented from shock and liquor that all he could do was stand there and gape at her. He didn't even seem to notice any pain yet.

She helped him appreciate the moment better by slashing the razor back across his throat.

This time he tried to scream.

But it was too late for that, of course.

She watched as he grasped at his throat, then as his legs collapsed under him, then as he clutched at the air for help.

All the time he was making gagging noises; all the time his chest was becoming soaked with his own blood.

In less than a minute he was dead.

The woman folded the razor, slid it back into her pocket, and started walking away.

In moments she was out of the blue glow of the neon above the back door. Then there was just the hard clear winter light of distant stars.

214

Her feet crunched ice as she walked down the alley.

Kathleen wanted to make some sense of it, of course, but there was no sense to be made. She had just killed a man and would like to kill others.

In her stomach, the snake shifted position once more, and again she thought of what it had been like carrying a baby to term.

But this was a far different thing she was giving birth to now. A far different thing.

She walked through the night to a bus stop where a bus that reminded her of a huge glowing insect picked her up and took her home.

CT Publishing

If you have enjoyed this book, we are quietly confident you will enjoy the following titles as well.

ED GORMAN
THE LONG MIDNIGHT

A PLACE TO DIE FOR...

Meredith Sawyer had grown up at Dr Richard Candlemas's academy—a place she has spent her life trying to forget. Candlemas was gifted with telekinetic powers and an undeniable brilliance, and so were the special children he recruited.

A MIND TO KILL FOR...

Meredith has tried to forget the energies the children unleashed with their minds... and the secrets that had drawn her sister into Candlemas's inner circle of favourites. Now, with her sister long dead, Meredith is a Chicago reporter, with Candlemas's school only a bad memory

A TERROR TO SCREAM FOR...

Then police detective Tom Gage investigates the bizarre murder of an academy teacher. His journey into the twisted alleyways of the past leads to the answers Gage needs ... and sweeps Meredith into a vortex of terror. For the truth about Candlemas foretells terrible destruction-and puts Meredith and Gage into a race with death.

Price: £4.99 ISBN: 1-902002-08-3

Available from all good bookshops, or post free from:
CT Publishing, PO Box 5880,
Birmingham B16 8JF
www.crimetime.co.uk
email ct@crimetime.demon.co.uk

ED GORMAN
NIGHT KILLS

The odd thing was how comfortably she seemed to fit inside there, as if this were a coffin and not a freezer at all. She was completely nude and only now beginning to show signs of the freezing process, ice forming on her arms and face.

But he could tell she hadn't been in here very long because of the smells...

Frank Brolan, successful adman, unwitting fall-guy. Someone has murdered a call girl and planted her in his freezer. Frank has to find the killer before the cops find him.

As the body count rises, with the killer leaving Frank's mark at every crime, Frank flees into the night and the city. He finds help in an unlikely duo—a teenage whore and a wheelchair-bound dwarf with a mind like a steel trap...

"A painfully powerful and personal novel about three outsiders—an alcoholic advertising executive, a man twisted and disfigured by spina bifida, and a runaway teenage girl—brought together in a noir unlike any you've ever read. Violent, melancholy, bitterly humorous, Night Kills is a 'relationship' novel of the classic mould. As disturbing and sad a crime novel as I've ever read."

—CEMETERY DANCE

Price: £4.99 ISBN: 1-902002-03-2
Available from all good bookshops, or post free from:
CT Publishing, PO Box 5880,
Birmingham B16 8JF
www.crimetime.co.uk
email ct@crimetime.demon.co.uk

ED GORMAN
CAGE OF NIGHT

TWENTY-ONE-YEAR-old Spence returns to his hometown after two years in the Army and falls in love with Cindy Brasher, Homecoming Queen and town goddess to a long line of jealous men. A string of robberies put Spence at odds with his obsessive love for Cindy. One by one Spence's rivals are implicated in horrific crimes. Spence wonders how much Cindy knows, and why she wants him, like her past boyfriends, to visit the old well in the woods...

"The book is full of Gorman's characteristic virtues as a writer: sympathy, humour, commitment to the craft of storytelling, and a headlong narrative drive. A real writer is at work here and there aren't many of those to go around."

—DARK ECHO.

"Cornell Woolrich would have enjoyed Cage Of Night."

—LOCUS.

"A book that combines romance, sex, violence, madness and an almost oppressive degree of grief, Cage Of Night is one of the most unique noirs ever written."

—PIRATE WRITINGS.

"Gorman is defining noir for the nineties."

—CEMETERY DANCE.

Price: £4.99 ISBN: 1-902002-02-4

Available from all good bookshops, or post free from:
**CT Publishing, PO Box 5880,
Birmingham B16 8JF
www.crimetime.co.uk**
email ct@crimetime.demon.co.uk

GWENDOLINE BUTLER

A NAMELESS COFFIN

Nobody took much notice when the handbag slashing began in London. A few women found small nicks in their handbags, others huge gashes. John Coffin had a feeling that the cases were going to lead to something far more unpleasant. A similar case in Scotland—of coats, this time—comes to trial in Murreinhead, and Giles Almond, a mild-mannered officer of the Court, is viciously attacked by a knife-wielding assailant.

Then the body of a missing Murreinhead woman is discovered in a rotting tenement in London, and the chase is on…

Coffin's investigation moves between the two locales and suspense builds as yet another murder victim is discovered…Where is the killer? And what is the connection between London and Murreinhead?

'[Butler's] inventiveness never seems to flag; and the singular atmosphere of her books, compounded of jauntiness and menace, remains undiminished'

—PATRICIA CRAIG, TLS

Price: £4.99 ISBN: 1-902002-11-3
Available from all good bookshops, or post free from:
CT Publishing, PO Box 5880,
Birmingham B16 8JF
www.crimetime.co.uk
email ct@crimetime.demon.co.uk

GWENDOLINE BUTLER
COFFIN IN OXFORD

"It was like a Chinese puzzle. In St Ebbe's was a flat, in the flat was a trunk, and in the trunk was a body. The body of a woman..."

Ted was brought round from the first attack, if you could call it an attack, with difficulty. He had been found shut up in a cupboard with a scarf tightened around his neck: his own scarf, to add insult to injury...

'Gwendoline Butler is excellent on the bizarre fantasies of other people's lives and on modern paranoia overlaying old secrets; and her plots have the rare ability to shock'

—ANDREW TAYLOR, THE INDEPENDENT

ISBN: 1-902002-00-8 Price: £4.99

JENNIE MELVILLE
WINDSOR RED

Charmian Daniels, on a sabbatical from the police force takes rooms in Wellington Yard, Windsor near the pottery of Anny, a childhood friend. The rhythm of life in Wellington Yard is disturbed by the disappearance of Anny's daughter with her violent boyfriend. Dismembered limbs from an unidentified body are discovered in a rubbish sack. A child is snatched from its pram. Headless torsos are found outside Windsor.

Are these events connected? And what relationship do they have to the coterie of female criminals that Charmian is 'studying'...? All is resolved in a Grand Guignol climax that will leave the most hardened crime fiction fans gasping.

ISBN: 1-902002-01-6 Price: £4.99

Available from all good bookshops, or post free from:
CT Publishing, PO Box 5880, Birmingham B16 8JF